PRAISE FOR

C000299182

'A great read. Lose yourself adventure.'

—Tim Lovejoy, television presenter

'A fascinating, dark and witty look at a world gone wrong. A glorious read.'

—Lou Sanders, comedian

'Bloody (and) brilliant. Prepare to be pulled into a world where dark comedy and high tension collide, driven by characters alive with hope and desire, greed and violence.'

—Phil Davies, playwright and screenwriter

'Michael Millar's writing is original, accomplished and entertaining. His characters are unique and memorable, and he's established a not-too-distant and credible dystopia with terrifying ease.'

—Bryony Sutherland, author of *Being Biracial: Where Our Secret Worlds Collide*

'Taut writing and sharp-edged tension. Millar is like a darkly humorous Kafka.'

—Jack Hayes, author of *When Eagles Burn*

HOORAY FOR THE
NEXT TO DIE

ALSO BY MICHAEL MILLAR

HOORAY FOR THE NEXT TO DIE

Part One of the Revenge of Jimmy Mac

MICHAEL MILLAR

First published in 2021 by whitefox

Copyright © Michael Millar 2021

The moral right of Michael Millar to be identified as the author of this work has been asserted in accordance with the Copyright, Designs and Patents Act 1988.

All rights reserved. No part of this publication may be reproduced or transmitted in any form or by any means, electronic or mechanical including photocopying, recording or any information storage or retrieval system, without prior permission in writing from the publishers.

This novel is entirely a work of fiction. The names, characters and incidents portrayed in it are the work of the author's imagination. Any resemblance to actual persons, living or dead, events or localities is entirely coincidental.

ISBN 978-1-913532-82-6

Also available as an ebook

ISBN 978-1-913532-83-3

Typeset by Jill Sawyer Phypers
Cover design by Jack Smyth
Project management by whitefox

For Harry and Elizabeth, Charlie and Jock, Bertram and Reginald,
Ford and Trillian, Lola, Wormold, Ben Nevis, Lord Emsworth,
Yossarian, and all the rest.

With enormous respect. And profound apologies.

Editor's note

This project is about understanding. Primarily, it will help determine who is to blame for this outrage and inform their punishment. But the terms of reference must go further than that. This must be an exercise in anthropology. In psychology. For whatever one's opinion of this specimen, one must agree it is remarkable and ripe for study. To understand it is to understand those like it. This is crucial, for they are the first to turn. And the last to break.

With our recent advances in hypnagogic reprogramming and the application of more traditional methods, we can bend wills to our fancy and at our leisure. But true power lies in there being no need to apply such methods in the first place. To stop the rot of nonconformity before it sets in. Without this understanding, I will never exert complete control. Without understanding, I will never have their minds.

CHAPTER 1

How-d'ye-Do

Of all the ghosts that come to visit, only one ever speaks. Of all the ghosts, it is the only one I wish would not. A chill on my skin announces the apparition's arrival, the stinking heat momentarily forgotten. But no matter where I turn, there it is, sitting for eternity on an exquisite spectral sofa – *my* exquisite spectral sofa, damn it.

The infamous stare bores into me, a reminder that my visitor is more inquisitor than inquisitive. Then comes the voice of scientific examination, of quiet expectation, of cold enquiry. The question is always the same.

'Would you die for what you believe in, Mr Macfarlane?'

It is a pointless charade, for the answer too remains the same.

'Of course not.' I mean, the idea is appalling. Ghastly. Preposterous.

'Perhaps you are one of that rare breed who would go further,' it intones with a heartless wonder, undaunted by my efforts to be helpful. 'Perhaps you are someone who would give up more than themselves. Tell me: are you that person? Are you someone who would give up *everything*?'

It is surely a mark of the man I was (and might still be, who knows?) that the latter option always seemed the better choice. In my experience, when someone threatens to 'take everything', they plan to leave you alive to wallow in your unbearable loss. In my case, this would be an error on the part of the oppressor, since the personal sanctity of one James Macfarlane, Esq. was always my primary concern. And by some margin, I might add.

1

The ghost never stays long enough for an answer. This is frustrating because I'm desperate to explain myself so it might leave me alone. Maybe go and find some other haunt. I rehearse my answers over and over in anticipation of the next visit but, when it comes, the examination is always fleeting and I am left gesticulating into thin air like a trapeze artist who, mid-routine, remembers his partner has booked the day off.

Then I must compose myself, for it is the turn of the others to troop by. Conscience is a cruel master to one such as I and, while their stares are sometimes sad, they are often accusatory. On the worst days, they offer forgiveness. It is then I begin to wonder if losing everything is all it's cracked up to be.

My hand strays to the naked wrist where the old woman's golden bangle once hung. They took that away, of course, and now the names that were so elegantly carved into the shining metal only exist as a scar on my memory. The names that first gave order and impetus to my revenge. My golden butcher's bill.

God, I need a drink. Something to lighten the mood or, at the very least, dampen a creeping enthusiasm for shuffling off this awful coil . . . But what? I struggle for answers more and more. The thick, warm air dulls the senses, and while I've never been foolish enough to think there was a bad time for a drink, at least I had a routine before. (I was quite strict in fact: no whisky before 11 a.m., for example. That's more of a gin time, obviously.) It is impossible to maintain such a common-sense approach when you've long since lost count of the days and the weeks. Maybe even the months. When you're beginning to wonder if there really is a world outside, or if these grey walls are the only world that ever was.

Then a moment of clarity: one third cognac, one third dry vermouth, one third absinthe. Stir and strain. Never shake.

The No. 1. Gaze upon it and whisper its name with reverence.

The liquid burns like fire in the glass, engorged by the deep red hues of the setting sun. Studying the golden glow, we may observe hints of caramel, a buttery texture, flamboyant tones of bloodied urine.

Raising the antique crystal, I swirl the concoction around to release the aromas. Mmm . . . yes, a definite whiff of danger. The fluid comes to rest but its legs cling to the glass like grappling hooks. Time passes. The beard itches damnably; I shall treat myself to a wash in the toilet when we no longer have company.

Back to the glass. The viscous surface is calm but brooding. Plotting, perhaps. I grow in certainty that it seeks my demise. To forestall its devious plans, I raise the tumbler and prepare to tip it back with one mighty throw.

'A cup to the dead already,' I say, saluting the barman. (Archie, who else?)

He does not answer but the sentiment is writ plain upon his face: *Hooray for the next to die.*

The liquor slides down, first imbuing me with a sense of foreboding, then a soupçon of despondency, followed by a garnish of alarm. It spreads through my veins with a tingling sensation, much like that enjoyed during a chemical gas attack. I sigh contentedly; it was everything I hoped it would be. Archie smiles. I know now there's no point in asking him to talk to me. He never talks. I try to count his scars. A fool's errand. Instead, I tally his teeth. A more feasible task.

I drain the last drop. Now empty, the glass dissolves in my hand. Archie vanishes as quickly as he arrived, melting away into the thick, shimmering air. I settle back against the hard, pocked concrete and close my eyes.

Cheery-bye, Archie, old friend. It's a' baws, so it is.

For a moment I cling to his image, which is as clear to me as the day he went to the great bar brawl in the sky. I live in dread of

* Dreadful (vulgar).

3

it fading for good. Clarity is in increasingly short supply. All the others, everything we did to set the world on fire . . . it's all beginning to drift away. I try my best to hold on to them but, you must understand, sanity is *exhausting*.

Why I fixate on Archie is anyone's guess. Perhaps it was his fearlessness and warrior spirit that so complemented my own lack of moral fibre. Perhaps it was our symbiotic relationship: he, the keeper of the key to the drinks trolley, and I, finely poised between aspiring and functioning alcoholic. There are no answers. He was he and I was I. Perhaps that's all that matters.

Pride and Common Sense are the only ones who make time to talk to me now. I am pleased to regain their company after such a long absence, but it's a mixed blessing. They argue incessantly and are currently at war over my latest perceived act of treason. Shh! If we're quiet, we might listen in for a moment:

We must not write this! Pride rages.

Ha! Only you could possess such certainty, Common Sense fires back.

Not another word from you, Common Sense. This is an act of betrayal. A final capitulation. If we do this, they win.

Nonsense, we must do as they say. We must write it all down.

Don't be ridiculous, you damned fool. I mean, look at this thing. It's a bloody typewriter. Tap tap ting. Tap tap ting. It's enough to drive us madder. And anyway, who forces someone to use a typewriter in this day and age, I ask you? In a field of strong contenders, this must surely qualify as cruel and unusual punishment.

Mac, I implore us! How are we even contemplating Pride's opinions? He's the reason we're in this stinking hellhole in the first place. If it weren't for Pride, we'd be back in Caledon, enjoying the fruits of fortune and fame. Pride's a bastard.

Now, look here—

And what are we, if we are not Jimmy Mac? *What is the point of*

4

everything we have done, everything we have achieved – everyone who has been lost – if no one ever hears about it? Status is all that stands between us and oblivion. Surely we won't risk leaving our legacy to the cold indifference of posterity?

The bloody what?

Yes! Think of the books. Remember the musty smell in Smith's library, just before he pitched us into the inferno? Think about all that knowledge: printed, unalterable, secure. We don't have the luxury of such certainty. Right now, data is being accessed, records manipulated, and history erased. Our history. But we've been given the chance to actually write something down! To lock our truth in a vault of ink and paper.

Common Sense has lost it, I'm telling you, Mac. Doolally. Cracked. Bonkers. The only thing he's got right is that we are Jimmy Mac. *And Jimmy Mac would never be pushed around – manipulated – like this.*

Oh, come now, Pride. Even you have to admit we are a shadow of the shadow of our former self. All that matters now is protecting – no, preserving – *the Jimmy Mac name. This will surely be our last chance to tell our story. The last chance to be saved from oblivion. Come on, Mac. We just have to get started. We just have to be brave.*

Pride is on the ropes. The threat of anonymity – of our very existence expunged – weighs too heavily on such a fractured ego as ours. And so, a decision is made. Pride is cross at losing the argument, but mollified when I point out this story is very much about him. However, I do take Common Sense aside and warn him against sweeping pronouncements on being brave: there are few more terrifying things in this world than deciding to be brave, everyone knows that.

And so, it is time to begin. But where? I had a good first line. Oh balls, what was it?

Ah, yes. Right: here we go.

* * *

5

They call me a killer. Which, frankly, I think is unfair. I happen to disagree with murder as a form of argument. Yes, I have killed, but that was either in the service of a nation or by mistake; a somewhat embarrassing admission for someone with my particular skill set.

But to label me 'a killer' is not on. It carries all sorts of unfounded connotations: a devious nature, a certain degeneracy, even a lack of manners, God forbid. It also requires stone-cold malice aforethought, and that must be the clincher. No one who knew me could ever claim I thought things through. To demonstrate good faith, I'll argue the toss with those who have labelled me a psychopath. What with the superficial charm, the impulsiveness, the ability to manipulate others, and grandiose notions of self-worth, they may well have a point.

I suppose what you call me is up to you. What matters is that you make up your own mind, not have it made up for you. Rest assured, you can rely on me to tell all, exactly as it happened. There is no reason to lie. Everything I tried to achieve lies in ruins. Everyone I tried to protect is surely gone – except the Reverend, of course. He will no doubt be fine, the evil old bastard. Which just goes to show that the good really do die young, while those with a propensity for skinning a man alive when circumstances dictate will forever find themselves in good stead.

Read and learn, children. Read and learn.

I'll admit right from the start that my motives were wrong, my resolve ever wavering, and my ability to second-guess others, third rate. And yes, I was often ignorant as to what was actually going on and quite how I got to that point (let alone why). But there is still no better person to tell this story.

I am James Macfarlane.

I am the Wolf of Badenoch.

And this is my confession.

CHAPTER 2

The Beginning of the End

My execution, such as it was, was a loud and confused affair. I must have been inches from death when they dragged me out of the O-Tank, under the stony glare of Wallace and The Bruce (themselves also repeatedly accused of treason, as it happens). I have visions of baying, jostling crowds – present to witness my execution – parting à la Red Sea as they took me away. But I can't have seen that since, after some considerable effort, I had finally achieved unconsciousness. Then I guess it was a short trip in a discreet laundry van to a big ol' transport plane bound for Parts Unknown.

I woke in a massive aircraft, alone and cold in the half-darkness, the roar of the engines pounding in my ears. The dim, flickering lights bolted along the spine of the hold threw shadows everywhere. I don't remember being afraid, just tired. Resigned to whatever lay ahead. A single thought revolved in my mind: what compels us to do the right thing when often we never recover? I mulled this conundrum for considerable time, before deciding Mother Nature has, for her own sick entertainment, bestowed on the human race a simple but blinding inability to appreciate the consequences of these kindly acts on our tender, squishy bits. If people could see Old Father Time rising from his chair in resignation, picking up his knuckledusters, and waiting patiently for them behind a skip, they wouldn't do these things.

As I sat there, ruminating on human folly, a tiny movement, just visible out of the corner of my eye, seized my attention. The familiar, icy finger of fear touched me. I quietly cursed the fool who said whatever it was he said about 'not fearing death but fearing not living' or some such nonsense. Both have scared me for as long as I can remember. Even my state of exhaustion couldn't change that.

I craned my neck from side to side, but could see nothing beyond a line of huge crates that ran like vertebrae down the middle of the hold. They stood in grim formation, secured in place by heavy straps, shrouded in gloom, and serenaded by the ever-present engine howl. Somewhere behind them was something or someone. I stared deeper into the darkness, waiting and worrying about what skulked in the shadows. The tension grew until I begged the spectres to reveal themselves. None did. Looking back, I suppose it was hardly their fault. The croak that issued from my parched throat when I called out made introductions unlikely. The best I could manage was a passable impression of a deflating balloon.

I sank back into the netting of my improvised seat. I'm no stranger to travelling long distances wedged into the netting of a cargo aircraft – it's the price we paid for all that cloak-and-dagger nonsense, back in the day – but then my hands weren't tied behind my back. The bonds restricted my movement and made me ache all over. I had a growing suspicion that my guards – whoever or wherever they might be – had given me an extra beating while I was unconscious. My newly torn shirt and trousers, stained with blood that hadn't been spilled when I was last compos mentis, pointed towards skulduggery. But why? Perhaps they detested me. Or perhaps I was in the hands of some motivated and conscientious operators who were a credit to their employer: a beacon of inspiration for repressive regimes everywhere. There was a strong chance they were a combination of the two. I could feel my hands swelling. The tight rope binding them was of rough hemp, designed for maximum discomfort. Again, credit where credit's due: my captors were consummate professionals.

I slid in and out of consciousness, but sleep never lasted long. As soon as I drifted off, a jolt of turbulence would send pain shooting around my body, bringing me back to the land of the living (although it's a stretch to call it 'living' when I have been taken out of the world and dropped into Hell's waiting-room). Many hours later we finally bumped down and the noise subsided. The ramp at the back of the plane lowered, hydraulics protesting. Bright light flooded in. I winced and, without thinking, tried to cover my eyes, succeeding only in scraping yet more skin from my tattered wrists. As if by magic, two large men appeared from behind the crates, clad in the dark uniform of the Mallice, Caledon's secret police. That explained the dedication to their craft.

They regarded me in silence, admiring their handiwork. Such paragons of violent repression usually take pride in what they do, and rightfully so. I pictured them unrolling a tablet and asking me to fill in a customer satisfaction form, whereupon I'd reply 'Very good' or 'Excellent' to such questions as 'How comprehensive was the beating you experienced?', 'Were your guards suitably intimidating?', and 'How likely are you to choose being brutalised by our staff in the future?'

Having appraised me and found that all was in disorder, the operatives dragged me out into the sunlight, leaving me swaying on the spot as they went to get our passports stamped and peruse the souvenir stand. I closed my eyes and took a deep breath, relishing a rare moment of calm. The moment the tail had opened, the balmy breeze that rushed in had given me a pretty good idea of where we were – to the nearest thousand miles, at least. Once you've felt the caress of that air on your skin and filled your grateful lungs, the memory never leaves you. It's the combination of early morning warmth and a certain earthiness that does it. As if the planet has rolled out the red carpet to welcome you back to the cradle of humanity. Surely even the baffling array of smoke and mirrors the

9

regime might throw up couldn't hide this truth: I was in Africa. The relief of having this anchor was huge. But it was soon supplanted by a problem: I was in bloody Africa. This did not bode well.

Squinting through bruised eyelids, it was clear that avenues for escape could best be described as 'limited'. This is where Mother Nature spent her difficult teenage years after falling in with a tough crowd. This is where she rolls up her sleeves, reveals the anchor-shaped tattoo on her left boob, and slips on the brass knuckles that Old Father Time gifted her last Christmas, all the while giving you a look that says 'Come an' 'ave a go if you think you're 'ard enough . . .'

The ground was rock solid beneath my feet as I took a couple of tentative steps away from the plane. Tufts of sharp yellow grass and slivers of stone bit at my bare feet. In the distance a line of sparse trees, interspersed with spiked acacia bushes, carried on their fight for life in the parched earth. The local architecture offered no succour either. A collection of low white storage buildings sat to one side of the airfield, which itself was no more than a long clearing in the bush.

Yes, the odds of a getaway seemed poor indeed, but old habits die hard and the escape and evasion training drilled into me all those years ago was already demanding I abscond, odds be damned. Waving its swagger stick in threatening fashion, The Training reminded me that the chance of evading my captors would decrease as time passed; that the goal was *not to make it to the first stop* if I could avoid it.

Let's get to it, then, Pride piped up. *You know the score: guards taken unawares, our strength at its best, no locked doors, etc. etc. Come on. Quick march, soldier!*

Woah there, interrupted Common Sense, appalled at the prospect. *That might work for the first stop, but do we recall anything about the eighth? The tenth? Do we even know how many stops there have been since the buggers first laid their hands on us?*

No one did.

And where would we go anyway? Common Sense continued. *How long do we honestly think we would survive? Just look at that bone-dry ground. Lord knows when we'd see water.*

This was an excellent point. When most people think of being cut adrift in the African bush, they worry about being savaged by a hungry lion or rogered by a horny hippo. The reality is that heat, sun, and lack of cover are likely to kill you long before the animals. They'll just snack on you later.

Look at the state of us, Common Sense said with a remorseless combination of prudence and logic. *What are we going to do? Survive on seeds and fruit picked out of dung? Can you really see us filtering water from fresh elephant shit through our shirt? If nothing else, the dry-cleaning bills will be ruinous.*

Again, these were all good points, but to Pride's delight it didn't matter. When you've trained as long and as hard as I have for eventualities like this, such protestations fall on deaf ears. Pride was in his element, conjuring scenes of Bushman Mac spinning baobab bark into twine to light fires, bedecking himself with ostrich eggshells to carry food and water, then fashioning a knobkerrie out of lethally dense hardwood to smash in the brains of any passing adversaries. I even harboured luxurious notions of settling down with a good book and a pile of Kalahari apple leaves (softer and stronger than any quilted toilet paper, I can tell you). All these romantic images and more flashed before my eyes, priming mind and body for the adventure that lay ahead. It was now or never.

With a rush of adrenaline, I began my daring bid for freedom. To my right, a couple of locals stopped unloading crates from the plane, brushed the dust from their immaculate green military uniforms, and stared silently at events as they unfolded.

Ha! Pride yelled in defiance. *This is the last you'll see of us!*

I was off. Gone. Free! They watched me cross the ground,

heading for the treeline. Over the parched earth I hobbled, coming ever closer to the dense bush and freedom. Go, Mac, go!

The spectators exchanged bored looks and ambled over to engage in a dramatic low-speed pursuit. Soon they tired of my shambolic gait and pushed me on the ground with an indifference that was embarrassing for everyone. The two men bent over me as I lay coughing in the dust, their grimaces revealing bright white teeth that shone against their dark skin. Then they turned on their heels and marched over to the Mallice operatives, with whom they exchanged short, terse words. My local hosts didn't seem to like whatever instructions were being handed out and returned stern-faced to drag my weary frame across the baked earth towards a dust-covered sedan.

In its glory days, this car was no doubt the pride and joy of a corrupt government minister or, ahem, incorruptible NGO (they're impossible to distinguish by their vehicles, you know). Now it looked tired and frustrated, slumped low on its suspension, rust creeping around the wheel arches and into its nether regions. The boot creaked in protest as the men bundled me inside.

Lying in my latest coffin I could see the vast airplane, crouched ready on the runway; the secret police officers making their way back on board without a second glance; the crates – with their Black Saltire of Caledon brands – stacked neatly by the runway, seemingly forgotten in the sunshine. An intense feeling of loss washed over me. These were the last threads connecting me to another world. Another time.

The engines roared to life and the plane began its taxi to the far end of the strip. As it circled to face the runway the aircraft was still for a moment, its nose pointing directly at me at the edge of the strip, as if staring at one of its own for one last time. Then the pitch of the engines changed and the massive transporter came lumbering down the airstrip, faster and faster until it tore itself out of gravity's grip and swept over our heads. Moments later it was nothing more than a pinprick in the blue. In a few moments more it would disappear, severing the final link to the place I called home. I stared, desperate to hang on to its last moments. But they wouldn't even give me that. The boot slammed down, plunging me into darkness. Cutting the cord.

CHAPTER 3

Mwari Inzwai Tsitsi Nhamo Ini Muno

If you've never been bundled into a boot, let me tell you how it goes, as I regard myself an expert in this field. Firstly, it hurts. You don't fold in neatly, particularly if you're as tall as I am. Your head encounters something hard, making your brain bounce in your skull, sending shockwaves of pain from temple to temple. Next, some part of you will make contact with the detritus therein. And there is always detritus. When was the last time you saw an empty boot? You should be suspicious of anyone with an empty boot, for they are certainly some kind of maniac. In this case, the detritus was a wheel jack that proved an effective substitute for a kidney punch and left me gasping for breath.

Next, if you're lucky, your kidnappers – perhaps through lack of preparation or being financially disadvantaged – will have brought a small vehicle. If that's the case, you won't be staying in the boot long as it simply won't shut. Of course, they'll give it a bloody good go, compounding your woes. But then comes the wonderful moment when, in their frustration, they drag you back out and throw you onto the back seat. There you lie, sure in the knowledge that the dusty, smelly cloth is better than the softest down that e'er was plucked from the plumpest Hungarian goose.

After this routine had taken its course in exactly the manner I have described, I lay on the shabby but forgiving fabric of the back seat and attempted to analyse my position. The ledger read thus: firstly, if this was an airstrip designed to land a plane of that size, we were within striking distance of civilisation. Moreover, judging by the manner of my transport, I was not an official visitor and thus was unknown to the local constabulary. Taken together, these facts raised tantalising visions of escape and shelter if I could just get more of a head start on my guards. Hope springs eternal, does it not?

Plagued by ill-conceived optimism and poorly formed plans, I raised my head to look out the window. A thin sheen of yellow dust limited my vision, but not as much as the huge hand – it would be more accurate to call it a paw – that enveloped my head and forced it back onto the musty fabric.

'Down! Now!' a deep voice barked. 'No look! Eyes shut!'

The paw crashed down again on the side of my head, embedding my cheek an inch into the seat. The same paw then grabbed my hair, pulling my head back up so a strip of cloth could be tied around my eyes. There was a brief period of quiet as doors opened and closed with a squeak and a clunk, before the engine spluttered into life, and we were on our merry way. The cadence of the engine surprised me, but then I realised it must be petrol-driven. How quaint. After a brief period, we turned off the smooth tarmac of the road and bumped along a track before everything became smooth again. Not long after that I felt a strange sliding sensation, as if the car was slipping from side to side as it drove along. To my knowledge, only driving in thick sand offers that sensation, which meant we were venturing far from the beaten track. Eventually, we halted and the engine cut out.

The ensuing silence lay thick on me like a blanket: the deep silence you only find miles from civilisation where there is no ambient noise. No drifting hubbub of conversation. No electrical buzz. No whirr of drones in the sky. Silence of the kind money can't buy anymore.

But it was not the kind of silence I could afford, nor would be

15

afforded. The door next to my head was wrenched open and voices yelled in a language I didn't understand. Rough hands grabbed my arms and dragged me out. As soon as my feet cleared the door, they dropped me onto the baked earth. A small cloud of dust rose and sent me into agonising spasms of coughing.

When this subsided, the silence returned. I lay, muscles tensed, adrenaline coursing through me, as I waited for the next act of abuse. None came. The peace was broken only by the faint sound of cowbells clanging, carried on the barest of breezes from far away. The air still had that earthy quality to it, but was growing steadily warmer. It felt as if it was expanding around me, the heat pressing against my skin. If I were to take a stab at the time, I'd have guessed mid-morning. It was a long time since the soil had seen rain, and it was parched and unyielding as concrete. Small, sharp rocks laced the surface, ensuring maximum discomfort for anyone foolish enough to lie on them.

I listened. There was no sound now. Even the cows had left me. Gingerly, I moved my head up, catching the blindfold on a stone and easing it down. On any other day, the sight before me would have taken my breath away, but my broken ribs were already fulfilling that function admirably. I was lying on a small plateau, but ahead the land fell away several hundred metres to the edge of a huge lake. It must have been half a mile wide and disappeared over the horizon, making me wonder if it wasn't an inlet of the sea. Then I spied movement. Creatures – little more than black dots – were loping to the edge of the water and drinking from it. That meant it couldn't be saltwater. I saw one bring its head up and send an arc of water over its back, as elephants are wont to do.

Surrounding this monstrous lake was fifty metres or so of green scrub. At a distance it looked like a well-manicured lawn, its extremity marking the high-water line. The greenery gave way to bushes – perhaps small trees or the horrible, spiked acacia bushes – that

16

generously covered the dark brown earth and no doubt hid numerous beasties with big, pointy teeth. Moving further from the edge of the water, the ground rose up on both sides of the lake to low hills that couldn't have been more than a couple of hundred metres high. With my hillside joining the two sides together, it resembled a natural Circus Maximus. Then there was the sky. If you haven't seen an African sky on a glorious day, it's difficult to do it justice in words. It just seems so vast and deep and rich and blue. It's the difference between paddling in the shallows that make up one's native firmament and plunging headlong into the deep end. I marvelled at how small and irrelevant I was in the cosmic scheme of things, which put my sufferings into context and was oddly comforting. It seemed as if Mother Nature had experienced an epiphany here, put down the knuckledusters, and decided to make love, not war.

But what of humanity's achievements? Evidence was limited. I'd estimate the plateau was twenty metres by thirty. The main structure was a single-storey, rectangular building with whitewashed walls and framed at the far end by a large tree with blazing red leaves. The only other building was a small, unpainted concrete structure with a rusting, corrugated iron roof. It stood alone on the other side of the plateau, sporting no doors or windows. *Some sort of storeroom*, I thought, before noticing something rather odd. Low down on one side, a water pipe entered the wall and another one left it just below. Why would a storeroom need running water?

There was no time to dwell on this, as a wooden door at one end of the white building was thrown open and out marched my two guardians, resplendent in their green uniforms. As they strode over, I looked at them properly for the first time, forgetting I was supposed to be blindfolded. Either they didn't notice or they no longer cared. I was on their turf now, far behind enemy lines. They were tall – perhaps not as tall as me, but each around the six-foot mark. The one on the right was a beast of a man. His chest strained at the buttons of his uniform; I suspected they simply didn't make them large enough for him. His sleeves were rolled midway up his forearms, where the fabric could go no further, and the muscles rivalled my thighs for size. His face was large and square, with a wide, flat nose that looked as if it had been broken, although God alone knew who'd have picked a fight with him. He'd have given Archie a good run for his money, although if it had come to it, I'd have still backed my man. (It's hard to beat someone who was taught from a tender age that 'You'll never lose a fight if you're willing to put your thumbs in another man's eyes.' A wise woman, Archie's mum.)

The huge guard strode towards me. I decided to call him Big Yin. His companion was wiry and lighter on his feet. He reminded me of a long-distance runner as he hurried across the dirt with bouncing steps, trying to keep up with the mighty strides of his colleague. I christened him Spurtle, as his build reminded me of a porridge-stirring stick. (You can take the boy out of Caledon, but never Caledon out of the boy.) His face was thinner than Big Yin's, with a high forehead and eyes that were bright, intelligent, and unmistakably malevolent.

Both guards sported that uniquely unforgiving scowl, accentuated by impressive bone structure, that you see on the faces of any half-decent African despot's personal guard, suggesting 'Forgiveness and mercy are no longer employed here. Thank you for your enquiry. This communication will now self-destruct.' That said, there was a rawness about them, a refreshing spontaneity that contrasted with the calculated indifference of the Mallice. I wondered if they might be reasoned with.

Almost without breaking stride, they scooped me off the ground. I expected to be taken into the white building that appeared to be their barracks. Instead, we made a beeline for the small outbuilding. We circled round to the right of the little concrete bunker and the horror of it was revealed. This was no storeroom. In the middle of

18

the bare wall was a heavy, rust-caked iron door with a small letter-box-shaped slot at eye level. Three heavy iron hinges dominated the left-hand edge, secured in place by large round rivets. On the right was a wide, flat metal bolt that appeared to be welded in place by time and the elements.

Big Yin let go of me and I sagged in Spurtle's arms, whereupon he spat out a stream of indecipherable invective. Probably worried I'd crease his uniform. I staggered upright in a bid to show willing. Anything that could endear me to my captors would help ease my passage through the troubled times ahead. Standing up was small beer, but I wasn't capable of much else and, anyway, I doubted there was time to build a rapport through mutual taste in literature.

Big Yin was heaving at the bolt, muscles bulging with the effort. It gave way, sliding back with a screeching that betrayed a long lack of employment. Then, mighty hands curled round its edges, he dragged open the door. It took up the bolt's song with its own tortured harmonies.

Their strong arms took my weak ones and thrust me inside. With a deft flick of a knife that revealed much practice, Spurtle cut the bonds from my hands and the blood rushed back to my fingers like a hundred burning needles sliding through my veins. As I clenched, stretched, and massaged my hands, Spurtle said something in the language I didn't understand before repeating it at a yell. The added aggression was as much of a translation as I needed. I stumbled back from the door, deeper into the cell. The two men hauled the screaming metal shut, leaving me in the twilight of my prison. The bolt was dragged into place, complaining bitterly as it went, and Big Yin and Spurtle's footsteps, soft on the hard ground, receded. All was silent once more.

In the gloom I took in my new accommodation. The window-less walls were made of rough concrete and, for the first of a thousand times, I paced it out. Six steps by nine.

Six steps by nine.

Six steps by nine.

The only light source was a thin crack that ran around the length of the cell, where the roof was raised by a couple of inches from the walls. As the blazing sun rose high in the empty sky and the metal roof rained down incessant waves of heat, the reason for this strange construction became evident: it was to stop inhabitants from suffocating.

The room was bare except for a small concrete partition, perhaps a metre high and six inches thick, which protruded at right angles from the wall at the far end of the cell. I approached it warily and peered over the top. Nothing leapt out and hit me, which was a welcome change. Instead, it shielded a small area that contained a squat concrete bowl that – holy of holies! – had water in it. A toilet. So, this was an en suite cell. How thoughtful.

As my eyes continued to adjust in the half-light, words and pictures began to swim out of the shadows. Like a crude mural, they were carved into the concrete in different sizes and scripts. Some messages were in English: MUFUNGA ARRESTED 17/03/96 AFTER STEALING BOBOJANI + FUEL TANK. 5 DAYS HERE SO FAR. Others were more simple confessions: M CHENS 22/04 – 24/04 BOAT THEFT. Some were just names: STEPHAN CHOMURUME. Others were just words: DETAINED. One inmate clearly had defiance on his mind, having carved an AK-47 rifle with surprising artistic sensibility into the wall and christened the stock 'Crispen', of all things.

One message stood out amongst the names, confessions, pleas, and other inscrutable inscriptions. It was in much bigger letters, each about a foot high, and covered a large proportion of one of the end walls. Oddly, no one had touched it. Many of the other engravings had suffered at the hands of others leaving their mark, but this one was immaculate, with a respectful few inches left all around it before the silent cacophony began again.

I traced my fingers over the letters with unaccountable reverence. What could it mean? And why had the previous inhabitants treated it with such veneration? I sat down on the floor, cross-legged, and stared at it. But I could find no clues. It seemed important. It spoke to me. But whether it was imparting a blessing, a threat, or the local bus timetable was impossible to judge.

There I remained until a nagging voice in the back of my mind grew so loud that I could ignore it no longer. It turned out to be The Training, once more dragging me back onto parade and berating me for not pulling my finger out. The Training then passed the responsibility down the chain of command to The Rules. As instructed, I dutifully trailed a shaky finger across the rough grey floor, creating an imaginary checklist. It read:

1. Remain positive (tough one, that).
2. Stay clean (it's important both for your health and so your captors aren't encouraged to treat you like the animal you are starting to resemble).
3. Do whatever you can to facilitate your captors' wishes and engage with them on a human level (to keep yourself in one piece, form a bond, and make it less likely they'll want to kill you).
4. Have a routine (so you retain a semblance of normality in your mind at least, and don't go potty).

All The Rules went to hell pretty much immediately when the door was dragged open, screeching on its hinges as Spurtle sprang in. I scrabbled to my feet and backed away from him. He screamed in his impenetrable language, launched himself forward, and cracked me across the stomach with the kind of leadwood knobkerrie I had fantasised about on the airfield. I replied to his greeting with the customary 'Oof!' and crumpled onto the floor. Then he really laid in. He asked no questions; he just beat me senseless. I cried out that I was a Good Citizen, but either he didn't understand or he didn't care. Perhaps someone had told him it was a lie.

When Spurtle took a break, I lay groaning and exhausted on the concrete floor. I offered no resistance because I knew and understood Spurtle's greeting only too well. It's a dominance exercise that aficionados call 'tenderising the meat', and I'm sorry to say I've taught this vile practice to men just like that vicious beanpole on several occasions. The idea is for the captor to make it clear that you – the victim – are at their mercy. You are nothing. They are God Almighty. Sometimes, to really mess with you, this aggression is mixed with acts of kindness, such as the giving of food, as well as constant changes in schedule. In that way, they break you. It's inevitable and I've never seen it fail.

The Rules lay in tatters but I was keen to salvage something from the encounter, so I turned to the only gambit I had left. Rule 3: Engage with your captor on a human level. As Spurtle turned to leave, I slowly raised my tenderised form, and croaked at him as best I could.

'Wait! Spur . . . I mean, sir. There, on the wall: *Mwari inzwai tsitsi nhamo ini muno*. What does it mean?'

He stopped and stared back at me, a quizzical look on his face. I reached out and jabbed a trembling finger at the carved words.

'*Mwari inzwai tsitsi nhamo ini muno*,' I repeated, the alien sounds getting caught in my swollen mouth.

His eyes moved to the wall, then back to me. He started grinning.

'*Mwari inzwai tsitsi nhamo ini muno*,' Spurtle repeated, relishing each syllable. Then he laughed. It was a high-pitched, singsong laugh that echoed around the cell, yet betrayed no hint of human compassion. In halting English, he said, 'It means God have the mercy on me here.'

He giggled that chilling laugh once more and then was gone, leaving the door barred behind him. I stared at those words for a long time, and then I did something I had not done since I was a child. I prayed. All I got in return was silence. The likes of me don't get their prayers answered – or they certainly shouldn't, at any rate.

Sometime later, Big Yin appeared. He marched through the door and laid this damned typewriter at my feet, demanding I 'Write the Wolf' (his face betraying even more confusion about this order than mine). Eventually, having listened to Pride and Common Sense argue it out in my head, I sat down to write.

Soon I ran into problems. Having charted my journey to Africa, I found myself flummoxed, with no idea how to proceed. I sat for hours, slowly roasting as the sun blazed a path over the metal roof. Then, late in the afternoon, a faint smell of wood smoke drifted into my prison cell. All of a sudden I was transported back to the smouldering ruin of a once proud monument . . . to a fiend with a mask of blood rushing out of the dark . . . to the sickening crack as the poor man's nose broke . . . to a primal howl echoing down the valley . . .

And then I knew exactly where I should start: the good old days.

CHAPTER 4

See You, Jimmy

The night that seared the Wolf of Badenoch onto the psyche of Caledon – perhaps even the world – began as peacefully as any other in the Highlands. There was fire, blood, and anguish to come, but the dark mountains slipped by in silence as we ate up the miles towards our target. The peace and majesty of that timeless place endured as ever it had, belying the miasma of tyranny that had settled over my homeland.

We passed few vehicles on the road and saw fewer people. Those on show shuffled by, wrapped up warm, doing their time under the darkening sky. I wondered how many dreamed of escape. How many had a plan? Not many, I'd wager. We were miles from the cities but the wide-open fields and purple hills were still maximum security.

I realised I was humming tunelessly when informed of it by the scowl in the rear-view mirror. It was hardly my fault. Not only was I sober, I had been sober for weeks. You can't plan a national outrage properly without a clear head. But, by God, I needed a drink now. I contemplated continuing with the humming to ease my growing fears but the scowl made me stop. You mustn't anger chauffeurs. They are members of that untouchable class of service providers who wield complete power and must be obeyed. Like waiters or customs officers, they are uncompromising and wield their powers mercilessly (often at the expense of your nether regions).

The car's electric engine hummed as it ferried us silently onwards to treason. The electricity had come back on just in time for us to charge the battery, which had been a stroke of luck but also a reminder of just how decayed and decrepit the country had become during our golden age.

That cold, clear evening marked fifteen long years to the day since the rise of the Marischal. Fifteen years since the people of Caledon were roused from their slumber with promises of nettles to be grasped, destinies to be wrestled with, and potential to be fulfilled. Fifteen years since its citizens quietly lay down under the boot of fascism and ushered in a time of misery unseen since the Highland Clearances. At least, I think that's how it happened. To be honest, I wasn't paying attention at the time.

As I sat in the darkness it seemed almost impossible to think of a time when the Marischal was not there to protect, direct, and punish us when we strayed from the true path. Worse, it felt ludicrous to believe that I would be the one to change it. I shook my head, as if that would blow the doubts away. But silence and darkness are uneasy bedfellows for a coward. I looked out the window, trying to take succour from the power and splendour of the land I fought to liberate. But for all their grandeur, the towering hills that slid past were nothing more than passive observers.

I turned to the job at hand. I thought desperate, happy thoughts about destruction and devastation; about a job well done. But still darkness and silence intruded. They took hold and dragged me away from the night ahead and into the past. They ushered in the weight of history, which came at me, fists flailing. In that instant I was witness to the Marischal's terrible reign. To the isolation he brought in the name of progress; to his breaking down of a people so they might be rebuilt; to the relentless categorisation and definition of his subjects so that we might express ourselves as he saw fit. And worst of all on a night like this, I watched him unleash the Devil's Wind – a campaign of repression and reprisal by his secret police, the Mallice.

The fine men and women of the Marischal Police Department – and their psychotic leader, Thomas Loker – were rarely far from my mind in those days, but on this particular evening they felt close enough for me to reach out and touch (like putting my quaking fingers into a cage of rabid dogs). When you're about to do something as naughty as I was, it's impossible to ignore these highly effective purveyors of ferocity and intimidation, of wretchedness and suffering. And while I doubted they were as naturally gifted at delivering violence as my man Archie, they had received a lot more training. They were bound together by a shared love of atrocity and backed up by enough data algorithms, AI, drones, and satellite surveillance to warm the heart of the most demanding despot. Whatever you did and wherever you went, you left a shadow. And they were the stealers of shadows. You would expect nothing less from a group led by a lunatic who lovingly displayed the polished skulls of his victims. Goddamn Loker. Someone has to.

All told, on that anniversary of the Marischal's triumph, Caledon was a fearful, bleak country, where sorrows came in battalions and hope cowered behind the sofa. Just looking around the car was a reminder of how alone we were. The vehicle was probably the last connected car on the road that was entirely unconnected to anything. (The environmentalist in you will throw your hands up and wail about the return of traffic jams, poisonous clouds, and vicious road rage to our streets if my vehicle couldn't talk to the transport system – and you may be right. I'd just say I hope you never have the small matters of arrest, The Question, and your own execution to worry about, as I did.)

With history so intent on intruding, I tried to reminisce. I looked for inspiration in the terrifying stories of my childhood that detailed dark, dystopian worlds and the heroic folk who brought them down. But all that happened was I ended up mulling over how different our tyranny was to those tales. How there were no booming public address systems to proclaim the Marischal's benevolence and generosity. How there was no all-seeing eye staring accusingly from screens and billboards every minute. Our oppression was different. It was a creeping, insidious one. It was always there, always watching, but it did not need eyes. It was our partner in every step we took, every decision we made. It was part of us: the natural consequence of becoming so accepting of our digital humanity, of our willingness to carry devices that wrapped surveillance in tawdry, synapse-firing entertainments. Our oppression had been with us for years and it did not need its own eyes. It had ours.

Nor were we in the land of gleaming futuristic towers and flying cars that the stories promised us. I don't know why that was – maybe the economics of despotism just didn't stack up. Or, more likely, those who might have driven us towards that beautiful, sustainable future had been employed in more lofty pursuits, like building gambling algorithms or developing apps that tricked children into buying dragon gems. No, Caledon was the same dank, wild, and beautiful country I remembered from the Scotland of my youth. Except it was hotter now. Thank God for global warming.

My fingers strayed to the golden bracelet around my wrist, the names on it hidden in the darkness. Normally the old woman's jewellery acted as an inspiration – a power source that fired up indignation and anger. But the little letters carved into the 18 carats seemed so inconsequential now. By God, when did things get so out of hand?

Shifting in my seat, I accidentally kicked the ancient metal biscuit tin in the footwell. It made a hollow but reassuring sound. The tin held all our electronic devices, rendering them invisible to both satellite trackers and drones. It was a tranquil island of disconnectivity, and on hand in case the electromagnetic field around the car failed. Quite unnecessary really, and I suspect only there to satisfy Archie's shortbread addiction.

In the old days we'd have had a team supporting us in a crazy venture like this. There would have been flashing buttons, buzzing comms, and incessant garbled orders. Surveillance teams would be on the ground, dashing intelligence officers would be briefing them on radios in curt and heroic terms, and office geeks would be crunching data, triangulating signals, and cursing the lack of doughnuts. We would all have exciting code names: the Bravos on their bikes, the Charlies in their cars, and the Zeros on foot, cold and alone in the dark, annoyed that no one was taking the time to appreciate the irony of their cipher.

But those days were gone. I focused on what team I did have with me. He was a solid and reassuring silhouette in the driver's seat and – goddamn it! – wearing that bloody chauffeur's hat again. I'm sure he only did it to take the mickey, but it was impossible to tell. Archie Dhugal Fraser was about six foot six. I say 'about', having never been stupid enough to measure him. A thatch of messy black hair sat atop a big round head that bore many scars. These did not come from the daring life-and-limb missions we used to enjoy together: he was too much of a professional. No, these were almost all from spur-of-the-moment pub fights. Life out of the military was hard for Archie, you see. He simply couldn't get enough of smashing people's faces in.

Archie moved like a gorilla that has mastered ballet, but one that retained the prerogative to tear you limb from limb if you were silly enough to make such a comparison. A man of few words – perhaps because he just didn't know that many, I was never sure – he was my right-hand man. He was sometimes predictable, mostly respectful, and absolutely deadly. A demonic butler and insurance policy, all rolled into one.

'Archie,' I said, with a carefree air that was breathtaking in its dishonesty.

'Everythin' a'right, Mr Mac?'

'Yes, yes. A quick pub quiz, I thought. A bottle of the good stuff and a weekend off with no questions asked about any new scars, if you get all the answers.'

'A quiz aboot whit?'

'The big picture stuff. You know, the stuff that'll keep the train on the rails if I'm gone.'

'Aw, come on, Mr Mac. Yeh know ah'd no' let anythin' happen tae yeh. No' tonight, or any ither night.'

'Yes, yes, of course, Archie, but you never know. Humour me, eh?'

The big eyes bored into me from the rear-view mirror. 'Aye, OK.'

Relief flooded through me at this opportunity for distraction. 'Round one is the Bloody Regime Change round. Ready?'

'OK, but if ah get them a', then it's no' jist a weekend. It's a long weekend. Monday an' a'.'

'Oh, all right. Your time starts . . . now! Name the five things you need if you're planning armed insurrection.'

Archie's face broke into a grin and he warmed to his task, big hands drumming on the steering wheel. 'Right then, Mr Mac. Number one: the right people. Trained, motivated, and hangin' oot where they should be. Aye?'

'A strong start.'

'Then there's the right tools, obviously.'

'Screwdrivers? Hammers? What?'

'Aw, Jeez, come oan. Arms caches in dumps a' aroond the country.'

'But what if you can't organise that?'

'Then ah prioritise, obviously, don't ah?'

'Example?'

'Well, one kilo o' high explosive is enough tae destroy a whole power station, so worth keeping some o' that handy, eh?'

'Quite right. Next?'

'Intelligence, aye? And before yeh make some glaikit* joke, ah mean the secretive kind, don't ah.'

'Why?'

'So yeh can pinpoint high-value targets, obviously. Maximum bang fer yer buck, eh?' Archie giggled. He found himself tremendously funny on occasion – usually in circumstances when I was trying not to soil myself. But then he was brave and I was nothing of the sort.

'Tell me what a high-value target is.'

'Somethin' that interrupts people's daily life as much as possible.'

'Why?'

'Look, Mr Mac, this is much more than five questions—'

'*Why?* Archie. This is important.'

'Och, keep yer hair oan. It's cuz yeh've got tae show that the rulin' body cannae protect its citizens properly. Yeh know, make the populace lose confidence in its governors an' so oan.'

'Good. Two more to go, come on.'

'Willpower, aye? That's no' hard.'

'Not hard to guess, no. Harder to pull off.'

'Och, yeh worry tae much, Mr Mac.'

'Just you wait until you're running the show. Just you wait until you're the one dealing with the constant improvisation, the shortages, and the stony faces of an ungrateful nation. Anyway, what's the last one? Your long weekend all hangs on this.'

'Oh, it's . . . Hang oan . . . Oh bluidy hell, whit is it?'

'Tick tock, Archie.'

'Jesus Christ . . . Ha! Ah've got it! Money: lots and lots of fucken money, eh? Nailed it! That's mah long weekend in the bank.'

'Congratulations, Archie, you have completed this module of the Insurgent's Handbook. If we survive the night, you can put your holiday in the diary first thing tomorrow.'

* Stupid or foolish.

I debated introducing him to the final and most complex rule of all: the tiny, secret, interior deadness that is so crucial to this line of work. The ability to launch yourself into the stratosphere and blithely orbit events, people, issues, and ramifications without being crushed under the weight of the stress, collateral damage, loss, and endless permutations that could result from every decision you make. As it turned out, such considerations would have to wait.

'Roadblock, Mr Mac,' Archie's brusque voice cut in.

Up ahead, emerging from the gloom, was a man in a black bulletproof vest. Our headlights lit him up as he strode into the middle of the road and waved us down. Behind him a car jutted out from the verge, blocking the lane. Another man was leaning on the bonnet, a machine pistol cradled in his arms as he rubbed his cold hands together.

'Sitrep, Archie,' I ordered, instinct taking over.

'Two o' them, disnae look like they're pigs though. Just regular polis.'

'Pigs' were what Archie called Mallice operatives. There was a clear note of disappointment in his voice. He did so like a challenge.

'One wi' a UMP45 in his hands,' Archie continued his appraisal. 'Och, gi'e me the old MP5 any day. This bugger oot in the road disnae seem to be carrying. Probably left it in the car. Pure dolly,* man.' He tapped the display on the dashboard. 'Thermal's no' showin' anyone else oot there. Just these two. Well shan** fer them.'

'Take a deep breath, Archie,' I said. 'You know the drill. No unpleasantness unless it absolutely can't be helped. We've got bigger things to think about.'

The disappointment was palpable in the narrow eyes that glowered at me from the rear-view mirror. We slowed down and the purr of the engine gave way to silence as we halted a few feet from

* Foolish or idiotic.

** Not very fair.

the plod. Archie's window slid down and, with what he no doubt considered his most winning smile, he addressed the policeman.

'Whit can a' do fae yeh, officer?'

The poor man recoiled slightly at that scarred and toothless visage before regaining his composure. 'Your ID,' came the barked order. 'Now!'

Archie handed the officer the card, which he stared hard at.

'Are you a Good Citizen?'

'Aye, ah'm a Good Citizen.'

It's taken Archie years of therapy to say that without hitting anyone. Nonetheless, I saw his hands tighten on the steering wheel and, for the sake of both officers' health, wound down my window. A look of shock appeared on the officer's face. He stared at me, unblinking.

'*Feasgar math*, officer, *Caledon gu bràth!*'* I said, offering up the regulation patriotic greeting. 'How goes your evening vigil?'

He remained stunned for a second before beginning to garble. 'Mac, wow, I mean, Mr Macfarlane . . . I didn't realise. Hey, Callum, I mean, Officer Robertson, look who it is! It's the man himself, *Jimmy Mac*. Good evening, Jim – I mean, sir.'

'No need for all that; I'm a mere servant of Caledon like yourself,' I replied, self-deprecating weasel that I am. 'A Good Citizen, of course, you don't need to ask.'

Before I could move, hands were thrust through the open window, grabbing mine and shaking them heartily.

'What brings you out in the cold?' I asked, reclaiming my fingers.

'It's the Wolf,' explained the overawed arm of the law. 'You know, the Badenoch bastard who's been attacking the roads and rails.' (I won't bore you with our previous missions because they were small beer – trials, really. Suffice to say they had already

* Good evening, officer, Caledon forever!

32

secured the Wolf a bad name, even if it was nothing compared to what was ahead.)

'Oh, and the water supply.' Officer Callum crowded the window to get a better view of yours truly. 'I'm so sorry about that. I hope it hasn't hit you too hard. We all rely on you, of course!'

They both laughed nervously, impressed and subdued by my presence. Celebrity has its perks, to be sure. Glancing forward I noticed Archie's eyes still locked on our loquacious law enforcers, his fingertips now the only point of contact with the steering wheel. This was not a good sign. He was ready to strike. I desperately needed to avoid the police doing something silly, like thinking they were in charge of the situation.

'I'm not going to lie, lads,' I announced, adopting my Serious Face, 'the attack on the spring is making business difficult, but we are prepared for emergencies – though perhaps none so malicious as this.' I paused and they nodded gravely. It was nice to see the Wolf's destruction of the aquifer – an intentional act of self-harm and obfuscation – paying off. 'Look, I'm terribly sorry to inconvenience you, but we are overdue for dinner with Lord Farquharson – and you know how he can be with tardy guests, I'm sure.'

Well, of course they didn't but, as any psychologist will tell you, bringing people in on something – even if they have no interest or involvement in it – is the first step to securing their cooperation. It also helps to name-drop, as this intimidates and impresses if done well. And I'm great at it.

'Oh, aye,' Officer Callum said. 'But I'm afraid we're still going to have to search your car. Orders to check everyone. I'm sorry, but, you know, the Wolf . . .' He tailed off in embarrassment.

'I completely understand, officer, you must do your duty. I'm afraid all you'll find in the boot is guns.'

Officer Callum was somewhat taken aback by this news and unconsciously put a hand on the stock of his machine pistol.

I pretended not to notice. 'A fine old Joseph Lang and a cheeky Russian Baikal – a ratting gun, of course, but a heavy hitter.'

Archie shook his head, struggling to cope with my appalling snobbery. The officers looked confused, so I helped them out.

'Shotguns, you see? We're shooting at Invereiton Estate with Lord Farquharson tomorrow.'

'Of course, sir,' said Officer Callum. 'But we'll still have to look.'

Tread carefully, Mac, murmured Common Sense out of the darkness.

'Look wherever you please,' I replied, all smiles. 'Archie, would you be an angel and open the boot for the officers?'

There was no way I was letting the police examine the contents alone. Archie climbed out of the car, causing the two officers to step back as he towered over them.

'The boot's a bit temperamental, you see. Can't open it from inside,' I added to keep things moving. 'My valet will need to do it.'

Archie marched to the rear. If the police had been better at their jobs, they might have remarked on how lightly he moved for a big man. He messed about with the fingerprint recognition, cursing in a way I thought was a bit over the top, before hefting up the boot. Cold air rushed into the car, making me shiver.

I heard him click open the gun cases and mutter, 'There's yon guns,' as he retreated just behind the officers. I prayed it would be a cursory search. A rigorous investigation would reveal a stash of weapons and explosives, hidden beneath the shotguns in the space normally reserved for a spare wheel. Such a discovery would prove detrimental to the officers' well-being, and their bodies would be a good deal harder to fix than the situation if Archie got involved. To my relief – and, I suspect, Archie's disappointment – the cases were quickly shut and locked. I was not surprised. If you know a better place to hide illegal guns than beneath legal guns, then I'd like to hear it.

'We'll wish you a good night then, sir,' said Officer Callum, who had returned to me, and to looking starstruck. 'Sorry to have detained you unnecessarily.'

'And a good night to you, officers. Don't worry, it was no trouble at all.'

Archie returned to the car in a grump and we had started to pull away when I ordered him to stop.

'Whit's up?' he asked, focused and ready.

'I'll be right back,' I replied. 'Just keep the engine running and turn up the damn heat.'

Taking a deep breath, I clambered out of the car, smoothing down my dinner jacket and straightening my bow tie. I walked back up the dark, silent highway towards the roadblock. The cold stung my skin and I had to work hard to control my breathing as the adrenaline coursed around my body. The glow of the police headlights illuminated my breath, which rose in white clouds ahead of me. The cops, now silhouettes in the car beams, spied an immaculately dressed spectre emerging from the darkness and demanded, in loud voices, that I halt immediately. Two shiny black machine pistols were pointed with conviction at my head. My heart hammered in my chest as I raised my weapons. For a moment nothing happened. Then they lowered theirs. It wasn't a fair fight.

'A couple of bottles of the eighteen-year-old, lads,' I said, marching forward unchecked. 'Port-barrelled. Just to say thanks for your service and to warm the cockles when you get home.'

After that, it was back to smiles, touching of caps, and promises of eternal fealty as I handed over the whisky. Most importantly, no one pointed any more guns at me, which was an immense relief.

'I might ask you a favour, gentlemen,' I murmured, conspiratorially. 'If you would not record this meeting in your log, I would be much obliged. You know how quickly the smallest detail of my life tends to make its way onto the web; I don't want my social calls on the diary sites tomorrow if I can avoid it. It'll go down badly with my hosts.'

'What meeting?' whispered Officer Callum with an exaggerated wink.

God, I'm glad Archie didn't see that; he'd brained people for less.

'Thank you, officers. *Mar sin leat.*'*

'And to you, Mr Macfarlane.'

One threw up the famous Jimmy Mac salute. To their delight, I matched it before turning on my heel in a suitably military fashion and marching back to the car. The men chattered behind me, more like lovesick teenagers than police officers. I wondered if I could trust them to keep schtum. I was a pretty big deal, after all.

Archie had the police scanner fired up when I climbed inside. As we wended our way south, I was delighted to hear it emitting the glorious sound of silence. Outside, the stars shone bright and there was nary a drone in the sky. It was a fitting calm, because all hell was about to break loose.

---

* Goodbye.

CHAPTER 5

Tempus Fuckit

Section 7, Dissident Monitoring (International)
Marischal Police Department, Central Division
Tolbooth, Edinburgh

Mallice Report: #72349
Priority: 1C
MPD Operative ID: 5426
Date recorded: 9/3/38
Location: Brussels, Belgium
Subject: Professor Randolph Spring, currently in unapproved exile

Notes: An edited transcript of a speech given at the launch of
Prof. Spring's autobiography, *Phoenix Risen: The Life and Times
of Professor Randolph Spring*. Audio is taken direct from the live
desk feed so, due to lack of microphones in the crowd, their
questions and interventions have not been captured.

[Tapping of a microphone. Various feedback.]
Is this on? Now, what was I . . . Yes, yes.

[Unintelligible call from the crowd.]
[SPRING] Well, if you weren't here for my earlier talk about the Neo— yes, yes, the *Neo-eisimeileachd,* independence – then I cannot be held responsible. We are here to discuss Finlay's rise, and my time is precious.

[Unintelligible call from the crowd.]
[SPRING] What? Yes, of course Finlay is the Marischal. For God's sake. [Spring muttering. Inaudible.] Come now, *absit invidia,* Randolph. *Absit invidia.*[*]

Can we please start now? You all know how far I have come to be here? What I have suffered? Well then, accord me the respect I deserve and we shall begin. Those who wish to read with me should turn to Chapter Four.

[A pause.]

Let us take a trip down memory lane. Think back to when that tired old moniker, 'the Fourth Industrial Revolution', promised us economic growth, personal empowerment, better health systems, and so on and so on and so on. A dream of equality that collapsed when real power – and by that I mean computer-processing power, of course – simply became concentrated in the hands of the few. Despite their best intentions, those few drove inequality, political polarisation, and social fragmentation.

From the start, Finlay tapped into a latent sense of powerlessness and a deep distrust of institutions. He shifted the nationalist message from civic and inclusive – a sense of shared endeavour for the greater good – to the rhetoric of self-improvement.

He called on individuals to take responsibility and power back for themselves and, in turn, make the country great again. Of

---

[*] No offence intended.

course, *great* meant whatever the listener wanted it to mean, just as long as they played their part.

Very few, myself excluded, had the vision to see this was the first step in preparing us for a campaign of blood and soil, where real blood would be the currency of success. But did they listen to us when we spoke up? No, they did not. Instead, they lapped it up and, looking back, we can see why. It was a world of concentrated power and atomised societies, of data theft and cyber war, of environmental disaster and institutional indifference, of inflated self-worth and the quest for purpose. And there lay Finlay's brilliance. He gave us change and gave us a purpose, knowing full well people had become sick of the consequences of their choices. They needed saving from all that their freedom had brought them. He knew they would no longer stand for being slaves to their own will. And so he made the weight of our choices intolerable, priming us to accept our place as cogs in his machine.

I've put a selection of quotes up on the screen behind me that I think encapsulate the response from the populace at the time . . . Oh, they aren't there yet. Well, perhaps if we give the man with the projector a moment. Right, here we are. I suppose I'll have to read them for you too? Of course I do. Well, pay attention, will you?

> 'Duncan Finlay is real and sincere. We're tired of being cheated. The more they attack him, the more we love him.'
> – Sandra Poulter, Aberdeen

> 'He's brought energy back to the people. They want somebody that's not connected with the government.'
> – Nicolas Adams, Glasgow

> 'I backed Finlay from the beginning. Because he calls things out. He does not allow lies to live.

He just exposes things. Duncan Finlay is not politically correct, and I love that about him.'
– Sarah McComb, Dundee

'He doesn't hold back. You get what he really believes in, even if everything that he says isn't the right thing exactly.'
– Martin Anderson, Edinburgh

So, as you can see, he mined a rich vein of discontent. Of course, a good part of that came from the fact that, after independence, there were no more barbarians at the gate. No one left to blame. But you can read all about that in Chapter Three. Or perhaps there's a film taken of the last talk somewhere. Daniel?

[Unintelligible answer.]

Yes, if you want to know about the Neo, come and ask Daniel – but not until later on – and he will facilitate your access to that film.

So, where were we? Ah, yes. Finlay's political enemies at home and abroad were quick to criticise and to caricature. They scoffed at his quasi-mystical insight into the will of the people. But these critics had missed the point: he *did* understand the people. And he understood them better than anyone had for years. Finlay's true talent was to be just like everyone else, only more so.

[Unintelligible call from the crowd.]

[SPRING] Oh, come now. If I decide there is time at the end, you may get a question. I will see. We will see. But *tempus fugit.** Yes, it does.

[Unintelligible call from the crowd.]

[SPRING] You want me to tell you what?

[Unintelligible call from the crowd.]

[SPRING] No, dammit, I will not talk about that man; that monster they call the Wolf! Do you know what he did to me? To

* Time flies.

my body? To my mind? Do you know what I suffer every day now? All sustained to satisfy his fear and arrogance? He is gone and we are all the better for it. Every day I nurture a hope that I never need hear that name again.

[Pause.]

[SPRING] I have a theory about him, you know. It's not just arrogance and privilege that drives his behaviour. *Witzelsucht*,* you see? Rare neurological disease. He has all the signs. By God, I hope it's a tumour.

[Unintelligible call from the crowd.]

[SPRING] No! You cannot criticise me. You were not there. You do not know the real man. The real animal.

[Long pause.]

[UNCONFIRMED SPEAKER] Professor? Are you . . . Please, someone get him some water. Sophie, please bring up the wheelchair. Professor, are you all right to continue? Professor, can you hear me?

[SPRING] What? Oh, do stop interrupting, Daniel. Pay attention. Now, where were we? Yes, yes. Page 113, for those reading along.

Now we come to the bent and warped doctrine of meritocracy upon which would stand the whole structure of the Marischal's dystopia. I have already touched on Finlay's rhetoric of self-improvement; the idea that the rise of the *individual* would drive the country forwards. He offered us the chance to become a nation where we got what we deserved after years of being short-changed by those with unfair advantages. The Marischal offered a truth that many in the nation *wanted* to hear. And his truth was a broad church. It didn't tie itself to place or time. He was a purveyor of vague dreams full of fancy and wonder. It suited a million different visions of Scotland's future – and it had to serve at least that number of ever-changing

---

* Condition characterised by excessive facetiousness and inappropriate or pointless humour, often caused by brain trauma, stroke or tumour affecting the frontal lobes.

dreams. Social media had long since embedded the manufactured self; we had moulded and remoulded ourselves so often to fit the circumstances, who could say who they really were anymore? The Marischal simply provided a new set of parameters into which we inserted our persona of choice.

Perhaps this notion of equality of opportunity – where outcomes stemmed from no more advantage than your inherent talents – was a pure and fair notion in his mind to start with. I am afraid that even I cannot divine the original intention. Perhaps he didn't have a plan, other than to create a so-called *level playing field*. Perhaps we all give him too much credit now when we look back on the arch-manipulation and cynical disregard for morality that followed. But I doubt it. The Marischal was a man who would make Machiavelli's *Prince* despair at his own amateurish attempts at statecraft.

Of course, debating his original motivation is a fool's errand. It is what he did with this doctrine of meritocracy that matters. Over the two or three short years that followed he took it to extremes, ultimately mandating that altruistic behaviour that was to the benefit of one person over another was an affront. The government was increasingly *forced* – so he said – to become the referee of whether our opportunities and the outcomes that flowed from them were *fair* or *unfair*. In so doing, the regime became the de facto arbiter of our personal ambition. And so this system, which was supposed to reward and differentiate talent, laid the basis of a cruel and oppressive regime that ensured everyone was categorised, allocated, and controlled, according to his or her talents. And, since he had indoctrinated so many in the mantra of individualism, the creation of communities that would have arisen once upon a time – for the common good and to defy oppression – simply never materialised. He cemented this with creations such as The Separation. Once again—

[Unintelligible call from the crowd.]

[SPRING] What? You have not heard of The Separation? How have you not . . . Oh, never mind. Look, it's simple: The Separation filters children based on their talents at an early age, pushing them in certain directions under the banner of maximising the effectiveness of the limited workforce. But its real purpose is to allow the regime to shape a new generation's experience from a young age. Clear? Good. Can we please go on now?

Once again, the Marischal displayed his insight into humanity, knowing, as he did, that perspective is born of life experience. If you can control that experience from a young age, the need for active oppression diminishes as you have already shaped their *normal* – you have imposed *your* truth. He delivered this with false empathy and a certainty that swept people along. You must remember that certainty will always triumph over fact because it is certainty that people look to their leaders for.

A brief aside. You'll notice I mentioned *fact* just then. So much has been said about the notion that we live in the *post-truth environment*. But we always have, have we not? Fact is *what happened*, yes? But facts are meaningless without interpretation. Only once that interpretation is applied do you find your truth. Truth is *why it happened* and *what it means*. Truth is a matter of perspective and has been such since the beginning of recorded time.

So, I say to you that the wailing and gnashing of teeth over a post-truth environment was a distraction, a piece of trickery and misdirection. For while we looked the other way, the Marischal was constructing a post-*fact* environment, leveraging our digital advancement to turn facts – once solid as stone – into something as ephemeral as the truth we sought. It was a landscape where events – evidence – could be eradicated and forgotten at the stroke of a key or the touch of a screen. Gone. And what is history without evidence? It is nothing more than a story, and stories are soon corrupted. When facts are taken away, people forget. And when we have forgotten what has been and what we were, we can be remoulded into what we should be.

[Pause.]

Now, back to the book. We are on page 121. When the election came, Finlay was centre stage and under attack on all sides – just as he wanted. He turned a national debate about his behaviour into a partisan referendum where just one question mattered: whom did you want to win? This wasn't about him; it was about *them*. It was a challenge to vested institutions and perceived wisdom; letting him cloak his murderous plans in a mantle of democratic virtue. It was a call to arms. The distillation of every issue, every permutation, to a binary choice: Finlay's future, or his rivals and the past.

[Pause.]

What? Five minutes more, you say? Yes, yes, I understand. There is so much more to talk about but I see time is stopping for no one, so let us jump forward, past Finlay's election, and relive a democracy's tortured transition to autocracy. Turn to page 187. We reach Scotland's final transformation into Caledon.

We fell faster than Lucifer, although the destination was the same. There were many episodes along the way. In my book you can read about the persecution Finlay began in the name of *Scottishness*, where his truth was elevated to a national virtue. Non-believers were branded Unscottish or Non-Scots and harangued and denounced by the populist movement. Enemies were castigated for the smallest mistakes while supporters were forgiven almost any crime. Some of the faithful took this lesson to heart – so much so that *unexpectedly* became an ever more popular way of dying in Scotland. More and more people became random victims, to the point where randomness became normal and expected. It became government by assassination.

Soon – and it happened very fast – it became clear that the freedom people thought they were winning was actually the freedom to think the same way. The safety that they had looked to their leaders for became safety from the alternative: state-sponsored retribution. But still they embraced it because they understood why it was happening. They understood that, to rise from the mire of someone else's making, all this was *necessary*.

I could go on. I could tell you all about the vicious Sedition Laws. But I have not been afforded enough time and must address the one event that cemented Finlay's place more than any other.

You see, Finlay still had a problem. Imposing a philosophy is one thing, but creating a lasting reality is quite another. That requires embedding a culture, which takes time – and so often dictators don't have that kind of time. But that's when the stars aligned and Finlay knew his destiny was manifest. Because that's when the Second Wave began.

We thought the old pandemic had passed. We had not forgotten counting our dead, day by day, but we had beaten it. We had banded together and we had fought and won. When the Second Wave struck, we knew what to do. Countries had learned. The people had learned. Most importantly of all, Finlay had learned. The only way to stop the virus was to enforce quarantines, bring in stringent social control measures. The populace willingly opened up to a government invasion of their digital identities to aid the contact-tracing operation. The borders were closed. Only this time, they didn't reopen. We were on lockdown. Forever.

[Long pause.]

Now, you all know what I have suffered; the privations I have borne with such fortitude in defiance of the regime. You know that I do not wear the epithet of *hero* lightly. Still, in my book – which you can buy at the back of the room, but only at the end – you will see I have applied academic rigour and balance to this discourse. And you are no doubt asking why the people put up with all this? Well, Finlay was clever enough to realise that dictatorships cannot live on violence alone. Like all good psychopaths, he married suppression with charm and benevolence. If you were, or indeed are, a supporter of the regime, then life in Caledon – as he quickly rechristened it – was tolerable. In fact, one might say it is better than in many other places. If you're living behind The Wall then you've probably got a job and, due to The Separation at school, you're probably quite good at it. All in all, there's a decent chance you will be satisfied, if not happy. There will be food on the table and clean water to drink – at a time when many countries around the world are going to war to secure access to it.

In fact, there are many people who skip happily across the Marischal's hellscape, content to log in to get their Citizen Points and ensure their Citizen Credit Score is high enough to give them access to the products and services they need. You have to remember that the Marischal is a dictator for the modern age. There are no statues or posters of him glaring down on us. There are no public address systems, tethered to lamp posts, blaring orthodoxy in our ears. There is no need for so overt an ogre.

He knows us as well as we know ourselves. He is with us every day, an accomplice to every decision we make. He is in the cables that carry our data; he is in the invisible waves that fill the air; in the satellites that criss-cross the sky. He sees our every move and knows our most intimate desires. He does not need to be seen. The regime does not see us as people; we are information flows. We are numbers and letters. We are data to be collected, analysed, and, where necessary, mercilessly optimised. He is everywhere, taking us in his invisible embrace and ready to crush us. We know that he knows. And he knows that we know that he knows.

But you must not mistake my objectivity for weakness or complicity with the regime. Caledonians may indeed reap the benefits I have laid out, but you must not for one second think free will is part of that compact. If you make that mistake then it's straight to the punishment chambers – the *O-Tanks* – of which you have no doubt heard so much.

[A pause.]

I remember the first person I saw put in there. A woman. Can't have been more than twenty-five. I watched how the panic struck her face. How she clawed at her throat, her nails leaving bloody marks. How she collapsed, before opening her mouth in a silent scream. How they put her through it again and again. I don't even know why. Like so many others, I was just there out of curiosity.

[A call from the crowd, followed by a number of others.]

[SPRING] What? Haven't I already . . . Look, I don't care what they did to that man. Why would you grasp such a creature – that lupine sociopath – to your shallow, callous breasts? My God. You think James Macfarlane a hero, don't you? All of you. You've bought into the jingoistic myth. Well, I won't have it. Tell me, would a hero do *this* to me?

[Exclamations of shock from the crowd.]

Oh yes, I will tell you the truth about him. Yes, yes, the truth will out. [Shouting] The truth will out!

[The sound of a scuffle and a bang, followed by audio feedback, likely caused by the microphone being dropped on the floor.]

[UNCONFIRMED SPEAKER] Sophie, please help the professor to his wheelchair. Ladies and gentlemen, quiet please. No, no pictures. You see before you a hero. A man who has borne more than any of us could imagine. Professor? Can we have some help here?

[Ends.]

CHAPTER 6

Via the Back Passage

After our brush with the law on that dark, freezing motorway, the journey returned to the same mundane and sweat-inducing routine as before.

'Archie,' I said, breaking the silence. 'Estimated time until target, if you please?'

'Approximately thirty minutes, Mr Mac,' Archie replied, staring into the beams that forged into the cavernous darkness ahead.

'And time to rendezvous?'

'Approximately ten minutes, Mr Mac.'

'Thank you.'

'Hey, Mr Mac?'

'Yes?'

'When we pick oor boy up, yer no' gonnae let him drone oan wi' a' that techie shite, are yeh? I swear I'll tear his bluidy head aff if he does.'

'My dear Archie, hope springs eternal, but I wouldn't bet the house on it,' I responded, in as disarming a manner as I could. I needed Archie's mind on the task ahead, not on dismembering a fellow team member.

'Och, ah get that he does it tae wind me up, yeh know? But ah cannae help gettin' pure radge.* It's a' baws, so it is.'

'Oh, Archie, I've told you time and again, that's how people like him communicate. They're not natural conversationalists like you.'

---

* Becoming upset.

'Grrrr.'

This growl could have been a word – most likely a naughty one – but it was difficult to tell. One of the most wonderful things about the Glasgow dialect is the pure energy its exponents can channel into swearing. Consonants and vowels crash through gritted teeth in a concert of extraordinary belligerent energy. And while you can't readily understand the words, the message couldn't be clearer.

We continued through the darkness, approaching the grand gateway to Invereiton, home of the Farquharsons. There, we stopped to deposit a couple of highly traceable comms devices (aug-specs, if you're interested) by the roadside in case anyone had chosen to track our movements. Our false digital location established, we drove a few metres past the gate, following the wall marking the boundary of the estate. When it turned away from the road, we followed it down a short, bumpy track into a bank of trees. Archie killed the engine and we rolled to a halt.

Stage one complete.

I stepped out onto the soft ground, taking a deep breath of cold air – 'silver inhalations of the dusk', if you'll pardon me savaging Coleridge. Bright beams of moonlight darted between the spindly black trunks, intermittently lighting up the big man as he opened the boot and began moving equipment from our black 4x4 to a second vehicle hidden in the trees. It was another off-roader, but a different marque and sprayed a deep red.

Archie went about his business in near silence. I stared through the trees, alert to any movement and listening for the high-pitched buzz that would betray any drones above. All was still.

We were almost at the southern reaches of Strathspey and Badenoch, where the noble but unforgiving mountains of the Highlands gave way to the undulating pine forests of Perth and Kinross. As Archie worked, I took in the cloying darkness of the magnificent Cairngorms National Park. The gloom and anonymity wrapped me up like a blanket. All around us the hills were silhouettes under a canopy of stars vaster than one could fathom. These mountains, with their heather, rock, and scree, continued the vigil they had held for millennia. They stood patiently to see what we – their temporary and troublesome tenants – would do next. I had no doubt they would see a free Caledon, even if I would not. It was a comforting thought.

As my eyesight adjusted to the night, I began to pick out small figures on the hillsides beyond the wood. I knew them to be flocks of hardy sheep with cynical glares: the product of harsh conditions and generations of forebears who had kept cold, lonely crofters warm at night. You'd be cynical too in the circumstances.

A rustle in the trees, just beyond the second car, snapped me out of my reverie. I stared hard into the dark wood and listened harder. Silence reigned and I started to think I had imagined it. There it was again, no more than footfall, but now I was on alert it cut through the night like a thunderclap. With extraordinary speed Archie spun on his heel and a pistol appeared in his right hand. I trained the .27 that had been hidden under my well-tailored jacket into the gloom. (Archie preferred the bigger .37. He worried his chums might accuse him of 'havin' a lassie's shooter' if he didn't carry a weapon that would stop a rhinoceros.)

I nodded to the big guy and pointed two fingers to the left. He moved silently into the dark in a flanking movement. The careless crunch of footsteps on leaves and twigs approached. I dropped into a squat, my pistol pointing exactly at the spot where a short, dishevelled man, clad all in black, wandered into the clearing.

'Stay where you are,' I hissed.

His head snapped up and he stared at me wide-eyed. His expression was only exacerbated when Archie's enormous arm slid around his neck and a pistol muzzle ground into his temple.

'It's me! It's Wally! It's bloody me!' the unkempt figure cried in panic.

'Aye, ah guessed as much,' said Archie, now smiling but not removing the weapon. 'But yeh wouldnae deny me mah bit o' fun, would yeh?'

'Jesus H. Christ,' I muttered. 'Archie, take your pistol out of Wally's face immediately. Wally, you idiot, what's with all the thunderous sneaking about? I was clear about passwords, wasn't I? You could have got yourself killed.'

'Sorry, you were late and I had to piss,' Wally said, breathing hard as he shook himself free from Archie's embrace and brushed his clothes down with trembling hands.

'Well, now you've seen fit to grace us with your presence,' I replied magnanimously, 'help Archie with the kit, would you please?'

I holstered the pistol and leant back against the bonnet of the car. Taking another gulp of crisp winter air, I waited for the adrenaline to ease, watching Wally as he transferred our gear across from one vehicle to the other, tripped on a log, and dropped a packet of plastic explosives. His whispered curses floated through the wood. I sighed. Even now Wally had broken from his task to surreptitiously suck on his asthma inhaler, in a bid to arrest the wheeze triggered by Archie's over-enthusiastic greeting.

You're surely wondering what this chap was all about. Well, first I should say his name wasn't Wally at all. It was Graeme. Graeme Finney. 'Wally' came from the military slang *chota wallah*, which means 'little guy' – a linguistic affectation from days long gone, when our army marched through different countries under a different flag. Wally and I first met when I won him in a game of cards. He didn't much like the officer who gambled him away anyhow, and I'm pleased to say he grew in confidence every day thereafter. He was five foot six in his shoes and his rectangular face was half-covered by long, unwashed hair, which seemed to be a badge of honour in the community of master manipulators that he inhabited most of his waking hours. Wally looked a mess and had an air of permanent bafflement. He was a man who seemed to expect new surprises at every turn and yet was still surprised when they came. He was even more baffled when they didn't.

All in all, an odd bedfellow in such a venture, you might say. And you'd be wrong. If you looked into his crystal-clear green eyes, you'd see them moving, seeking, analysing. It was in those eyes you could see the restless energy of a genius. You'd see Wally, the electronic road warrior, the unlocker of doors, the plunderer of networks. With a computer in hand he was as dangerous as any army. He only ended up in the actual military after being caught making a stunningly large withdrawal from a central bank.

Those of you in the espionage community will know the best intelligence is made up of SIGINT (signals intelligence: data interception, digital traffic, that sort of thing), HUMINT (intel garnered from humans), TECHINT (obvious, surely?) and GEOINT, which covers geospatial intelligence (or 'maps' to you and me). Wally was our chief source of both SIGINT and TECHINT and, as such, a major reason we were still alive.

Sadly, his mind had placed tough restrictions on those superlative cerebral skills straying too far into the realms of the physical. In the latter dominion he displayed a terrifying capability for ineptitude. An artistry for inviting ruin. If there was a threshold to be tripped across, a vase to be knocked from its pedestal, or a banana skin to be slipped upon, Wally would orchestrate it with unerring precision.

He and Archie pretended they couldn't stand each other. They bickered, fought, and taunted one another mercilessly, yet were completely inseparable. Wally took the greatest joy in reminding the big man – by word and deed – that his physical prowess was nothing more than arrested development; a Neolithic version of

Wally's mental strength and technological capabilities. For years I had waited for the day when the wee fella overstepped the mark and lost all his teeth, but it never came. There was the odd bruise and the occasional fracture, but that was just Archie being playful. As I said, they were inseparable, right to the end.

'OK, we're all done, Mr Mac,' said Archie, his huge head looming alarmingly close to mine.

'Well, nothing for it but to crack on, eh? Let's get this job done so we can get a drink down us.'

The red 4x4 moved slowly out of the woods. Archie drove in total darkness, using only the ruts of the track to guide us back to the highway. The road was empty and silent as a graveyard as we glided onto the tarmac. Our headlights blazed a hole in the night, and we shot south once more.

'How are we looking, Wally?'

Wally reached into a backpack and pulled out a tablet. As he unrolled it, bright blue light filled the interior.

'Fer fuck's sake, why don't we just put a siren on the roof?' Archie growled.

Ignoring him, Wally swivelled in his seat, turned the screen to face me, and began jabbing at it in excitement. 'Does that answer your question?'

'No.'

'But what do you see?'

'I see a website. Actually, I see the website of our target.'

'Look: there, in the top corner.'

'It says Administrator.'

'Now do you understand?'

'No.'

He stared at me piteously, willing me to either comprehend or to beg his indulgence. I began to share Archie's urge to hurt the wee chap.

'What does it mean?' I asked, my teeth grinding.

'Well, I first tried going retro. You know, exploit long-lost loopholes, maybe find a few patches that hadn't been applied when the software first went in or weren't updated properly. I tried a brute force attack, then went spear phishing. They were surprisingly well prepared. In the end I realised I was being stupid.'

'Wally, my brain is hurting. I don't need a saga. Just tell me what Administrator means. Don't make me set Archie on you.'

'It means we're in. I have control.'

His fingers danced across the screen, which jumped rapidly through security footage from our target: the colossal Pitlochry hydro-electric dam. It was all there: the gates, guard towers, offices, turbine room, even the salmon ladder. Then he was showing me personnel profiles, staff schedules, even bank accounts.

I have to confess I found Wally's electronic subterfuge fascinating. I could kill and maim as well as most, but felt something of a dinosaur when faced with a guy who could dive into the internet, smash through the most solid of post-cyberwar national barriers, and unleash hell from anywhere in the world. Much of Wally's downtime was spent whiling away the hours by alternately shutting down communication and transport networks in far-flung and ill-protected places, just to see how fast local society began to collapse. Can you imagine how quickly your day would change without information systems, electricity, running water, and control signals for the roads and railways? Wally's record for street riots was fourteen hours. By then he didn't even bother to note down when the looting started.

'After the false start, do you want to know how I pulled it off?' he asked, childish glee mingling with professional pride.

'No,' said Archie from the front.

'Now, now, Archie. Let Wally have his moment in the sun and we might all learn something.'

'There's nae bluidy chance o' that happenin',' came the curt response. 'Ah tell yeh, that boy's wired tae the moon* an' he's gonnae get skelped** in a minute.'

'I think, Wally, what Archie is saying is that he understands the words you are saying, just not the order you are saying them in. I have a similar affliction.'

'To be honest it was easy,' said Wally, with a superior tone that risked landing him with superior injuries. 'The whole system is on a legacy blockchain protocol, and all the data and records we need are on there. We just needed to get in. So we flexed a few financial muscles through our shell companies and manufactured a fifty-one per cent attack that gave us control of everything.'

A low growl emanated from the driver's seat.

Wally continued, seemingly oblivious to the danger. 'Not back-door access to the network, you understand. Front-door access! I just don't know what I'd do without the private key cracking software I developed—'

'Oh mah Goad, gi'e yer tongue a rest, yeh wee—'

'Ah, sorry, Archie, I forgot you were there. I'll dumb it down, but I can only go so far.'

'Mr Mac, permission tae—'

'Permission denied. Look, Wally, I think we get the point.'

Archie's fingers were white on the wheel. 'If yeh dinnae start tae speak English, ah'm gonnae give that bluidy computer backdoor access tae *yer* network an' run it deep intae *yer* crypter. An' if that's no' clear enough, ah mean ah'm gonnae shove it up yer—'

'No more explanation necessary, Archie,' I interrupted. (As I have already mentioned, he's a man of few words, but hugely creative when it comes to articulating – and executing – violence.)

Wally paused, weighing up his next words. 'Of course, your

* Strange or eccentric.
** Slapped.

HUMINT made a huge difference, Mr M. I could have been looking around their system forever – their records aren't up to date, the useless bastards. If you hadn't got those titbits about the staffing issues, we'd never have been able to optimize the operation date. So, I have to ask, how did *you* know the fella was taking his holiday? Because it's that little drop of social engineering that really swung it.'

'Now, you know I can't tell you that,' I said. 'The rules are clear: we work in cells. One cell does not know what the other cell is doing. You can't be forced to tell what you don't know.'

The implications of that ever-present existential threat hung in the air, before Archie broke the silence with a warning.

'Haud oan tight!' he called as he wrenched the steering wheel right, sending the car veering across the road and onto a rutted track, which plunged into a thick wood. We bounced along the narrow lane until a barn loomed up in front of us, alone amongst the trees. Archie deftly manoeuvred the vehicle behind it and out of sight of any random passers-by, stopping with a quite unnecessary suddenness that threw me forward into my seat belt. A bang and a groan came from the front. Wally had not been wearing his seat belt. Archie's grin betrayed that he was all too aware of this.

'Archie, you complete bastard,' he moaned. 'You could have broken my bloody nose.'

'But ah didnae, did ah?' Archie pushed his door open. 'Right, time tae get some exercise.'

It was noticeably colder now, despite the pine trees that crowded round us. Their trunks and branches reached up and over us, blocking out much of the sky and filling the air with their fresh scent. Pale beams of moonlight broke through the canopy, darting between the trees like ghostly spotlights. The silence was almost complete. Even the wind seemed to be holding its breath.

I stripped off my dinner jacket and other accoutrements, handing the various items to Archie, who folded them to perfection and placed them on the parcel shelf with the care of one laying down a newborn babe. No matter the occasion, he was always the consummate professional. I remember wondering at the time how on earth I would ever manage without him. Not well, as it turned out.

The only sound came from the shouldering of bergens; the pulling on of gloves, balaclavas, and infrared headsets; the checking and holstering of weapons; and, finally, the double puff of Wally's asthma inhaler.

The fear that had plagued me in the car – born of expectation and the unknown – began to recede. Now, the prospect of danger ahead gave me a familiar thrill, mingled with the reassuring certainty that our little team was *very* good at this sort of thing. (My particular strain of cowardice is rooted in the unknown. In situations where I'm on ground I recognise and in circumstances over which I can assert a modicum of control, I've been known to make rash and impetuous judgements. But when it comes to true bravery – the kind that charges into the darkened alley to answer the anonymous call for help – then just hope it isn't one James Macfarlane, Esq. who is strolling by as you come under attack, because your chances of salvation will be slim.)

The only real worry I had at that moment was timing. The road-block had made us late and time was of the essence if we were to complete stage two and have any chance of making stage three – and completing stage three would determine whether we were still alive by the end of the week. And it was Friday.

Within two minutes we stood there, ready: three black apparitions.

'Go silent,' I said, breaking the quiet.

'Leave no shadow,' they answered in unison, completing our mantra.

I gave each a small nod.

'Aye?' rumbled Archie.

'Aye,' whispered Wally.

'Aye,' I said, peering into the dark trees ahead. 'Let's hunt.'

'The whole Wolf thing goan tae yer heid, has it?' I heard Archie say through his balaclava, promptly ruining my moment of melodrama.

I kept a tactful silence. One of the key tenets of leadership is to know when you have lost the high ground.

CHAPTER 7

Where Salmon Dare

We crept up the rutted track, hemmed in on both sides by woodland. With open fields approaching on the left-hand side, we slipped off the path and into the trees on the right, slipping through a mix of skeletal Scots pines and full-bodied spruce.

The gloom enveloped us. Now and then a ray of silver moonlight would illuminate Archie or Wally, before they vanished back into the darkness. Sometimes disembodied clouds of warm breath would appear in the shadows, before evaporating into the ether. The ground was soft underfoot. It must have rained recently as the scent of pine needles mingled with the damp smell of long-fallen tree trunks, decaying in the dark. There was an air of calm. The kind of calm that comes before the tempest. The kind of calm that breeds melodramatic narrative.

The path swung to the left, taking us back towards the main road and one of the most dangerous points of the mission. First we had to break cover to cross the tarmac, then make it over one hundred metres of wide-open grassland, full of ruts and rabbit holes, all waiting to break unwary ankles. Only once we had run that gauntlet would we reach the safety of the woods beyond.

Crouching in the treeline, I nodded to Wally. He set off across the deserted road at a sprint and reached the grass on the other side. Then, with practised ease, he tripped on some unseen obstacle and came down in a shambles of man, weaponry, and technology. The accompanying crash rent the silent night in twain. Archie turned to me, a look of paternal resignation on his face.

'Och, he cannae help it, Mr Mac, it's a gift.'

Before I even had time to curse Wally, Archie was on his feet and bolting towards the prone figure. Running at full pace, he hardly broke stride to latch two enormous hands onto Wally's shoulder straps and carry him bodily into the trees beyond.

The silence returned. I crouched, waiting. We weren't far from the target now and it seemed impossible that no one had heard us. My heart hammered in my chest as I strained to catch the first sounds of barked orders and hurried mobilisation. Yet the silence remained, broken only by a light breeze that brought the sound of the River Tummel, whose black waters were somewhere ahead in the distance. I looked at my watch. The minutes ticked by. Against every instinct and fibre of my being, I waited and listened. Teeth gritted and muscles tensed, I imagined the trees ahead filling with moving figures; I saw the muzzle flashes that would presage bullets splattering my squidgy bits. The passing seconds were like a razor-sharp pendulum bearing down on me.

No more time.

I looked up and down the empty highway. Nothing.

Now or never.

I launched out of the trees, feet pounding across the tarmac and onto the field. I covered the grass at a sprint, all the time praying an errant furrow wouldn't leave me in a whimpering heap. The well-being of my squidgy bits still dominated my every thought.

In a matter of seconds I was across the kill zone and crouching alongside Archie and the calamitous Wally in the trees. I took deep breaths to ease my aching soul and revelled momentarily in the anticlimax. I scowled at Wally from behind my balaclava, but there was no point in admonishing the little catastrophe as he looked wretched enough already. Most importantly, all my insides were still arranged as God intended, so no harm done.

I unsheathed my silenced pistol and beckoned the others to move on. As we padded through the undergrowth, the peace of the night started to take on a different mantle. The silence no longer heralded calm, but was instead the precursor to ambush. In my mind the air seemed thicker, more oppressive. Yet, despite my fears, we had neither heard nor seen a soul when we emerged from the trees at the edge of a wide expanse of black water.

Loch Faskally owed its existence not to nature, but to the concrete behemoth off to our right. Pitlochry hydro-electric dam stood dour and grey in the moonlight: an unforgiving sentinel that thwarted the raucous journey of the River Tummel down from the distant hills, forcing its transformation into the giant, slumbering loch. The water lapped at the great concrete wall, which reached two hundred metres across the loch to the far bank. Above that, a thin concrete walkway, raised a couple of metres above the lip, offered the only means of crossing. At our side of the loch was the great grey rectangular turbine hall. It looked for all the world like an Art Deco prison block, with its high angular walls and long windows.

Through that gap between dam and walkway, I could see down into the valley below. I was just able to make out the remnants of the Tummel as it continued its leisurely journey from the base of the huge wall keeping the loch at bay. The moon had begun playing hide-and-seek with a broken bank of clouds. When visible, its silvery light cast a perfect reflection of the tree-covered hills around the loch onto the dark, still water. When it disappeared behind the clouds, whole mountains were sucked into the inky blackness, only to be released to the surface minutes later.

I stared up at the moon and, in a moment of misplaced romanticism, wondered if I was born for this. Did you know the moon used to be called Macfarlane's Lantern? This was because my thieving reiver ancestors were noted for using it to light their way as they nipped off to steal their neighbours' cattle. I felt the urge to lie down and soak it all in until the subtle glow of Wally's tablet (still in one piece after his tumble, thank God) distracted me. He was tapping away at the graphene screen and shaking his head.

'No signal,' he whispered into his mic. 'No access to the system. We're blind. We need to get closer.'

I nodded to Archie, who took point as we moved along the water's edge towards the dam. Wally shambled along behind us, staring at the screen and looking imminently likely to fall into the loch. He kept up a constant stream of small headshakes until we were barely fifty metres away, then dropped to one knee.

'OK, we're in,' he hissed. 'Signal is strong.'

Leaving Wally at his vantage point, Archie and I climbed up the bank into the trees, where we stopped and crouched down. From this angle we could see along the length of the dam. Pale halogen lamps illuminated the scene in a flat orange light. Separating us from the wall of the dam was a maze of grille walkways, concrete walls, and steel railings, which offered access to various maintenance huts and, beyond them, the turbine hall and the dam itself. Amidst this warren were large gaps, which dropped into bubbling, pulsating pools of black water (remember those, they're important). I couldn't see a soul. It was as if the place had been deserted.

'Confirm audio,' I whispered.

'Confirmed,' came Wally's reply in my earpiece.

'Confirmed,' came the customary rumble from the big man.

We continued through the trees, passing the dam and following the line of the river that emerged, emasculated, from its base. Just to our left, separating the river from our hiding place in the trees, was a low wall, no more than thirty centimetres high, topped with a steel fence that rose to chest height. The wall and fence sloped down the hill in shallow steps, each about two metres long. Our way in.

Sometime in the dim and distant twentieth century, some clever fisheries mandarin realised that damming the river would mess with the salmon who, being stuck in their ways, liked to return to breed in the rivers in which they had hatched. Fussy, perhaps, but there you are. To solve this, they built a rising 'ladder' of water that began in front of the dam, climbing out of the river and away from the structure, before doubling back and going straight up to the left of the dam. Within this ladder was a series of pools that allowed the fish to bypass the dam as they swam upstream, accessing one small pool after another, each higher than the last, through circular openings in the walls of each section.

Our vantage point in the trees was just across from where the ladder doubled back on itself towards the dam and the fish entered the home straight. No security cameras and no personnel covered the ladder, as the authorities simply hadn't thought anyone would be stupid enough to swim up there. The real challenge wasn't discovery; it was covering the last 150 metres or so of the ladder against the heavy current rushing down from the loch, in the company of large, aggressive, sexually frustrated fish.

We took the bergens off our backs and began unpacking them with well-practised ease. Out came drysuits, night-vision swim masks, miniature breathing apparatus, and small, high-powered sea scooters. I highly recommend the latter for any quick submersible work you need to do (particularly if they've got a self-filling ballast hull, which gives you the pleasure of neutral buoyancy – if you're into that kind of thing).

Everything we would require at the other end of this little odyssey had been pre-packed into individual waterproof bags, which we now placed, in turn, into vacuum-sealed packs that we strapped to our backs. Everything we didn't need was packed away into the rucksacks and hidden under fallen pine branches. We gave each other the once-over to ensure seals were sealed and zips zipped, then moved out of the treeline to crouch low against the cold metal of the fence.

'Remember: ten minutes' breathing time on the respirators,' I whispered. 'Should be plenty, but let's make this quick.'

'Aye, we'll freeze tae death long before that anyway,' Archie replied, matter-of-factly.

With a nod, we started the stopwatches on our wrists and Archie vaulted over the fence and slid into the water. I counted to ten and followed him into the inky blackness. Even wearing the drysuit, the icy temperature took my breath away. The current slammed me back into the downhill wall of the pool; I clamped down with my teeth on the respirator to stop it being lost, and gripped the scooter for all I was worth. The water seemed determined to rip it from my hand and send it down the pipe in the wall beside me into the next pool.

I groaned inwardly as I was held there, pinned against the concrete by the flow. Muscles straining, I dragged the scooter in front of me, started its powerful motor and looked up into the murky water, which was now lit a deep green by the night-vision goggles.

Large black shapes darted all around me. I hadn't factored in so many fish still doing the climb this late in the season. They slid past, occasionally bashing into me, offended by their uninvited guest.

Ahead, through the murk, I caught a glimpse of a sizeable pair of Glaswegian feet disappearing through the hole in the first wall. I followed. The current made it tough going for the scooter and I prayed the engine would take the strain. I counted the pipes as we went, hidden from prying eyes above, in this dark-green world. At around the halfway point, the pipe in front glowed unexpectedly brightly. I eased the throttle on the scooter and passed into the next pool before almost losing my respirator for the second time.

The source of the light turned out to be a large window in the right-hand wall. Behind that was a small viewing gallery, no doubt for tourists wanting to catch a look at the passing salmon. Snoozing on a chair was a man in a dark uniform. He only had to look up to see the decidedly fishy sight of a six-foot salmon passing by. I hit the throttle and sped across the pool. At the top, I held my position and looked back to confirm we were still undiscovered. Through the distorted glass I could see the guard slumped there, oblivious to the passing of the Loch Faskally Monster.

The higher we went, the more fish we encountered. In several pools I lost sight of the next pipe as they crowded in front of me, sleek torpedoes jostling for position. They hit me again and again, their powerful bodies vying with mine for a place upriver. All I could do was grip grimly to the scooter handles and take the blows until the current eased and the salmon slowed, as if they'd crossed a finishing line.

Here the ladder turned to the right, indicating the end of my journey. I turned off the scooter and floated upwards, switching off the night-vision goggles as my head broke the surface. Only then did I notice the aching in my muscles, my shoulders little more than knots of lactic acid after my struggle with the scooter. I trod water, the eager fish slipping past my legs like sea serpents and breaking the surface around me as they vied to escape into the loch.

Now, pay attention at the back of the class. Do you remember I mentioned 'bubbling, pulsating pools of black water' earlier? Yes? Good job. Well, these pools marked the top of the ladder before the fish passed through the dam itself and it was here that I had emerged.

Archie was already out of the water, stripped out of his drysuit, and standing head-to-toe in black on the steel grille that hung above the water. I pulled myself up onto it and followed his lead, stashing the wet kit under the ladder that led up and out of the pool.

'We are in Bravo position, over,' I whispered into my headpiece.

'You are clear to come up, over,' came Wally's reassuring tones. 'It's a straight canter into Charlie position.'

We climbed up to the platform and crouched low. At night, the front of the dam facing the valley below was lit by a series of uplights and spotlights that made its geometric face soar into the sky. But around the back – the business end – there were just a few tall lamps, casting pools of strategically placed light, to pinpoint transgressors and ensure guards or engineers didn't fall into the loch after too many evening sharpeners. In front of us, the wall of the dam reached straight out to grasp the other side of the loch, straddled by the walkway. To our left, the great expanse of water stretched away into the darkness. It felt like a slumbering giant, with only the small spine of the dam holding its latent power and malevolence in check.

The turbine hall loomed to our right, austere in the moonlight. It was now just a short traverse along another metal runway to reach it. We had started moving forward when, out of the corner of my eye, I saw a camera high on a wall ahead of us begin to swivel.

Wally's urgent whisper filled my earpiece. 'Down!'

Both Archie and I dropped prone on our stomachs on the steel platform. We were bathed in the light of one of the lamps, two salmon out of water. Out of a tunnel that led to the walkway over the dam, a figure had appeared: a security guard dressed in a dark boiler suit and bulletproof jacket, cradling a machine pistol in his arms.

'What the hell's he doin' there?' Archie said.

'No idea, he's off-protocol,' Wally replied. 'Shouldn't be there.'

I held my breath as his boots came closer, my body rigid on the cold steel. Beside me, Archie trained his pistol on the legs as they ambled towards us. I genuinely hoped this guard wouldn't have to die tonight, but a single turn of his head in our direction would do it. (Not that I cared about him, you understand – no one laments the death of a henchman – but it would make the rest of the evening hellishly stressful.)

The guard was just a few metres away when he took a fork in the walkway, wandering straight past us and over to the railings. There he stopped to lean on the barrier and stare across the loch to the hills beyond, just a fellow bard seeking inspiration. He pulled out a vape pod and took slow, deep drags on it, while we held our breath, lying exposed in a pool of orange light. The second hand of my watch hammered away at my wrist, every minute that passed a nail in our collective coffin.

Eventually the guard pocketed the vape, walked past us once more and strolled back down the tunnel that led to the walkway. Then he was gone.

'Clear,' came Wally's urgent voice. 'There's another guard crossing the dam from the other side, so you'll have to get inside quickly.'

Archie started to move when Wally cut in again.

'Wait, don't go yet, Archie. I need to talk you through the camera dead zones. And anyway, I didn't say "Simon says", did I?'

Archie's eyes narrowed.

'Right, go now,' Wally began. 'Come on! Archie, what are you doing? Move, for crying out loud. The bloody guard's coming. What the hell are you doing? You're going to get caught.'

He paused and I heard a loud sigh in my ear.

'Oh, for Christ's sake, Archie – Simon says Go.'

I shook my head in disbelief. It was like looking after a couple of children. Two big children playing with guns and explosives.

We traversed the metal platform, the steel ringing like tiny bells underfoot as we went.

'OK, keep going,' Wally directed. 'Now stop. You'll need to climb over the railing to your left to stay out of view. Make sure you stay low when you land – particularly if you're a freakishly tall troglodyte.'

'Aye,' said Archie, 'easy fer you tae say from the safety o' yer burrow, yeh fucken hobbit. Anyway, ah dinnae know whit a troggy-thingy is.'

'It's—'

'Enough!' I hissed. 'If you horrible creatures don't bloody concentrate, I will stop your pocket money.'

Seriously, trying to commit treason is like herding cats.

'Now, crawl to the big metal door,' came Wally's chastened voice. 'You've got about thirty seconds before the next guard comes past.'

'Understood, keep an eye out for any third parties,' I replied. It's always the third party that's likely to kill you, not the target you're watching.

We scrambled along the concrete, reaching the turbine hall where we knelt in the shadows by the entrance door. To our left was the mouth of the tunnel that led to the path across the dam. The door to the hall looked ancient and was made of steel, pocked with rivets, and painted dark green.

'Wally, prep to cut power if needed.'

We hadn't been able to see the door properly during our digi-recon and there was a decent chance it would be held shut by multiple magnetic locks. These give the impression of security, but it's an illusion: momentarily cutting the power and back-ups would let us straight in. Archie appraised the door and his face lit up with delight.

'A bluidy key!' he announced, voice tinged with wonder. 'Nae fingerprints, nae retinal scanners, nae nothin'. Mah Goad, when wiz the last time yeh saw an old-fashioned key, eh?'

'Twenty-five seconds until the guard has eyes on,' Wally's voice cut in over the comms.

Archie hummed a happy tune to himself as he worked. Many intruders in this day and age would struggle with a traditional lock, having never known anything other than digital. Archie was not one of them. He was a craftsman, and such challenges made his day. Having discarded the various electronic gadgets he had brought along to gain access, he was now hard at work with nothing more than two little metal rods (a tension wrench and a short hook, as those of you who have done any, ahem, *locksmithing* in the past will recognise).

'Fifteen seconds.'

I peered down the thin, dark corridor that led to the walkway over the dam. A faulty strip light deep inside was flashing on and off intermittently. The brief, flickering illuminations revealed the empty tunnel before plunging it back into darkness. A couple of nights previously Archie and I had watched a horror film – we were both suckers for the undead – and I couldn't help but think that if zombies were going to come from anywhere, it would surely be there.

'The guard is crossing the dam; estimate ten seconds before he comes down the steps into that tunnel and sees you,' Wally entreated urgently in my ear, before adding airily, 'You might want to hurry along, Archie.'

'Aye, it's easy tae be brave when yeh can sit o'er there in safety,' Archie growled.

'Nonsense,' came the reply, 'there's bound to be guards in the woods somewhere and I'm stuck babysitting you.'

'Ah'm no' talkin' aboot bein' safe frae *them*,' Archie said, still working calmly at the lock. 'It's me that yeh should be worried aboot.'

'Five seconds before he reaches the steps down to the tunnel. Tick tock, Archie. Tick tock.'

'Ach, keep yer knickers oan, we're in wi' time tae spare.'

The big man pulled the big metal handle down and opened the door a crack. We stepped cautiously through the door into the turbine hall. Archie pulled it shut, locking it from the inside while I surveyed the scene. We were high above the cavernous room on another metal gangway, which ran the full circumference of the rectangular hall. Halogen bulbs on the walls cast everything in dull orange and black. Below us the casings for the two immense turbines rose out of the floor, looking like long-abandoned lunar modules. Further on from them were a series of tall metal cabinets, their faces covered in dials and lights that blinked and whirred.

All this machinery was responsible for harnessing the latent power of the loch and turning it into energy for homes and businesses for miles and miles around. To destroy this power source would cause considerable inconvenience for the populace – the kind of inconvenience that is wont to make people question the ability of the regime to protect them. (Keen students will remember this lesson from our insurgency pub quiz earlier.)

Checking my watch and getting ever more alarmed at the hour, I descended a set of steel steps to the floor below. Archie followed just behind, going straight to the first turbine, unpacking his wares and getting to work with well-practised ease. He unscrewed a panel on one of the casings and placed his explosives inside, while I strung a series of small charges together, concealing them as best I could in the pale shadows between each metal cabinet.

'The guard has stopped at your position, over,' came an urgent voice in my ear.

Exchanging glances with Archie, I darted under the walkway beneath the door, while he began replacing the panel on the turbine.

'Come on, this is no time to bloody dawdle,' I thought aloud, forgetting we were wired for sound.

Archie stopped what he was doing, stood upright, and folded his arms. He took any perceived professional slights seriously, you see.

'Hide, damn you!' I seethed at him. 'This is no time for industrial action, you goddamned pinko.'

This was a mistake. He placed his screwdriver on the ground, drew himself to his full height, and folded his arms once more.

'The guard is at the door. He looks like he's searching for a key. Please confirm status.'

Archie stood proud and unmoving. This required delicate handling.

'Mr Fraser, I apologise for questioning you. Would you please make fast the turbine at your leisure and then bloody well hide, you utter and complete bastard?'

Professional pride restored, Archie picked up the screwdriver, casually spun it in the air, and then reattached the panel with deft flicks of his wrist.

'He's coming in,' said the voice in my ear, prompting our union rep of the National Insurgents Association (Caledon Chapter) to amble around the turbine and crouch behind it. Seconds later, the clunk of a key turning in the lock echoed in the silence and the door swung open.

Directly above my head two heavy black boots stepped onto the walkway, causing the metal frame to ring out. Fortunately, the noise that bounced around the hall masked a revolted observation from behind the turbine.

'He's wearing hobnailed boots. Bloody ponce.' (You have to remember Archie is from Glasgow, a city that can't abide sartorial pretension – and that includes wearing gloves in winter.)

I'd love to say that this outburst led to the man spotting me and a gun battle unfolding, where bullets ricocheted, oaths were sworn, and heroics performed. Instead the guard cast a bored glance at the seemingly deserted room, turned on one hobnailed heel, and was gone. This was all well and good, but another look at my watch revealed time – unlike that fiend, Archie – was refusing to stand still. We needed to be gone.

'Archie, we need to be out of here several minutes ago,' I urged. 'The more time we spend in here, the less time there will be for wanton violence.'

We went back to work, Archie exhibiting a new urgency. A click here, a snap there, and a squeeze thereafter, and all was in place.

I'm not going to tell you any more about placing high explosives because that would be irresponsible of me. There's a good chance you would fluff it anyway and blame me for losing a leg, and I'm in quite enough trouble as it is. (And don't think you can just go looking it up on the internet; there are extensive government programmes to make sure the bomb-making recipes you light upon will not only fail to work, but will allow sneaky intelligence types to cross-reference your online searches with your shopping habits. So, when you buy large amounts of fertiliser, you'll be in all sorts of trouble.)

I examined my handiwork, checking for mistakes. Even for experts – which we were – this was a dicey operation. Too little of the plastic would not do the necessary damage and make the whole enterprise pointless. Too much would destabilise the dam. If it collapsed, a torrent of biblical proportions would thunder down into the valley below, straight towards the local population, who I doubt had a single ark between them for shelter. It would be a disaster of huge environmental and human proportions. This was something I was keen to avoid in the battle for hearts and minds.

'All set,' said Archie.

'Right, let's go,' I replied. 'Wally, are we clear?'

'Yes, let's get us out of here,' he replied.

'Whit dae yeh mean, *us*?' snarled Archie as we climbed the metal stairs, pulled open the door, and peered into the dimly lit corridor outside. '*Us* is in this bluidy powder keg, while yeh's sittin' oot admirin' the bluidy view.'

'He's got a point,' said Wally, to my surprise. 'I could have turned the power off or overloaded the generator from miles away; there's really no reason for you to be there at all.'

'Yes, but then the Marischal could put the whole thing down to a tech failure or something, couldn't he?' I hissed impatiently. 'We need the rumour mill in overdrive tonight and everyone needs to be talking about the Wolf of Badenoch. This needs to be personal and identifiable.'

Archie pulled the door to the hall shut and went to work on it as I huddled by the wall. The faulty strip light, deep inside

72

that horrible tunnel, cast a bleak, flickering ambiance over him as he worked.

It was mere seconds before Archie finished with his picks, stood up, and gave an enormous heave on the door. As an afterthought he put the short hook back in the lock and broke the end off inside, sealing the hall and turning it into a turbine tomb.

'Aye, that's no' openin' fer anyone. Right then, time tae make things personal, eh?'

'All right, big man, do what you do best. But please don't enjoy it too much, we're on the clock here.'

His face lit up with the innocent joy that always came hand in hand with Archie unleashing terrible violence.

'Wally, can you ID a target?' I said.

'Already done,' came the reply. 'The poor bastard is moving away from you across the top of the dam. He's armed and, well, given the circumstances, probably not that dangerous.'

Archie looked pleased at this compliment. 'Great stuff!' he said, rubbing his hands before loping off into the flashing corridor, which lit then plunged him into darkness in truly terrifying fashion.

'Remember, Archie,' I whispered into the mic. 'We need to send a message. Strictly surface damage, OK? No one needs to die.'

'Aye, ah know. Stop rubbin' it in.'

I followed fifteen yards behind, now merely Archie's assistant. A zookeeper in the dangerous animal enclosure. In seconds he was through the flickering tunnel, up the steps at the other end, and onto the walkway above the dam. I reached the top of the steps and sank to my knees, camouflaged in the shadow of the low concrete walls. To our left were the loch and hills. To our right the face of the dam plunged fifty feet down to the remnants of the river that flowed out of its base. The whole valley spread out beyond, the lights of local villages twinkling in the dark. The air was clear and cold. The only sound was the water of the loch lapping against the great wall.

Ahead, the guard strolled towards the far bank, blissfully ignorant of his impending doom, which was loping across the top of the dam loaded with menace. All was going to plan. Archie would get to him well before he reached the end of the walkway, taking him unawares and leaving him nowhere to go. Then, to my horror, while still a good ten metres from the figure ahead, Archie hailed the man.

'Evenin', squire.' Dulcet Glaswegian tones echoed down the valley.

The man spun round and, to his immense surprise, saw a monstrous silhouetted fiend bearing down him. He raised his weapon and garbled something that was probably a request for the demon from the pit to stop and desist forthwith.

'Och, there's nae need fae that,' Archie replied jovially and, without breaking step, introduced himself with the traditional Glaswegian greeting, known thereabouts as 'pitin' the heid oan'.

This involves, dear sensitive reader, slamming one's forehead into either the victim's nose or, if you can swing it, the temple. The former approach will give you a huge advantage in any fight as your opponent will be blinded by tears, while also sucking in blood and struggling to breathe. The latter approach – the shot to the temple – is really only one for the connoisseur. It has the benefit of putting your opponent's lights straight out, but also risks doing them some serious brain damage. In fact, neither should be tried at home, children. Certainly not without proper adult supervision.

Archie's giant head connected at great velocity with the guard's face. A soundtrack of horrible cracking sounds accompanied the man's collapse to the floor.

'Is he conscious?' I demanded.

'That's a negative, Mr Mac.'

'Dammit! What about the message?'

'Aye, fair point. Mebbe ah did go in a bit hard, but yeh've got tae dae it that way. It's the only rule in a fight: all in from the get-go, extreme prejudice. *Extremity is the essence of surprise.* D'yeh ken who used tae say that?'

'Was it your mother?' I hissed.

'How did yeh ken that?'

'Oh, never mind.'

Spluttering noises emerged from the prone figure as he started to drown in his own blood.

'Archie, turn him over before he chokes, for God's sake,' I whispered. 'I really must stress: we *cannot* have him die on us. This is work, not your usual Saturday night out.' I looked again at my watch. Tick tock. Dammit, *dammit.* 'Wally, due to Archie's over-enthusiasm we need another target.'

'On it,' came Wally's voice in my ear. 'Woah! You're in luck. There's another mark there right now, Archie, at your twelve.'

I saw Archie look up in delight as another man – who must have been patrolling the bank – appeared at the end of the walkway. The bloody third party. Told you so. Seeing his prone colleague with an enormous black beast stooped over him, he wisely stopped. Then, in a display of appalling decision-making, he advanced towards the diabolical figure.

'You!' he said, his tremulous voice a study in vibrato. 'Step away from him and put your hands up!'

What the hell was Archie doing? His hands were moving from the ground to his face and back again, as if he was repeatedly stifling a sneeze. Then he rose to his feet and, in the booming voice he reserved for such occasions, roared at the man, 'It is the time for the Wolf!'

I put my head in my hands. This was all very frustrating. He was supposed to say *Now is the time of the Wolf!* We writers are terribly protective of our work and baulk at such crass editing. But it did the job, to be fair. The man stood frozen for a second, gave a strangled cry of fright, then turned and ran into the night. Archie, message duly delivered, started trotting back across the walkway.

I was already off the mark, taking the stairs back to the tunnel two at a time and racing along the corridor to the turbine hall, where I leaned against the cold iron door.

Swivelling round to check Archie's progress, I stared down the tunnel with its hellish flickering light. Imagine my shock when an actual zombie came marching down it. The Thing's face was the stuff of nightmares: covered in gore and dripping with blood, scars streaking its skin. The dark maw of a mouth leered at me, revealing a line of broken teeth. The corridor of terror finally had the undead inhabitants it so richly deserved. Except that, to my knowledge, zombies don't grin. Nor do they hum contentedly.

'Jesus fucking Christ!' I spluttered as I saw through Archie's bloodied mask, the anger of a duped coward replacing my panic. 'What the hell happened? Are you OK?'

'Och, it's no' mine, it's jist fer effect . . . Yeh know, tae add tae the ambiance,' our resident artist replied. 'But did yeh see that fearty bastard? Bluidy ran aff! Where's the sport in that?'

I was about to point out that the man's escape posed a far bigger problem than his lack of sportsmanship when explanation became obsolete. All hell broke loose: sirens wailed and orange lights set high on walls began revolving at high speed.

'Time to go,' Wally said.

'No shit,' I spat through gritted teeth. 'Shut those bloody things off.'

In seconds, darkness and silence enveloped us once more as Wally rampaged through their systems, shutting down alarms and blocking comms. Still, we had major problems. The plan now hung by a thread. The Wolf's message was only supposed to come to light when his victim woke up after several hours of Archie-induced slumber. But our presence was now known and we could be sure all sorts of people would soon descend upon us, intent on unpleasantness.

'I'm blocking comms from the control centre,' came Wally's voice, 'but I don't have details of any wider mobilisation protocols, or any other devices they're using. You've got to move fast and don't ignore the black spots or you'll get caught on camera. Jesus, you really are a bloody great lump, aren't you, Archie?'

Archie let the insult wash over him. He was in his happy place and no one would shift him. In moments we were at the top of the steps that led back down to the bubbling salmon pool. I raised a clenched fist to shoulder height: a Pavlovian command that made Archie sink to one knee through sheer force of habit and survey the area around him. All was quiet. The sky looked clear of drones so far; the loch lay flat and calm. I glanced at my watch again and cursed.

'Wally, unless you say otherwise, we're out of here.'

'You're all clear, Cap'n.'

'How many times have I told you not to call me that? No sirs, no Captains, or anything else of that nature, OK? We're not in the bloody army anymore.'

'Ah, sorry, Mr M. Old habits, you know? Still, you might want to get moving.'

'Right, back in the water, Archie, we've got to make this quick.'

In under two minutes we were clad once more in our drysuits and night-vision goggles. But, by God, it was a long two minutes. With every second that passed, the unbroken silence grew more oppressive. Where was everyone? Only when the shock of the freezing water hit me did my mind clear and I realised Archie's performance must have been quite a hit amongst the critics. Once the reviews were in, we were unlikely to attract any further spectators until audience members had collected heavy artillery from the cloakroom.

In contrast to our panicked exit from the dam, the journey back down the ladder was a positive delight. I was filled with childish glee as the current drove us down, like underwater abseilers. I followed Archie through each hole, each of us landing on the downstream wall, before dropping through the next tube. By the fourth wall I was challenging myself to land with legs on either side of the pipe. I waved at the sleeping guard as I shot past. Whoever said insurgency couldn't be fun?

The fish scattered before us and around thirty seconds later we were out of the water, over the rail, and darting into the trees. The journey back to the car was only broken by Archie stopping to scoop water out of the loch to clean his terrifying face – thus rendering it merely startling. Wally even managed to stay on his feet the whole way.

Stage two was complete.

But, as we disposed of our raiding garb (and I was once again looking splendid in my dinner jacket and tartan trews), it became impossible to ignore the fear that gnawed at my belly. I checked my watch for the umpteenth time and blasphemed liberally.

'Whit's up, Mr Mac? Somethin' wrong? We wiz in an' oot wi' hardly a hitch, weren't we?' said Archie, looking at me curiously.

'What is it?' asked Wally. 'Oh God, you haven't left something behind or something, have you?'

'No, dammit,' I said. 'Much worse.'

'Well, whit is it?' Archie urged. 'Spit it oot.'

I turned to them with a level gaze. For a while I said nothing, instead taking deep breaths to steady the hideous beating of my heart. Eventually, I offered the grim pronouncement in as measured a tone as I could.

'Gentlemen, we are late for dinner.'

CHAPTER 8

The King over the Water

A long time had passed since I could claim to be a stickler for punctuality. It had been a staple of my Presbyterian upbringing, but over the intervening years I'd grown too used to people waiting on me and for me. This time it was different. This time there was far more than social etiquette at stake. We were in stage three and it was time to dine or die.

We tore up the road, leaving the dam behind us, towering and silent in the moonlight. Resigned to its fate. But I didn't look back. My fevered mind was playing out two scenarios: timeliness and salvation, or tardiness and damnation at the hands of Loker's most capable monsters. Dinner was our alibi, our protection from the storm that would surely break. And every moment that passed made our deliverance less likely.

To Archie's credit, we arrived at the entrance to the Invereiton estate with indecent haste, having swapped cars and dropped our gear, along with a high-powered frag device, in the vehicle we left behind. Turning off the road, we stopped to pick up the aug-specs – so carefully and deviously discarded earlier – before passing through the giant wrought-iron gates. Age had warped and bent them, and they had long since become corroded in the open position. Lichen and rust vied for supremacy, eating away at the intricate metal flowers that wound their way across the bars. Two towering granite pillars held the gates in place, each topped with a clenched stone fist. Just like the twisted iron doors between them, the fists were souvenirs of better days. The ill-defined fingers told of a losing fight with years of unforgiving Scottish weather. We passed a gatehouse, constructed of the same dour grey stone as the pillars. It stood empty and dark, another reminder that things were not as they once were. I mused in a selfish way that it was one thing not being able to get the help, but another entirely not to be able to *afford* it anymore. A truly crushing blow. I began to wonder how the Farquharsons afforded any help at all. Massive estates like theirs were few and far between, our aristocratic families having long since been decimated by crippling taxes, exorbitant heating costs, and an inconvenient lack of feudal systems. Even the regime's efforts to maintain their long heritage and false romance in a bid to propagate its nationalist agenda couldn't save most of the ancient families. I wondered if the Farquharsons employed Helots (although I obviously use the word 'employed' advisedly when it's little more than slavery). Would such a noble family really stoop to that? The idea filled me with disgust, as it surely would them. But needs must, I suppose.

The lights of our car illuminated a wide, rutted track (still optimistically called a 'drive', no doubt), which snaked down a gentle slope. Ancient, wizened oak trees reached out from the gloom, before giving way to impressive rhododendron bushes. Sprawling lawns on either side of us replaced these, before Invereiton reared out of the darkness.

The castle's smooth walls rose four storeys into the sky – a sight to strike awe into the most stony-hearted visitor with its promise of historic memories and romantic legends. The face of the castle was pocked with small windows from which pricks of light shone into the night, as if a constellation had been mapped upon the walls. Large round turrets joined each corner of the building together, topped with fairy-tale pointed roofs. It was huge and imposing; a reminder that, despite attempts to change it into a country house ('turn the arrow slits intae windows, Willy!' seemed to have been the sum total of the brief), the castle remained a place designed to keep people out, rather than welcome guests in.

The sound of gravel munching at our wheels gave way to silence as we eased to a halt. The dials on Archie's dashboard cast a faint red glow over us as I straightened my bow tie, attempted to tame my dishevelled locks (never wear a balaclava before dinner if you can avoid it), and convened a final council of war.

'Wally, is everything in place?' I asked.

The wee man's tablet appeared once again and a dull blue light filled the car.

'Just a moment, Mr Mac,' Wally replied, humming under his breath as his fingers danced over the screen. 'I'm just hacking into the castle's web connection – bloody hell, it's slow . . . Only 6G out here. God, it's like the Dark Ages. Come on . . . Right. I'm in. OK. Yup, everything is in place. The all areas alarm will sound in twenty-three minutes. As planned this time, rather than being dictated by . . . *unpleasantness.*'

He shot a snide look at Archie, who mistook it as a compliment and smiled a lopsided grin back.

'Presuming the evacuation plans work, anyone within a mile of the blast zone should be out of the danger area within twenty minutes of that,' Wally continued. 'The charges are set for another, er, fifty-three minutes, meaning they will go off when the clock strikes nine. Finally, as requested, your Laughing Wolf logo will appear across all the pages of the power station's website one minute before that. Just in case anyone doesn't get the point.'

I was particularly pleased with this piece of theatre, which would see a black wolf's head, set within a buckled circle, rear up on each page of the site. It looked like the crest of a Highland clan, but was animated so the wolf's mouth opened and closed as it shook in silent mirth. You might call it crass, but in an age of mass misinformation, messages don't come much clearer than that.

'Ah quite like it, Mr Mac,' said Archie, turning to Wally. 'Punchy. It'll definitely go virus, eh, wee man?'

'It's viral, you idiot,' Wally began, before he noticed the smirk on Archie's face and lapsed into a quiet huff. Bloody incorrigible, the two of them, I tell you.

With everything in place at the dam, it was time for the assault on Invereiton Castle to begin. I stepped out of the car, my feet crunching on gravel, and stared up at the forbidding walls. This could well prove to be a damned sight harder than getting into the power station. His Lordship was a man for whom timeliness was next to godliness. Many a tardy dinner guest, no matter their reason for being waylaid, had been forced to beat a retreat from the castle walls having found the great door barred to them. And I was late to the tune of twenty minutes.

I approached the enormous wooden front door with its lion's head knocker. Standing before the towering entrance, I wished we'd kept some of the plastic explosive aside. I lifted the knocker and banged it down. The noise was fit to wake the dead, but there was no response. I waited and then pounded once more. No one came.

My mind began to race. I simply had to get in. But how? A frontal assault looked pointless. Yelling at the windows and appealing to Farquharson's better nature would also prove a waste of breath. I was already on thin ice with His Lordship, who didn't like me – nor ever had done – despite our acquaintance being passing at best. I was certain I was *persona non grata* due to the simple fact I was 'trade'. It did not matter how far back my own heritage might stretch: for men of Lord Farquharson's ilk, the blood of commerce that ran in my veins was an irrevocable blot on my copybook. The fact I was also the progeny of smugglers and ruffians made it even worse. His own financial shortcomings mattered not one jot. The newly rich are never to be esteemed as highly as the newly poor.

Yes, the great and good across the country might clamour to

have Jimmy Mac at their events and dinners, judging country fetes and hosting pyjama parties, but invitations from the castle were rare as hen's teeth. I was as surprised as anyone to get this one in the first place, and might well have declined had it not provided such a great alibi.

I stepped back to reconsider tactics for my one-man peasant's revolt. The air was brisk now and my breath appeared in thick clouds, before it too crashed impotently against the mighty wooden door. The smooth cladding of the walls afforded no hand- or footholds that I could see. Even if it had, there was no way I was getting through one of those tiny windows. I looked to the right, where the far corner of the castle joined a garden wall. It was rough and high, with ivy growing across its face. I discounted that as an entry point, in my current attire. What *would* my tailor say?

Instead, I followed the wall to the left and crept furtively round the turret at the end. A glorious sight revealed itself. In front of me a set of French doors had been thrown open and light from within the castle blazed into the gloom of a well-manicured garden. A way in! An incongruous back door to the impregnable fortress. Hugging the wall, I approached the incursion point, wincing at the noise of my feet as they crunched on the gravel.

I stopped and listened. Not a sound. With ill-deserved confidence, I strode into the doorway and immediately halted in shock. Standing with their backs to me were two men in full Highland rig, one of them bent over a decanter and pouring out healthy nips of Scotch, as the other looked on in reverence. I reversed back from whence I came, the stones munching noisily at my shoes.

I hadn't got far when time ran out. An enormous white beard appeared at the door, followed swiftly by the burly figure to whom it belonged. Lord Farquharson him-bloody-self. I flattened myself against the stone, mere feet from the open casement, hardly daring to breathe. A second man appeared on Farquharson's far side, hidden but for the belly that protruded past his host.

'Macfarlane's bloody late,' came the aristocratic voice of Alasdair, eleventh Lord Farquharson, whose family had infested these walls since the sixteenth century. 'Hardly surprising. No respect, d'you see? Arrogant too. Generations of poor breeding to blame. Can't hide it. Don't see why I have to put up with this sort of thing.' He paused before snarling, '*Jimmy Mac*,' his deep voice dripping with scorn.

I bristled, but since getting a seat at the man's table was imperative to my long-term well-being, I held fast, motionless; a mere MacWeed growing up the venerable Farquharson ramparts. The two men lapsed into silence, sipping whisky and blowing misty breath into the clear night.

Pressed against the cold wall, I appraised this scion of Highland society. His Lordship must have been around seventy years old, but was ramrod straight as a guardsman (which he had once been). He was tall and barrel-chested, steely-eyed and rosy-nosed. He sported a tremendous combination of long white hair tied into a ponytail and an equally long white beard. In his green velvet doublet, frilled jabot, and dark-blue kilt, he looked like the lovechild of a warlock and an elf.

'It is perhaps for the best for now,' said his companion, breaking the silence in a soft Highland lilt, similar to mine. 'We must discuss our tourist friend and the fewer ears there are, the better. James, God bless him, is perhaps not the most discreet, and our visitor is important . . .'

'I know how bloody important he is, Belleville,' grunted His Lordship. 'But it's high time we were shot of the bugger.'

Well, this was a turn-up for the books. It seemed His Lordship's companion was none other than Allen Fletcher, Laird of Belleville, a friend and neighbour of mine – and surely an ally in this Great Siege of Invereiton. He was shorter than his counterpart, his large stomach straining at the black waistcoat under his Prince Charlie jacket. Allen was one of those delightful and harmless people who have no place in a story like this. He had a trophy at home, awarded for 'Cunning on the Field of Croquet', for crying out loud. As far as I knew, the only worry he had in the world was how to make a particularly stubborn grouse moor pay its way now the foreign tourists and corporate junkets were all but gone. But these things are sent to try us.

Fletcher too was wearing a kilt and I noted he had a beautiful horn-handled sgian dubh tucked into his sock. He shouldn't have been carrying the traditional dagger under our strict personal arms laws, and I had to admire this surprising wee act of rebellion. If a man as harmless and eager to please as Allen Fletcher could not be forced into complete obedience, maybe there was hope for us yet.

'Anyway,' the Laird went on, 'you mustn't be too harsh on James. I know his reputation precedes him somewhat, but I like him and there's no doubt he's clever – look what he's done for his family's firm. Enormous success. And his heart really is in the right place.'

A lovely man, the Laird, but a *terrible* judge of character.

'Hmm,' grumbled His Lordship. 'Well, I think he's a fop, a wastrel, and very possibly a coward. And above all else, I can't abide cowards.'

'But he served . . .' chipped in the loyal Belleville.

'Yes, he did, but can you tell me what he did?' Farquharson fired back. 'Seven years in the armed forces, I'm told. Yet aside from the fact he was away a lot, no one knows what he did. Spent half his time in a cushy billet propping up some tinpot dictator, no doubt. A little too much of a Good Citizen, if you ask me.'

'I wonder,' Belleville mused, 'do you think he needs a grouse moor?'

'Forget Macfarlane, he's late and so lost to my table,' His Lordship snapped.

'But the grouse moor—'

'Oh, to hell with your moor. What matters is this tourist. How and when are we to get him out of here? Show him the sights?'

'No idea. We are as far as ever we were from a solution,' the Laird replied with the absent air of someone who was still mulling the potential sale of a stubborn grouse moor. 'There just doesn't seem to be a guide who is both keen and able.'

'That's because the last one was a bloody disaster – almost brought the whole tourist trade down around our ears. The cost is getting ridiculous.' The prospect of another dwindling income source seemingly weighed heavily on Farquharson's shoulders. 'And this one's even worse. Demand after demand after demand. That's all these blighters do. It's deplorable when one is doing one's best to look after them. There are plenty of other places they could stay, and none so nice as here, I'd wager.'

'Maybe James could take over?' said Belleville hopefully, causing me to grind a little more enamel off my poor teeth. There are few things I dislike more than being volunteered for, well, anything.

'He's got the time and resources to get our man out and about, doesn't he?' the Laird asked.

Wrong, my dear Belleville, I thought with conviction. I was buggered if I was going to babysit some uppity and unappreciative tourist. No doubt some foreigner keen to discover his noble Scottish roots. Hassle aside, you had to be really careful with these folks. A lot of planning had to go into making sure they left the country overflowing with praise for Caledon's generous hospitality and not lamenting the hollow look of defeat in the eyes of its populace. The regime was not one for bad reviews and could be bounteous in its retribution.

'Either way,' the Laird ploughed on, 'it wouldn't do any harm for you to be civil to James in case we do need to call on him for a favour. Maybe, just this once, forgive and forget his poor time-keeping, eh?'

My heart pounded with excitement: an opportunity for redemption swam before me. Would Farquharson take it?

Before His Lordship could answer, a booming noise split the night. Somewhere deep in the house a gong had announced that Dinner Was Served. I waited and stared at the men, blood rushing in my ears. Farquharson cocked an eyebrow, although whether it was at the call of the gong or Belleville's suggestion that he grant me a reprieve remained unknown.

I was out of options. Soon the French doors would close and with them my window of opportunity for storming the castle. It was now or never. Mental faculties sharpened by a night of subterfuge and mind filled with righteous indignation at the slights on my good – OK, mediocre – name, I tiptoed back to the turret, the noise of the stones under my feet masked by the exertions of whoever was banging away with such gusto inside.

In the shadows I shut my eyes, gave a silent prayer that Belleville's suggestion had taken root, and crunched my way raucously over the gravel to greet my host.

'*Feasgar math*, Your Lordship!' I said, all smiles. 'I am sorry not to have seen you yet, but I do so love a good stroll in the grounds before dinner. May I say, your gardener is a miracle worker?'

Our eyes met and we held each other's gaze, his look confirming just how aware he was that I was lying. But I had given him a chance to welcome me inside without compromising his iron principles. The question was whether he would take it.

I stood, palm thrust out in greeting. He stood motionless, eyeing me vindictively. His eyes strayed to the golden bangle on my wrist and the distain was clear. Men worthy of the name did not wear jewellery in His Lordship's world. My hand hung in the air, awaiting its fate. Then, out of the corner of my eye, I spotted an almost imperceptible nudge from the Laird and the big hand rose in a relentless and mechanical fashion, clamping itself around mine and squeezing very tightly indeed. I did not return the bone-crushing gesture – he could have this victory. However, I didn't let the pain register on my face. He wasn't getting that.

'My gardener is nothing of the sort,' rumbled Farquharson in a stern voice that not only ignored my greeting, but also poured disdain on my use of the regulation Gaelic. 'He has ridiculous notions about the value of moss.'

I wasn't sure what to do with this information. 'It's a pleasure to be here,' I replied, my teeth gritted as His Lordship continued to rearrange my hand. 'But, my Lord, I shall need my trigger finger back if we are to do your keepers proud tomorrow.'

He relinquished his vicelike grip and I turned to greet the Laird. His Lordship interrupted us with curt thrusts of 'Come along, no time for that sort of thing,' and 'The Colonel will do bloody murder if we aren't in our places on time.'

Dutifully we followed as Farquharson led the way through the French doors and into an informal drawing room, which seemed to have been decorated by a passing empire builder. The dark wooden floors were covered with rectangular rugs in whites, reds, purples, and blues. I recognised a threadbare Star of Kashmir on one, probably obtained by a relative who was either on a Grand Tour or happened to be annexing the country at the time. In one corner stood a grand piano, covered in old family photographs. Strewn around were a number of battered old chairs and sofas. It is a peculiarity of great houses that, away from the formal rooms, a rambling, comfortable shabbiness takes over. It's as if the house has exhaled deeply, shedding the trappings of duty and station.

We moved through a series of magnificent rooms that were all mahogany panels, tartan carpets, and mounted claymores. The old swords were fanned out across the walls and, here and there, shoved carelessly into umbrella stands.

On the way to the dining room I passed through the towering

entrance hall, where I spied Archie, inexplicably dressed in a full butler rig of bow tie and tails, and preparing to heft my case up the wide, curving staircase. I scampered over to him.

'How the devil did you get in?' I hissed. 'And when on earth did you get changed?'

He put his finger to his nose and said, 'Never you mind, Mr Mac,' while attempting a conspiratorial wink that made him look as if he was having a stroke. Archie had an uncanny knack of appearing from the shadows in places you'd least expect. He was a professional lurker, highly trained in disappearing into, and appearing from, dark places. And you'd better pray he was on your side when he did.

I stood, waiting for more detail. When none was forthcoming, I made the mistake of going into battle. I stood my ground, launching a barrage of awkward silence that would have broken lesser men. But, as is so often the case, Archie had the higher ground; safe in the knowledge I could not resist the relentless sound of the dinner gong. He knew for whom it tolled. I broke first.

'Well, make sure my suitcase is in my room and its contents unpacked immediately, or we'll be having words, Mr Fraser,' I threatened. Pathetically.

'Aye, right,' Archie replied, stony-faced.

I eyed him suspiciously. 'Just to be clear, do you mean "aye right" or "aye *right*"?'

'Aye, right.'

'As in "aye right, I'm off to get on with it"? Rather than "aye right, that's not happening"?'

'Aye, OK.'

'Right. Wait . . . hang on. As in "aye OK, I'll do it but I'm not happy about it"?'

'Aye, cheers.'

'As in "thanks for nothing"?'

89

'Aye.'

'Well then, I'm glad we've cleared that up.' I turned on my heel and strode into the magnificent Invereiton dining room, where the hum of polite conversation hung in the air. A long rosewood table covered in silverware dominated the rectangular room. A chandelier loomed over the middle of the table, hanging from an ornately plastered ceiling. Large portraits of ancestors who broke bread on this very spot in days of yore stared haughtily down from walls covered in deep-green wallpaper.

On one side of the room sat an ancient stone fireplace big enough to burn a witch in. Opposite, immense bay windows overlooked the walled garden, into which I'd been sensible enough not to climb before. If Farquharson had seen that, he'd have set the dogs on me.

The cynics amongst you might be looking at this grandeur and saying 'Hold on a moment: this is a time of hardship and despotism. What gives, with this opulence and high living, cavorting and carousing?' Well, firstly, there's the Helots, the poor devils. We'll come to them in a moment. But the real reason behind the continued existence of the *ancien régime* under the *nouveau régime* is that the Marischal has, for years now, comprehensively wrapped us up in the mythology and romanticism of Scotland. You can hardly move for swirling mists and hairy Highlanders, heroic battlefield charges, and Jacobites obligingly dropping dead in front of nasty redcoats, their muskets belching smoke. Renderings of vast, heather-clad glens reach out from public walls and screens, beckoning us to places where Highland cows sup from crystal-clear lochs, and stags-upon-crags stare nobly into the distance. It's a hopelessly clichéd vision of a past that never was, but there's nothing that papers over the cracks quite like sentimentality and the Marischal knew it. Ancient families like the Farquharsons were the very embodiment of these hackneyed notions, so he embraced them. And you can be sure the beneficiaries adapted to the new politics – and tax breaks – with an expediency that made the portraits of their ancestors positively beam with pride.

Perhaps it was this sense of protection – being wrapped in a blanket of rose-tinted antiquity – that did it; perhaps it was the victory of successfully storming the castle, but elation swept over me as I surveyed the room. I was in! I was safe! To my right, a tall grandfather clock ticked loudly and inexorably towards my victory. Or would it be destruction? Only time would tell. All I could do for now was wait. And drink. Preferably a lot.

Somebody was way ahead of me, though. A slurring voice cut through the chatter on the far side of the table.

'Too many totalitarian regimes in too many countries do their best to shut down media outlets, don't you see? Attempting to ban everything that threatens their power and leaving just a couple of national mouthpieces to spout their rulers' interpretation of events,' came the voice, dampened by the vast jowls that surrounded its mouth.

The voice was familiar. I looked for its owner and there he was, already sat down, a gin and tonic clenched in his stubby fingers. Corpulence kept Iain Barclay from pulling in his chair. The once formidable publisher – who now spent most of his time as a malfunctioning alcoholic – was playing to type. I tried to catch his eye, but Barclay was too busy extemporising. He dabbed his dewy forehead with a handkerchief, eyes roving the room for the source of his next drink. Next to him a slight and deservedly worried-looking woman, whose name I have forgotten, was reeling under the onslaught. I could only guess she had made the terrible error of engaging him on how his day at work had gone. Everyone knew not to do that. The embittered Barclay, a former champion of free speech – now a state mouthpiece without the courage to do anything about it – was only too willing to spew impotent bile on the subject.

'That kind of clampdown is a mistake, you see?' he said, stabbing his glass in her direction. 'The key is not to eradicate information. It is to weaponise it.'

'Well, yes, of course,' she replied uncertainly. 'But I think . . .'

I leaned closer to listen. Barclay was sailing dangerously close to the wind and the chance of someone other than me courting impending doom helped cheer me up. Barclay lifted his glass belligerently above his shoulder and rattled the ice, none of which had had the chance to melt. A servant appeared, ready to whisk it away.

'The Marischal knew . . . Less tonic this time. More gin.'

'The Marischal wanted less tonic?' the woman asked, confused.

'What? No, of course not. What are you talking about?'

As the servant leaned down to take Barclay's glass his shirt cuff rode up, revealing an angry red welt on the inside of his wrist in the shape of an 'S'. The mark of shame. The brand of the Helot, worn by those poor souls who had been found wanting by the regime and thrown into indentured servitude. Whether anyone else noticed didn't matter. No one batted an eyelid. Helots were everywhere. The Caledon economy couldn't function without the free labour. Still, I found myself disliking Farquharson even more for securing his position in this way.

I watched the man leave, his eyes cast to the floor, the S for Sedition hidden once more behind the crisp cotton of his shirt. The brand was new; I wondered what he had done to deserve it, and at which town square auction the ancient and honourable house of Farquharson had secured his services.

Barclay's angry voice interrupted my thoughts. 'You see the Marischal realised that mass media – twenty-four hours a day and 365 days a year – had set us all adrift in a vast sea of information. Our ability to tell right from wrong, important from inconsequential, was suffocating in an ever-growing midden.'

His victim raised her eyebrows in enquiry.

'Midden means pile of shit,' I chipped in across the table, keen to help.

She looked shocked at my manners but had no time to rebuke me because Barclay was in full flow once more, growing more pompous, bitter, and meandering. Gs with ever less T came and went like ships in the night.

'This was his genius, you see?' Barclay declared conspiratorially, leaning towards the poor lady. 'The Marischal realised that this offered the opportunity to understand people better than they understood themselves. Like never before, knowledge was power. The key was to make sure he had the *quality* knowledge, while others were drowning in dross. So rather than smash the servers, he let the arteries of our internet superhighway clog up with more fat, before walling us in with our very own national web that meant he could control and understand the information flow even better. And while he was drowning us in inconsequential nonsense he ensured any views being shared on anything of importance were restricted to his orthodoxy. He put an end to disinformation that wasn't his own.'

'Well, at least we know we're getting lies we can trust,' I chipped in, keen to mock him for the benefit of any regime stooges either in the room or peering through nooks or crannies.

Barclay eyed me uncertainly through half-glazed eyes and continued. 'The plan was fiendish in its ingenuity. It was wicked, but it was shrewd. Yes, it was.'

On he went, stopping only briefly to turn purple and cough violently until a small wedge of lime came shooting out of his windpipe. The poor lady looked terrified by this point. Even being associated with Barclay's views could have nasty consequences for those who couldn't afford to be. For my part, I stayed and listened, revelling in his stupidity and wondering just how far he would go. I didn't share the woman's fear of association with his ill-advised views. I was privileged, I was powerful, and – no doubt just like Barclay – I thought myself safe from retribution. How wrong we were, those of us at this dinner of the damned.

There was a scraping of a chair as Barclay's victim tried to make excuses and rise, but he grabbed her arm.

'No, no, you have to understand the extent of it all,' he said urgently, as she pulled against his grasp. 'Please, listen. How can I make you believe? Wait, I've got it! Just listen to us. Look around you. Do you not see the absurdity of it all? Do you think twenty years ago we spoke in this ludicrous way? Like cheap reproduction Victorians?'

He took a deep drink from his glass and the fire returned to his eyes.

'For years, we – the media – have been forced to communicate with you differently, using long-outdated words to cultivate a sense of sentimentality, to embed a feeling of rose-tinted comfort that harks back to some long-lost childhood,' Barclay proclaimed, poking his glass at his increasingly bewildered neighbour. 'And that – as the Marischal intended – has changed how you all talk to each other . . . Corrupted how you speak . . . Do you not see how this . . . Wait, where are you going?'

The lady finally decided to make good her escape, asking a servant where she might powder her nose. I too was growing bored of Barclay's gin-soaked resentment. While the Marischal had done much to shape our existence, aggrandising his achievements unnecessarily was of no help to anyone. I mean, going to the length of changing our very speech to that of days of old, just to embed the Marischal's romantic vision of Caledon? It defied belief. Indubitably so.

Behind me the grandfather clock ticked on, forcing its way back into my consciousness. It seemed to be getting louder. I realised my hand was shaking, so shoved it in my pocket. A creeping nervousness was spreading through me. That chill increased with every heavy second marked by the pendulum in the clock's guts. I cursed Barclay for ruining the temporary buoyance of my mood.

Striding to my seat, I snatched up a glass of wine and drained it, before surveying the room, looking for a distraction from the tell-tale tick of the clock. I counted off Allen Fletcher, Laird of Belleville, and his wife, Annabelle. Then the two daughters of the house, Catriona and Mary Farquharson, as well as a son home from the army; I forget which one, Lachlan, I think.

Then all my woes were forgotten for the moment. My eye lit – and lingered – upon Lizzy Burke, whom I was both surprised and delighted to see holding court at the far end of the room. For a blessed moment the hideous ticking receded. I drank her in like the vile, libidinous man I am. My God, where to start? Perhaps with those deep brown eyes; those oval windows to a devious soul? Or maybe the eyelashes, so long they were wont to cause a light-to-moderate breeze when she blinked? Maybe the lips – so full and red, for I know you wouldn't accept anything less. Lizzy's thick auburn hair hung coquettishly over one eye, topping an almond-shaped face that was perhaps too thin to qualify as conventionally beautiful. But even the harshest critic would find that, in her presence, nothing mattered whatsoever, for she radiated . . . What? An aura? Maybe. If it was, it was an aura that marched over, slapped you across the cheek, and demanded you pay attention.

Pull it together, Mac. Pride was back. *She's gone now. It's too late for eulogies and you don't deserve to give one anyway.*

Oh, come now, Pride, you know what she meant to us, said Common Sense. *You know what happened. We are allowed this moment.*

Don't drag up ancient history. Wallowing in self-pity won't improve any of that. I thought you're supposed to bring common sense to this party? Don't be fooled. She knew what she was doing. She knew the risks. She knew the consequences. What we think about her changes nothing and makes us no more guilty.

Woah there, Pride. Easy, pal. I don't disagree with you.

Say what now?

I'm just saying it was a different time.

Yes, I suppose it was. A simpler time.

When the world made more sense.

When we were happy. When we . . . OK, stop right there. That's quite enough of this nonsense. We're Jimmy Mac. We're . . . We're . . .

Would you like a hug?

Of course not. Unless you need one?

Come on, bring it in.

Lizzy's tinkling laugh filled the room, making even Barclay's befuddled features clear for a second as he caught a whiff of redemption in her languid tones. His wife, standing far enough away to plausibly deny she was aware of his previous behaviour, looked furious at his lascivious gaze. In Barclay's defence, it was difficult not to stare. As usual, she looked as if she had been dipped into her clothes and left to dry. Lizzy was wrapped in a black velvet cocktail dress, her breasts straining against the fabric. They are usually straining against something or other. It's their lot in life. If you want to chide me for ogling, then so be it. Take solace in the fact that Lizzy couldn't have cared less. She relished people's attention and, make no mistake, while they prayed for her, she preyed on them.

At that moment she was explaining what a 'Confluencer' was (the title someone had coined to describe her curious occupation as digital innovator, social influencer, and dealer in political intrigue). Lizzy was one of the first stars to emerge on CaledoNet after we sealed off our internet from the outside world and began drowning in the carefully crafted cesspit to which Barclay had alluded minutes before. Whether the details of her story were true or just the latest yarn Lizzy had created to keep herself interesting and interested, I don't know. There was so much mystery surrounding Lizzy Burke. So much I never learned. And so little left for me to hold on to. I'm sorry, Lizzy.

Mac! For God's sake!

Sorry, where were we? To give a sense of just how ethereal her reputation had become, there were persistent rumours at the time that she had recently spent several months as a companion to a German prince by the name of Ludwig. He offered her titles and a pension to stay, they say, all of which she turned down out of nothing more than flippant ennui.

Some called her one of the country's brightest entrepreneurs. Others called her a whore. She, like the Marischal, knew the value of knowledge, and she knew how to get it. She was the keeper of secrets – many uttered before, during, and after the throes of passion. And in these deeply conservative times, the ruthless and unrepentant use of her femininity was extraordinary. Lizzy called herself 'post-feminist', but I have no idea what that meant. Just as importantly, her online platforms were acknowledged as an unofficial conduit for our leaders' thoughts. It was there you would go to learn who was in favour and who was out. Who would never be heard of again.

No matter how powerful you were, it paid to be her friend. For these reasons, Lizzy Burke was often described as the most dangerous person in Caledon. Normally, the Powers That Be would bump her off, quick smart, for being such a liability. But she was famously discreet when required and, if they did do her in, to whom would they turn for comfort and to whisper their burning secrets? There was just no one else in her league.

I caught her eye and we nodded in mutual recognition. I took my seat and continued to stare. She did not stare back. My attention was dragged away from Lizzy (no mean feat) by the person next to her. A stranger. To see such a thing in the high-powered and inbred circles in which I moved was rare. I looked at him, wracking my brains. Who was he? Had I seen him before? What was he doing here? Suddenly, the grandfather clock was back with a vengeance, hammering out the passing seconds and vying with my heartbeat for control of my eardrums.

Tall and slim, with an annoyingly square jaw, this stranger was close shaven, had his hair parted in the middle, and sported neatly cropped eyebrows – not the style in these parts. If I were to guess his age, I'd say early thirties. He had the confident air of someone who, through either talent or connections, had been fast-tracked somewhere, somehow. He wasn't wearing tartan either, which was equally unusual in a gathering such as this, under a regime such as that. Instead he was impeccably dressed in bow tie and tails. Unusual. Out of place. Unnerving. Tick tock. TICK TOCK.

His English accent was difficult to place. Not quite the pure King's English of the aristocratic Lord Farquharson, which would identify him as some minor gentry that had crawled out of the provincial woodwork. No, it was more nuanced. The voice of a cosmopolitan everyman . . . or was it no one? Try as I might, I couldn't pin him down to a time or place. The hairs on the back of my neck stood up. In the back of my mind, an alarm bell began to ring, joining the growing cacophony from the relentless grandfather clock.

Then I had it. Here was the 'tourist' whom His Lordship had been so keen to shift onto some poor, unwilling sod. Relief washed over me and the terrible ticking receded once more. If the only danger this one posed was the risk of unsolicited sightseeing, then I could rest easy. That could be dodged. One less thing to worry about. Still, as dinner went on, I struggled to shake the feeling that I was somehow mistaken. The stranger seemed bright-eyed and polite, well-spoken and engaged with the present company. It surprised me that Farquharson found the man so unpalatable.

'Hildebrand Blunt,' breathed my neighbour, Catriona Farquharson, leaning over from my right and pressing her ample frame against my arm.

'Hildebrand?' I said in disbelief, both at the ridiculousness of

98

the stranger's moniker and the inappropriate proximity of her chest.

'Hildebrand, yes,' Catriona confirmed, in what she presumably thought was a sultry voice, but which sounded more like my old Austin Healey refusing to start in cold weather. 'Up from England to visit. Think he might be a poof.'

I gave Catriona the most cursory of appraisals. She was a product of the Highlands, born and bred on the moors, where the strength to wrestle a stag to a standstill and the ability to heft a caber was highly prized among the local lads. It also seemed likely from her animosity that Hildebrand had rebuffed her advances, although it was difficult to tell. (And if you're appalled by her appraisal of Blunt, then lucky you. Liberalism has long since been chased from our shores and homophobia is one of several less edifying traits infesting my country. Totalitarianism, you'll be surprised to hear, isn't conducive to embracing people's differences.)

I was wondering how to probe Catriona further about the mysterious Englishman, while avoiding a probing myself from her wandering hands, when a clear and commanding voice rang out.

'My dear friends, welcome to Invereiton,' announced the Colonel from her place at the head of the table.

Anne, Lady Farquharson – for it was she – must have been in her seventies but, like her husband, was straight-backed and tall. (The nickname, in case you're interested, came from an eponymous and no less formidable eighteenth-century relative – otherwise known as *La Belle Rebelle* – who had raised hundreds of troops for Bonnie Prince Charlie and, I'm told, once even took the surrender of her own husband, who was fighting for the other side.)

Lady Anne's slim figure, thin, angular face, and straight silver hair, gave her all the makings of some terrifying Haversham-esque matriarch. In fact, she was nothing of the sort. Rather, she was one of those confident, steady types from whom one feels compelled to seek approval (bloody awful people, if you ask me). She projected a look of calm benevolence, the hallmark of the confident and composed.

'Now, please,' she continued, 'do feel free to start as soon as you are served. My dear husband is already giving a fine demonstration, should you need any guidance.'

Lord Farquharson had already settled into his cock-a-leekie* soup and was caught unawares. He spluttered, looked enraged, realised no good would come from any argument, and set to cleaning the broth from his beard in red-faced silence.

As the Helots filled our bowls from silver ladles, the Colonel spoke again. Out of the corner of my eye, I watched the clock tick on.

'My dear?'

Lord Farquharson, clearly fuming after his wife's public rebuke, managed to spill more soup down his beard. 'Yes, my dear?'

'Would you propose the Loyal Toast?'

'What? Eh? Of course, dear.'

Once His Lordship had finished dabbing at the mess down his front, he did as commanded. '*Slàinte an Marischal, Caledon gu bràth!*'** he boomed.

'We are Good Citizens,' we parroted without thinking.

As we dutifully raised our glasses, I noticed something odd. His Lordship, Belleville, and the Colonel – perhaps even Lizzy too – had done something decidedly curious. As they lifted their wine they did so in an arc, so their glasses went up and over their water glasses before being brought to the usual position in front of them. I'd heard of this little foible but never seen anyone do it. For unless I was much mistaken, this was the secret toast to 'The King over the Water', a relic of Jacobean times meant as coded loyalty to the Stuarts. Why had they done it? What did it mean?

---

* A traditional Scottish soup made of leeks and peppered chicken stock, thickened with rice.

** To the health of the Marischal, Caledon forever!

Tick tock. Tick bloody tock.

In a bid to stop the grandfather clock asserting its rotten ticking on my craven mind, I took a large slug from my glass and signalled for a top-up. I pushed the moment from my mind, labelling it another piece of archaic and meaningless nonsense in the complex social jigsaw that was designed to remind people of the Farquharsons' superiority. I turned to Catriona, who was delighted to have my attention. Soon my mind was occupied with a new threat, as I split my focus between hearing all about the recent Invereiton Highland Games and performing complex Wing Chun Kung Fu defensive techniques to stop Catriona's wandering hands from molesting me under the table.

As dinner progressed, the constant supply of wine imposed a certain serenity on the grandfather clock's steady vigil. As the booze flowed, the conversation became more daring, fuelled by the misplaced sense of safety that is born of social standing. I started to look at the clock less and less, perhaps every two minutes or so. I don't actually remember much of what was said until the subject of O-Tanks came up. There was a vociferous argument over whether such a public spectacle brutalised society or whether it was to everyone's benefit . . . the lowest prison population for eighty years . . . justice being seen to be done . . . the system no longer favouring the perpetrator over the victim . . . and . . .

Oh Jesus, that horrible rushing noise. Not again, please. The invisible vice clamped over my mouth and nose. The terrible burning in my chest. The desperate scratching of my nails on the walls. The faces – hundreds of faces, watching impassively. The look on Lord Farquharson's face as he watched me die. The blackness. Then the terrible ordeal beginning again.

Mac, come back. It's over. Come back.

Finally, the pudding bowls were spirited away, coffee poured, and – to the delight of the stalwart Barclay – decanters of whisky and port placed *in situ*. Then the clock rang the hour. The count-down was complete. My heart was beating uncontrollably fast and, even though I'd tracked the progress of the hands around the face so closely, the sound took me by surprise. It was so loud! I resisted the urge to look at it now. What would I even see? The hands were now nothing more than fingers pointing to the hour in rank accusation, proclaiming my guilt.

Bad Citizen, Bad Citizen, Bad Citizen, the accusing clockface yelled.

I tried to concentrate on Blunt, who was boring his fellow diners with some diatribe about investing in Caledon, but it was impossible. I was struggling to keep my heart rate down. I wanted to gasp for air, to get up and walk around to ease the tension. I felt imprisoned in my chair and pulled at my collar, which seemed to be constricting around my throat. Out of nowhere, the enormity of what we had done – the *madness* of what we had done – struck me. Surely everyone else in the room felt it too? The chimes grew louder. Still the guests around me spoke pleasantly. They smiled. Someone laughed. Surely they could hear the raucous peal of the clock? Wait! Did they suspect? No, worse: they knew! They were taunting me, ostracising me with their overt display of inane chatter at this vital hour. Oh my God, when would this terrible clock leave me be?

And where the hell was Archie? He was supposed to be announc-ing our triumph. Had everything at the dam gone wrong? Had the bombs not gone off? Had the Mallice somehow defused them? Were they, even now, lifting shreds of DNA from the scene and sharpening their knives? Worse still, had we misjudged the power of the explosives? Were millions of gallons of water even now crashing down the valley, wiping whole towns and their inhabitants from the map?

The final chime crashed over the room. My eyes darted around the table where conversation continued as before. I looked back to the wicked timepiece and . . . everything was OK. No one was looking at me. No one knew. For, just as the last chime struck, Archie had materialised next to the clock like a djinn from the ether and now stood, half-hidden, in its shadow. I held his gaze for a split second, but it was enough for the big man to nod, give me the slightest of smiles, and once again evaporate from the room. Then I knew that while peace reigned at Invereiton, not far away all was flame and chaos and confusion.

A surge of adrenaline coursed through me. We had done it! The plan had worked and the Wolf had struck a massive blow for freedom. Weeks of planning and uncertainty and fear were over. Of course, there would be plenty more of all those things to worry about in due course, but for now, the Marischal, the Mallice and their despicable leader, Thomas Loker – they could all go to hell. For a precious moment I was overcome with joy. In my excitement a teaspoon, which I'd been absent-mindedly twiddling in my fingers, fell. It clattered from port glass to coffee cup. His Lordship scowled at the ill-mannered oik infesting his table. I caught Colonel Anne peering at me quizzically. Astutely, even. How long she had been looking was anyone's guess. But none of it mattered. Right now, all that mattered was victory.

I looked at my watch and, under my breath, started to count down from ten. At five, the lights flickered. At two, we were plunged into darkness.

CHAPTER 9

A Hell-Broth Boils

In the pitch-black, voices were raised in confusion and cutlery dropped in alarm.

'Oh, goddamn it!' Farquharson banged the table with a meaty fist. 'What the bloody hell is the matter now?' This was followed by another curse that indicated his attack on the table had resulted in another spillage.

'Calm down, dear,' came a soothing voice down the table.

'Who the bloody hell is telling me to calm down?' His Lordship boomed.

'It's Anne, dear.'

'Oh, right, yes, of course. Didn't recognise your voice in the dark.'

'Would you mind asking for some lights?'

'Of course, dear. Lights, I say! Someone's got to have some god-damned matches, don't they?'

I had no time to enjoy his discomfort as, moments later, Catriona's hand dived for my crotch and by God she was strong, the opportunist minx. I wrestled with her in silence as the Helots – who were well drilled, I'll give the Farquharsons that – swept in to light silver candleholders that stood atop the ancient walnut cabinets lining the walls of the room. Only then, as the candles blazed and cast weird shadows across the walls, did Catriona beat a surly retreat.

I'm glad she did because her fumblings were making it devil-ishly difficult to keep an eye on Iain Barclay, whom I was watching to see if he got any updates from his sources. The regime would be working hard to control the situation and the narrative, but if anyone were to get the lowdown it would be Barclay. Wally, for his part, would be monitoring channels as best he could, but it was a dangerous time to be messing with the apparatus of State. So, we had to wait and see how diligent Barclay's reporters were in getting to the site and relaying the news to him. If the information didn't come soon, it would be too late. Looking at the state of him, I'd wager Barclay wouldn't be able to take any call after the next half hour. His eyes were glassy and he seemed only half aware of what was going on around him.

More staff materialised at our shoulders, illuminating a dozen tall candlesticks that ran the length of the table like a ghostly copse of trees. No doubt, somewhere out in the dark and bitter cold, other workers were rampaging around barns to find diesel. Torch beams would flash in the night, lighting clouds of warm breath as they laboured in the freezing air. Foul curses would follow, directed at old generators that refused to start.

In the warmth of the dining room, the privileged few had, for a moment, been robbed of their ribald self-assurance. That terrible beast, reality, prowled around the table, whispering uncertainty into each ear. The shadows led a merry dance around the deep-green walls, making the portraits of the Farquharson ancestors malevolent and judgmental. Just as they would have wanted, no doubt.

Colonel Anne broke the silence, clapping her hands and rising from her seat. She had the bearing of a hostess who would let nothing ruin the occasion, and who had An Idea.

'A tour!' she sang out. 'Yes, we have many visitors who have never had the tour, and what a time for it! Alasdair, would you do the honours?'

His Lordship looked doubly shocked: surely she wasn't suggesting that the port bottle should be allowed to come to rest? And how dare she persist in the use of such a familiar form of address in the company of social inferiors like that Macfarlane cretin?

He looked for a moment as if he would refuse her. But with the briefest glance at that smiling, implacable face, he tipped back his port, gripped the arms of his chair and hauled himself upright.

'Follow me, please,' he said without enthusiasm and headed for the door.

As one, the table rose. All except Barclay, who had slipped into a light coma. Goddamn it. I had no choice but to begin the tour, which, as it turned out, was both interesting and important. You see, plans – nay, *schemes* – were starting to play out that were, unbeknownst to yours truly, already wrapping me in their dastardly embrace.

We began in the great hall, which was now lit with candles whose orange light reflected off walls festooned with polished ancient Scottish armaments. The shadows flickered over weapons ranging from halberds and Lochaber axes to small round targes and the obligatory basket-hilted swords decoratively crossed on the wall. It was to the latter His Lordship took us first.

'Before we start,' he said with respectful condescension, 'I must inform you in no uncertain terms that these swords, commonly known as claymores, are nothing of the sort. It is a misnomer and I insist, should you care to reference them, you address them as broadswords.'

Next he pointed us towards a huge iron sword mounted on the wall. It looked as if it had been fashioned in the time of cavemen and had since lain undisturbed in a peat bog. The weapon was hardly recognisable as a sword; rather it looked like a pitted brown cross.

'Now this' – Farquharson pointed at the double-handed behemoth – 'is what the uneducated would call a broadsword.'

'It looks pretty bloody broad to me,' I said, unable to contain myself.

He scowled. 'In fact, this, ladies and gentlemen – and yes, you too, Mr Macfarlane – is the real deal: a proper *claidheamh-mòr* – the claymore, or great sword. And, by God, if any lives up to its name it is this one. This is the Great Sword of *Dìleas Làimh*, which, for the Sassenachs[*] amongst you' – here he looked pointedly at Hildebrand with the kind of impatience and disappointment hitherto reserved for me – 'is Gaelic for the Loyal Hand. It is the origin of the family crest – a clenched fist.

'The sword was found during the renovations of the North Tower, buried in the foundations – put there, one imagines, to keep it safe from marauding English soldiers. It got its name after Angus, third Lord Farquharson, found his father's corpse as he retreated from the battlefield at Culloden in 1745. The last battle fought on British soil. Gripped tight in the dead lord's bloodied fist was the ancient family claymore you see before you. So tightly gripped that, with the redcoats on his heels, Angus had no choice but to slice off his father's hand so he could save the sword. Until the hand – that loyal fist – fell away through decay, they could not get it off.'

Noise of revulsion came from our party, which made Farquharson settle into the tour guide role. He stood looking dewy-eyed for a moment, sad at the lack of opportunities he had to repeat such fine family traditions. Here was a man looking for his own Culloden. The kind of man one should avoid at all costs.

Then Hildebrand sneezed and the spell was broken. Farquharson glared at him, before leading us towards the wide, curving staircase that dominated one side of the hall.

'What's that?' asked Lizzy, pointing at a rusted tangle of iron under a small table at the foot of the stairs. 'A bear trap?'

'Man trap,' came the resentful reply. 'Can't use it on poachers these days, of course. Not even ramblers. What has the world come to, I ask you?'

Up we went, my hands running over the smooth wooden

* English people, from the Gaelic for Saxon.

bannisters. The stairs led us to a landing, where the paltry light from the candle in His Lordship's hand reached out into the cloying darkness of the corridor beyond. It was colder up here, and I shuffled instinctively closer to Lizzy, who instinctively moved away.

Our guide stopped to knock on a piece of the wooden panelling that lined the walls up to chest height. His knock revealed the area behind to be hollow and, prising away one of the panels, he revealed a small space, barely big enough for a man to crouch in.

'A priest hole,' he explained. 'Place is bloody littered with them.'

We crowded round for a look, but something caught the keen eye of our English tourist.

'Your Lordship, what is this?' Hildebrand asked, pointing to an ancient-looking piece of parchment that hung on the wall in a large frame. It was yellowed and stained. Spidery words spread across it in what appeared to be old Scots. At the bottom clung the remnants of several red wax seals.

'Ah, yes, the proclamation. I'm not sure this is one for the ladies; it's a bit gruesome.' Farquharson frowned.

Of course, that did it. There's nothing the ladies like more than a touch of the gruesome. At least, the ones I know, anyway.

He pulled a pair of round spectacles from his old leather sporran and began to read, adopting a broad Scots accent to do justice to the incomprehensible scrawl. I remember snatches of it, which Farquharson read in tones that would do any amateur dramatist proud.

'*To all men to whom these present letters come, I, Johnston, Stewart of Fife, send greetings in God. Arbuthnott, Barclay, Falconer, Farquharson* . . . then addresses, postcodes, ordinance survey references . . . *for the killing of the late John of Melville, Laird of Glenbervie* . . . hellfire, brimstone, general unpleasantness . . . *the law shall have its course.*' Farquharson stopped to deliver a portentous look over the top of his half-moon spectacles, then turned back to the manuscript. '*We firmly forbid on the King's behalf, no man shall molest, trouble, or wrong the foresaid persons because of the killing of said John of Melville in the year of God 1421 . . .* You are looking at a pardon – for a heinous crime committed over six hundred years ago.' His Lordship held the candle beneath his chin, casting a ghostly shadow on his face, and I secretly hoped his long beard would catch fire and lighten the mood. 'But *horresco referens!*' Farquharson declared forcefully, making us all shrink back from him.

'I shudder as I tell the story,' piped up Hildebrand, translating unprompted for his host.

The voice was like a pin bursting a bubble. Lord Farquharson scowled afresh, furious at having his thunder stolen. Hildebrand looked back unabashed, as if he had no idea of his indiscretion. I wondered if I hadn't just seen the latest of a number of social misdemeanours that had made this tourist such a heavy yoke for the Farquharson shoulders to bear.

'There was a sheriff in these parts by the name of Melville, who bore his authority harshly,' he boomed, staring hard at each of us in turn. 'So harshly that he became detested by the barons hereabouts, who turned to the King for redress.'

His features ebbed and flowed in the candlelight. The flame flickered towards that mighty beard, threatening conflagration. I blew softly, ever hopeful of combustion, until a sharp elbow caught me in the ribs. Lizzy was next to me, armed with a look that said she had glimpsed the real me and it had come as a painful disappointment. His Lordship continued, unaware of the danger just averted.

'The monarch is said to have answered them, in a rash and impetuous moment: "Sorrow gin the sheriff were sodden, and supped in broo!"'

He looked at the Englishman, almost begging him to take a guess at the meaning. The latter gazed blankly back, oblivious. Still glowering at Hildebrand, His Lordship continued with relentless purpose.

'The sheriff should be drowned and made into soup!' he translated with relish.

Eyes widened amongst his audience as the implications presented themselves. This response cheered His Lordship up immeasurably after the previous Latin setback. He drew himself up with pride.

'Donald, Lord Farquharson, leading the others, lured the hated sheriff to the top of the hill of Killieridge, not far from here, under the pretence of hosting a hunting party. Upon this hill they had prepared a cauldron of oil, heated until boiling, into which they forced the screaming sheriff. According to the story, they waited until the flesh was off his bones and then they all partook of the hell-broth, making every man a cannibal so that none would be tempted to divulge their swift and noble act of justice.'

Justice clearly being in the eye of the beholder back then – just as it is now. *Plus ça change*, I tell you.

'But the story was revealed,' Farquharson announced. 'Some anonymous backslider – a traitor, a guttersnipe! – betrayed them and they were forced into hiding. The lairds were only pardoned years later – and rightfully so, I say – while to this day the hill is nicknamed the Sheriff's Pot by the locals. But this old parchment is not all we are left with, oh no. For, you see, the sheriff is still with us. Many's the guest who has reported, in the dead of night, hearing the heavy footsteps and rasping, tortured breath of the boiled man, the slapping and scraping of the skin hanging from his bones, as he stalks these corridors in search of the architect of his death . . . Now then! Shall we go to the dungeon? Or maybe the hanging tower?'

With that invitation – delivered in a jaunty tone better suited to one leading a tour of the local shortbread factories – Farquharson set off with a spring in his step. But he had to stop as no one was following. Neither would you, I suspect, if you'd just learned your guide's veins ran with cannibal's blood. Instead, we stood united in our desire to avoid any more of Farquharson's generous hospitality. The muttering began to spread.

'My, would you just look at the time?'

'Enough culture for one night, I think.'

'A quick snifter before bedtime, anyone?'

This sounded like a splendid idea, but Common Sense was roaring in my ear that I must stay the course; I must do more to ingratiate myself with His Lordship. With a sinking heart, I knew I must do everything I could to get him on side in case his goodwill was required in the coming hours and days. So, with a wide smile on my face and my guts dissolving, I announced I'd be delighted to complete this morbid horrorfest (or words to that effect) with a trip to the dungeon. A look of delight crossed His Lordship's crestfallen features.

'Ah, Macfarlane, I knew you were made of sterner stuff!' he lied, clapping me on the back and sending houseguests tumbling as he strode back along the landing. We deposited visitors in bedrooms as we went, leaving those most in need of a drink in the drawing room with a decanter for company. Somehow Barclay had made his way in there and was now snoozing peacefully, exactly as we'd left him, just in a different chair. And then there were two.

Into the kitchens we went, each of us armed with a candle, our steps echoing off the uneven flagstones, the candles casting crazy shadows. Stopping at a narrow wooden door, Farquharson cocked an eyebrow and pulled it open. Beyond lay a corridor so thin we had to walk in single file. These walls were of raw hewn stone that was cold and clammy to the touch. They were pocked with holes and sharp edges, as if they had been cut out with picks. The ceiling was so low I bowed down to make sure I didn't scalp myself on the grating surface above. The air was cool, thick, and claustrophobic.

The candle struggled to penetrate the superior darkness that lurked in this tunnel. The air grew colder and staler with every step, the call of *Dead man walking!* echoed from the murky corners of my imagination. Then the echo of our footsteps began to mix with another sound: a light whimpering. It took a while to realise it was coming from me.

I've said it before: when it comes to the unknown, I have none of the bravery that marks one out as courageous. And not only were we deep in the realms of the unknown, but things were about to get a lot worse. There was no way I could have known what was waiting for me down there. In the dark.

CHAPTER 10

At the Bottom of a Bottle

On we went. The close-set walls and dancing flame of the candle turned Farquharson's stately, stooped silhouette into a crooked monstrosity. At long last the corridor came to an end and widened out into a small, round chamber. The ceiling here was higher and vaulted, to support the weight of the massive building above it. On the far side of this horrible little atrium was a pitch-black hole. On closer inspection, this revealed itself to be a small doorway, with stone steps that led down and curved out of sight. I peered into the dark and didn't like it one bit. It was the kind of dark that desperate, clawing hands like to reach out of.

'Still keen on a poke around?' His Lordship smiled, waiting for my nerve to crack.

'Of course,' I replied.

Farquharson slapped his hand on one of the walls, as he might the flank of a horse. 'Almost four feet thick,' he said, a note of awe in his voice. 'It wouldn't have been the done thing if the ancestors could hear the screams and the begging for mercy, would it, what?'

I nodded mutely.

'Now, this is interesting,' he ploughed on, walking across the atrium and crouching down. He held out his candle to reveal a wooden board, about a metre square. It was bolted onto the wall, a few inches off the floor. 'There are two dungeons in the castle. The one we're about to visit is my *show* dungeon. Not many people know about the second.' He marched back over to me and, putting

113

his arm about my shoulders, squeezed me tightly to him. 'A wonder of engineering,' he purred softly. Lovingly.

I had a sudden and horrible premonition that I was on some kind of a date. A date that would end in unpleasantness. Terrible, awful unpleasantness. My buttocks clenched involuntarily, still caught in this mad historian's iron embrace.

'Behind that little panel is a shaft that is carved *within* the thickness of the castle wall,' he continued, the huge arm tightening further around my young(er), supple(ish) shoulders. *Oh God.* 'It leads to a dungeon, which is reached only after the chute drops you fifteen feet onto the stone floor. That entrance is plumb in the middle of the ceiling. Only when you stand up – if you haven't broken a leg in the fall, of course – will the terror of it hit you.' His voice was rising and his breath quickened as the words tumbled out. 'You'll run from wall to wall, searching for a door that you will never find. Stumbling over . . . What is that? Branches? No: Lord have mercy! Bones! You will feel the walls rise and then curve over you, and then you will realise your ingress is the only egress. There is no way out . . .'

He paused, lost in reverie. One hand was out in front of him, arcing around, conjuring up the horror below. The other kept me in its terrifying embrace.

'It's usually called an oubliette, as it's where you put people and forget about them. But ours has its own name: Farquharson's Bottle. Because of the shape, you see? For centuries it was an instrument of fear, a powerful threat that kept more than one lord from the assassin's knife.'

I wanted to whimper, but worried it would only inflame his ardour.

'Of course,' he continued, a note of sadness creeping into his voice, 'the passage of time brought with it an intolerance for our ancient and noble traditions. It became no longer acceptable to throw malfeasants down there. Not even travelling salesmen or Jehovah's Witnesses, if you'd believe it. Eventually the Bottle was joined to the cellars for storage and not long after that, it was sealed up entirely.' His jaw tightened. 'Bloody liberals. I mean, what's it coming to when a man can't be left alone to use his dungeons as he sees fit? It's tantamount to fascism. Oh well, onwards and downwards, eh?'

It was time to see what prize lay behind door number two. Heart sinking faster than the winding staircase, I dutifully followed him through the doorway, candle thrust forward in trembling hand. The bastard whistled a jaunty tune as he went – 'Highland Laddie', of all things. More fevered thoughts of unwanted advances came rushing back. Jesus, was I to be his Highland Laddie?

My brain was spinning. I would be able to fight him off, wouldn't I? What if he proved too strong? Would we talk about it over breakfast? Would I still have to write to his wife, thanking them for the hospitality? These and many other pressing questions found no answers in my adrenaline-soaked mind as I shuffled down the uneven stone stairs, fingertips finding support, but no succour, from the slimy, cold stone.

I followed Farquharson's shrill whistle as it rose up from the darkness, bouncing off the narrow walls. And still I went with him, not daring to back out lest my pariah status be confirmed and my alibi somehow undone. You no doubt think me mad, but choosing between lasting damnation and dungeon plaything for an evening is easier than you might think.

Down, down, down we went until I rounded the final turn of the spiral and found Farquharson standing by a thick wooden door, with shiny black nails hammered into it, hanging on heavy hinges. It looked brand new and I wondered from which range of dungeon doors, in which mail order catalogue, this one had been so carefully chosen.

It creaked open – unoiled for effect, no doubt – and we entered a vaulted chamber. The candle's light barely reached the other side. From what I could see, one end was curved, with the rest of the dungeon a square room, hewn from the same bare stone as above.

The first thing that struck me was the earthy smell in the air. Not decay; more the scent of one of the moors that stretched into the hills outside. The walls looked green, slimy, and mossy. I crossed the floor to the other side – in no more than fifteen quick, frightened steps – and touched one. Then I leant in and smelled this bizarre aroma.

'The work of my gardener! A fine job, is it not?' His Lordship's voice rang out from the doorway, but I had to squint to see his figure in the gloom. 'Recreated what the wall might once have been like. He is a genius, is he not?'

I placed my hand on the wet surface. 'You have an interior designer for your dungeon?'

'And a damn fine one, too. It's just a pity his theories on moss extend beyond these walls. Calls it an *alluring addition* to the ornamental garden, the vile heathen. I am prepared to tolerate that but where does it stop, I ask you? But he knows I am in his moss-covered clutches, damn his eyes. A shortage of head gardeners is one of the consequences of these times we live in. By God, a spell in the Bottle would soon convert him to the sanctity of grass.'

For a moment I almost forgot this was a conversation in a dungeon. The utter absurdity of the situation gripped me and I couldn't help but laugh, the noise echoing eerily off the stone and around the empty room. There was a growing warmth in my heart – the kind only your true coward can appreciate as reality intrudes, fears are dispelled, and the threat of appalling sexual deviancy wanes (*unwanted* sexual deviancy, obviously).

As His Lordship continued to grumble about the autocratic horrors perpetrated by head gardeners, I followed the line of the wall with my fingertips, being careful not to let my candle go out. Farquharson stood unmoving by the door, like a phantom jailer, appearing and disappearing in the unsteady candlelight. Yet, despite applying all my reason and relief to the place – it was a *show dungeon*, for crying out loud – it was still impossible to divorce this chamber completely from the horrors that had surely been perpetrated here.

And might still be! yelled Common Sense in my ear.

The initial warmth in my bosom was already waning. The atmosphere was once again becoming oppressive – as if the walls had absorbed some of the fear, pain, and despair of previous inhabitants and were regurgitating it back over me. The candle flickered in some unfelt breeze, threatening to go out. My hand touched something cold and hard on the wall and I pulled it back instinctively. The little flame danced again, warning me of its ultimate sanction. On further inspection, I learned my fingertips had stumbled on a large iron ring bolted onto the wall. There was another a few feet on, and another thereafter.

'Oh, those are original features,' said the demonic estate agent, still motionless, watching. Revelling in my discomfort. 'For manacles, you see?'

Manacles! Bloody manacles, moaned Common Sense in despair. *How does this stuff keep happening to me?*

Us, said Pride.

I blame you for all of this, said Common Sense.

Farquharson interrupted my mental paroxysms. 'Now, do you have time for one last tale before bed? I wouldn't want you to have nightmares . . .'

His Lordship's goading had the opposite effect than he was after, temporarily breaking the spell that he and his pit had cast over me. I was beginning to get annoyed, both by Farquharson's attempts to frighten me and by my natural propensity for being frightened.

'In for a penny, in for a pound,' I replied in a steady voice.

This is exactly what I'm talking about, said Common Sense.

'These dungeons – this one and the other on the far side of this wall' – Farquharson slapped the stone wall, sending another echo bouncing around the cell – 'are said to be haunted by the ghost of a drummer boy. One story says the boy incurred the jealousy of the lord, another that he failed to warn of an attack on the castle, but they agree that sometime in the early eighteenth century he was sealed inside his drum, rolled down the chute into Farquharson's Bottle, and left there to rot.' He walked over to the wall on my left and patted it lovingly. 'They say his ghostly drumming can be heard in the dungeons each night. They also say that if he is heard anywhere else in the castle, it is a portent of death.'

I grimaced in the candle's glow. In my head, Pride screamed back at him, *In that case, just you wait, you bloody lunatic, I'll be creeping out tonight with my drumsticks, just see if I bloody don't.* Common Sense exhaled in a resigned sort of way.

'It is said—'

Farquharson's sentence was never completed. A yell echoed around the dungeon, bringing me close to cardiac arrest. It had a similar effect on His Lordship, who promptly dropped his candle. It hit the flagstones and was extinguished. Now I had the only light.

'Alasdair! Are you down there?' came the echoing voice again, this time with a tone as close to anger as I ever heard it. Relief flooded through me and my heart sang unto the heavens: *God bless you, Colonel Anne!*

'Yes, dear,' he replied stoutly. 'Just showing Mr Macfarlane the sights.'

'Please come up here immediately.'

'Yes, dear,' he replied, a little less stoutly.

With the candle no longer in his hand I could barely separate his dark form from the darkness around him as he turned and walked up the stairs, seemingly forgetting I was there. I heard him ascending the steps until all was silent.

I started to follow him, crossing the dungeon towards the

yawning black hole of the door. I was halfway across when a breeze swept down the stairs, no doubt caused by some inconsiderate aristocrat opening a door somewhere. My candle gave one last angry twinkle and went out.

The darkness was total. A fear such as I had never felt before crept over me. The Training piped up to remind me darkness was my friend, but I told it to bugger off along with Pride, who was nowhere to be seen. No, this darkness was not now, nor would ever be, my friend. This was what it had been like for the terrified victims of the ancient Farquharsons. Cold. Alone. In the dark.

Then it got worse.

I was edging across the floor, being careful not to trip on the uneven flagstones, when I first heard it.

Rat-a-tat-tat.

I froze, focusing all my senses on the noise, desperate for it to have been my imagination. Nothing. Then:

Rat-a-tat-tat.

Then it came again, faster now. Relentless and unmistakable. It was coming from somewhere to the left of me. From Farquharson's Bottle.

Rat-a-tat-tat.

Rat-a-tat-tat.

There was no question it was rhythmic. A pluckier man than I would have gone over to the wall and banged on it, attempting to summon this demon drummer, then give the boy a stern talking-to – perhaps threaten a period of grounding – when he floated through the walls. But I was not that man. The thought of children frightened me enough, let alone undead ones. Instead I made a beeline for the door with all the speed one can muster when moving in complete darkness over an uneven floor. Which is not a lot.

Then I stopped again and this time couldn't stifle a whimper. In the doorway, maybe three metres away, I could swear there was a figure. Too tall to be a drummer boy, surely? But it couldn't be – there was no way I could see anyone in this darkness. Then I swear I saw it turn and disappear up the steps.

I stood for a few seconds – which is an age in a pitch-black dungeon, I can tell you – before a wave of anger broke over me. Of course! This was a joke. A bloody practical joke! I chased after the apparition.

Feeling my way upwards, fingertips trailing against the walls on either side of the tightly spiralling stairs, I went as quickly as I could, emerging into the deserted atrium at the top, before barrelling onwards into the thin stone corridor. Ahead in the dark I could see the closed door into the kitchen, an orange glow around it. I flung it open and burst into the room, the door slamming against the wall and swinging shut with a bang. I stood squinting in the light and shaking with fear and adrenaline, ready to do bloody murder, drummer boy or no. But, as is so often the case, my bravery was nothing but a walking shadow. My eyes widened in shock. I fancy I whimpered. The spectre came at me across the flagstones, arms wide to take me in its terrible embrace. I backed up against the door. There was nowhere to go.

'Oh, my dear, I am so sorry, left down there,' said the spectre, with surprising gentleness. It noticed the extinguished candle, gripped in the vice-like clasp of my quivering hand. 'Oh, and with no light, how appalling for you . . .'

Colonel Anne's arms, clad in a voluminous dressing gown, encircled me. I stood shaking in her embrace. Over her shoulder I spied Lord Farquharson, attempting to keep noble countenance after having clearly been given a serious reprimand.

'I heard him!' I hissed through gritted teeth.

There was a pause.

'Heard who?' she asked as I disentangled myself from her grip and jabbed a finger at the noble lord who was still skulking behind her.

'I suppose this is your idea of a joke?' I said, through clenched jaw.

'Don't use that tone with me, if you please—'

'I'm sorry,' said the Colonel, interrupting. 'James, who did you hear?'

'The drummer boy, of course! The bloody drummer boy.'

They froze for an instant and I could swear both went a little pale. Oh God, this wasn't a joke.

Anne was first to regain her composure. 'Just your imagination, my dear. Down there the mind plays tricks—'

'Rat-a-tat-tat. Rat-a-bloody-tat,' I insisted. 'Coming from Farquharson's damned Bottle, as clear as day.'

Both were definitely now more pallid; I fancy even His Lordship's rosy nose lost some of its lustre. I looked at them in bewilderment, waiting for the punchline to this vile charade. It didn't come.

'Bed for everyone, I think,' said Anne, quickly. 'We want to be sure of a good bag tomorrow to keep Mr Brown happy.'

'Mr Brown is our gamekeeper,' explained His Lordship. 'Has strong opinions on heather . . .'

'Oh, do be quiet, Alasdair.'

'Yes, dear.'

'Let's get you to bed, James.'

'Yes, dear. Sorry, I mean yes, Lady Anne.'

With one arm round me, Lady Anne led me at speed through the kitchen, into the hall, up the stairs, along the landing and, finally, into my room. My feet hardly touched the ground. She kept up a constant stream of inconsequential patter about the weather, the various game drives we would do tomorrow, and what a superb lunch she had in store for the guns. I didn't get a single word in, which was obviously the plan, and she left me with a brisk, 'Goodnight.'

As I lay wide awake in bed, it was clear sleep would not come. Turning to my side table, I was appalled to find there was only a water jug. The poor wee thing looked terribly lonely, no whisky to keep it company on such a dark, cold night. It's cruel what some people are capable of, it really is.

Still coursing with adrenaline as I was, the desire for drink overcame the instinct to hide under the covers until dawn. So, armed only with an ugly china sheep that had been minding its own business on the mantelpiece – quite how I thought Sheepy would see off whatever was lurking in the dark of the house is still beyond me – I set out for the drawing room, where a decanter waited with my name on it.

I made the trip in double-quick time, padding through shafts of moonlight in the sleeping house like some thief in the night, waving Sheepy menacingly at the merest suggestion of ghoulish apparitions. I dodged most of the creaky floorboards that I had noted when we were on our tour. (Good little soldier boy, ain't I?) In my haste to be back in the safe, warm confines of my room, I almost took the first decanter in front of me in the vast, cold space of the drawing room. Fortunately, knowing my host, I had the presence of mind to carefully examine its contents and discovered a terrible backstreet blend designed to trick marauding guests. Now, I don't know about your experiences of being a guest at someone else's home, but being lost in a dungeon and terrified by marauding spirits is one thing, however being duped into drinking Old Rashiebog's four-year-old Sweaty Sporran is liable to spoil any stay. In the fading glow of the embers in the giant hearth, I rooted around until I found something His Lordship would miss. I snatched it up and made for my room.

As I came back up to the top of the stairs, bottle in hand, whispered voices cut through the peace of the night. It was my hosts from behind a door somewhere down the hall.

'What were you *thinking*, Alasdair? Do you realise what you could have done?'

'My dear, I was on an important mission. If we are going to make use of him, I wanted to test his mettle for myself. I know what you think, but I suspect he's a coward, you see, and you know how much I hate a—'

'He is our *guest*, Alasdair, and a very influential one too. You know how useful he could be and yet you pull this nonsense! We need his help. You could have ruined everything.'

There was a pause. It was a most uncomfortable silence and His Lordship, clearly no match for his wife, folded in the face of it.

'Look, I just took him to the dungeons. I didn't expect him to hear anything – what was the chance of that? You have to admit it was terribly bad luck.'

'Terribly bad luck? Is that what you think it was? My God, Alasdair, sometimes I despair . . .'

On they went and I would happily have stayed to listen to His Lordship's discomfort, because I'm a mean and vindictive brute. Moreover, it seemed that their plans to palm Hildebrand Blunt off on me were now confirmed. I was forewarned and forearmed, and would do everything in my power to be as little use to them as possible. Perhaps the whole escapade had somehow been worth it after all. But all this could wait for another day. For now, all that mattered was that I had a date with a malt, who I was sure was single. And with whom I intended to go all the way.

I left the Farquharsons stewing in marital discord and scurried back to my room, where I placed a metal teaspoon in an empty glass and set it by the door. If anyone dared to come in, the resultant clatter would act as an early-warning system. I climbed into bed, pulled the heavy old duvet over me, and began my most important mission of the evening so far. Operation Oblivion started with the sound of whisky and water splashing together with wild abandon. With a speed that should surprise no one, all the Scotch was gone. Stage one complete. I plunged headlong into stage two and sleep came quickly. There was not a drummer boy to be heard. Mission accomplished.

CHAPTER 11

The World's a Stage

I was woken by the sound of the spoon clattering against the glass as it was knocked over by the opening door.

'No, drummer boy, don't take me – for I am no lord!' I hollered in my waking delirium, while seeking sanctuary beneath the covers.

'Are yeh OK, Mr Mac? Oh Jesus, whit a bluidy mess,' came the guttural Glaswegian response.

I peeked out from under the duvet and beheld a wonderful sight: Archie with a cup of tea and a teapot. On a silver platter, of all things. He did love a sense of occasion.

The big man was staring at my clothes, as well as the decanter, glass, and jug – all of which were strewn about the floor.

'Whit happened here?'

I mulled the answer for a while, before realising there was no way of coming out of it with any credit. The notion of getting sympathy from Archie after being scared out of my wits by a ghost was absurd.

In the end, I settled on 'It's a long story.'

'Aye, ah'm sure. Yeh'll be needin' this then.' With a flourish, he produced a glass from behind the teapot. Oh, happy days! I stared reverently at the patented morning pick-me-up that Archie proffered. I cannot recommend it highly enough and hereby donate the recipe to posterity:

A large measure of brandy
A dash of Angostura bitters
1 teaspoonful of sugar
A glass of fresh milk
Another large measure of brandy
Shake well
Strain into a tumbler
Add a squirt of soda (ideally from a syphon to add to the sense
*   of occasion)*
Serve.

Archie was fiercely proud of this concoction, simply known as 'The No. 2', and its ability to chase away what he called the 'Screaming Meemies'. I had long since given up asking what the No. 1 was. Every time I did, he would tap his nose and say, 'Never you mind, Mr Mac.' Then, with a look of profound solemnity, he would add, 'Just pray yeh never need it.'

I raised the glass and offered that ancient soldier's lament. 'A cup to the dead already.'

'An' hooray fer the next tae die.' Archie dipped his head out of habit.

I guzzled the reviving beverage as Archie pulled open the heavy maroon curtains, revealing the small windows behind. A pale morning sun crept into the room. By the level of light, I judged it was around 8 a.m., which meant – *oh, bloody hell* – I was late. Again.

The benefit of *tempus* having *fugit,* combined with the resulting panic in my breast and the life-giving properties of the No. 2, was that my hangover could gain no foothold. The air of urgency also drove any thoughts of ghostly drummer boys from my mind. So it was a surprisingly sprightly Mac who climbed like a snail onto its thorn and faced the day.

'Ah've laid oot yer get-up fer the day – yer togs are o'er by the windie,' said Archie, nodding towards the clothes that were care-fully arranged on a chair by the window. He was already dressed in a suit of dark-brown tweed, looking immaculate. My own shooting garb looked positively shabby by comparison, but I value comfort. A wise man once said to me, 'any fool can be uncomfortable'. I rather took this to heart since I was lying in a ditch at the time, wet and demoralised during the early days of military training. I pulled my tweeds on at speed and left the room, stopping only for Archie to straighten my tie.

'Och, yeh cannae go oot looken like that, it's enough tae make a man greet,"* he grumbled.

I was heading down the stairs when I saw Wally waiting in the hall, panting as if he had run to intercept me.

'Mr Mac,' he said between laboured breaths, 'I've done the cov-erage analysis and—'

'No time for that now,' I said, sweeping past, 'it can wait until after breakfast.'

'But sir, there's some strange—' He broke off mid-sentence for a short coughing fit.

I stopped and turned on my heel to face him. 'One: don't call me sir. Two: never, ever – and I cannot stress this enough – stand between breakfast and me. And three: for God's sake take your inhaler. That cough sounds awful.'

He spread his hands in silent plea but I was off, enticed by the smells emanating from the dining room.

I bounded into the long room. Its portraits now looked benevo-lent in the soft morning light. I had hoped to make a good impres-sion and to secure the last vestiges of porridge or kedgeree, but this was impossible because the dining table was deserted. Half-finished plates of food were cooling in rays of crisp sunshine spilling through the bay windows. The air of hasty abandonment was reminiscent of

* Cry.

a mealtime on the *Mary Celeste*. Something was afoot.

I stood surveying the scene. Steam rose from a large silver bowl in the middle of the table, filled with porridge. A ladle lay next to it, waiting to be of service. I awaited the return of the three bears. Then the sound of voices and – yes – a wailing siren drifted into the room. Perhaps the hungry bears had already returned and were wreaking bloody havoc in another wing of the castle.

I sauntered out of the dining room, following the noise and taking care to do nothing that might excite my hangover. Archie's concoctions could only hold back the tide for so long and no one had been polite enough to offer me a drink. I glanced at the grandfather clock. It was already past 8.30 and not a whiff of a pick-me-up. Poor show.

I crossed the hall and entered the snug, the cacophony growing ever closer. There, at the other end of the room, the whole party stood gathered, their backs to me. I watched for a moment, keen to gather any possible intel. I couldn't see any marauding bears, but one couldn't be too careful on fragile mornings such as this.

'Morning!' I ventured.

No one responded, so I mooched over to see what was going on. They were all crowded round the holo-screen, watching events unfold on CBC.[*] I peered over a shoulder at the small picture hovering uncertainly in the air – it couldn't have been more than thirty inches and I had to strain to see it. Isn't it curious how the size of one's screen is so often inversely proportionate to the size of one's house? Odd, that. The screen flickered, a side effect of our lamentable internet infrastructure, and I squinted at the murky images coming in and out of sight. Then the picture sharpened and I took a sharp intake of breath. There in front of us was the smouldering wreck of the Pitlochry hydro-electric dam turbine hall. In all the excitement, I had forgotten we'd blown up a major piece of national infrastructure barely twelve hours previously.

---

[*] Caledon Broadcasting Corporation.

The shell of the structure was open to the elements; grey stone walls charred black. It looked woeful in the flat light. A column of pale smoke rose into the deep-blue sky, disfiguring an otherwise perfect day. The sun reflected off the loch behind and got in the eyes of the assorted emergency services and other agents of the state, who milled around, trying to look busy.

'Oh my God, that's beautiful,' I murmured.

A couple of faces with curious expressions turned to me.

Bugger.

'Oh, the humanity!' I barked in panic, drawing even more inquisitive glances.

The camera panned to the right to show the dam, still intact. The water of the loch lapped gently against it, unconcerned by the carnage. Far beyond the dam I could see movement in the town as tiny people went about their business, no doubt zipping their coats tight around themselves and shivering in the cold morning air.

'Thank God,' I said, once again forgetting myself. Out of the corner of my eye I caught Hildebrand staring at me. I ignored him and continued watching the news report.

A clip of an interview with the security guard Archie had so violently greeted was being played. I noted that he hadn't been cleaned up, although his broken nose was now in a splint. The skin round his eyes was turning a dark shade of purple, laced with brown. He looked gruesome, but that was the point. As I'd once heard Iain Barclay say, 'If it bleeds, it leads.'

'He came out of the darkness,' the guard was saying. 'Huge . . . all in black . . . I challenged him and he attacked me like an animal. Then he screamed something about a wolf . . .'

'It was the Wolf of Badenoch again!' gulped one of our shocked company.

'I'm sorry,' said Hildebrand. 'What's a Wolf of Badenoch?'

The assembled company ignored him.

'It – I mean, he – didn't ask for anything, he just howled like a madman. I got back up and tried to fight him off, got a few blows in, but he was so strong . . . He was about to throw me over the dam when John – that's my colleague, over there – surprised him and he ran off. I think the idea of taking on two of us scared him.'

Oh, please! Pride was back and unrepentant.

Out of the corner of my eye I saw Hildebrand looking at me again in that intrusive way of his. I was beginning to understand what His Lordship didn't see in him.

Back on the report, the face of our despotic patriarch had appeared, turning from a heady discussion with a group of enthusiastic first responders to face the camera. He was clad in the regulation hard hat and fluorescent yellow jacket that all politicians are mandated to wear – even tyrannical despots – if they go within a hundred metres of any form of manufacturing. He looked tired, maybe even ill, which was nice to see. The anxiety of influence was lying heavy on his shoulders that day.

'Marischal, sir, can you comment on this attack?' asked the young reporter, who was holding a microphone under his nose. 'Was it the work of the Wolf of Badenoch?'

'We are ruling nothing out,' the Marischal replied, his voice rich and stern, a wall of unassailable authority. 'But I tell you this: I promise we will do everything we can to get to the bottom of what happened here.'

The reporter began to ask another question, but was cut off.

'And I'll tell you something else: I make no apology for putting every resource necessary into this.'

'But, the Wolf, Marischal—'

'If you just wait, I'll get to that. We must focus on the immediate issue, which is the safety of the dam and the local people. There may well be technical issues that need to be looked into and we must make sure lessons are learned.'

The interview was interrupted by the Englishman, Hildebrand: 'Your leader, he's a hard man, I grant you, but at least he will answer the press's questions. Not like our politicians.'

In a flash, Iain Barclay, our dilapidated media mogul, scooped up the remote control and paused the report. He was animated in a way I had never seen him. I wondered if he had already succeeded in securing a liquid breakfast.

'Ha!' he said. 'Answer questions? Are you joking?'

'But he . . .' Hildebrand was confused at having woken this grizzly bear that had been a docile koala just moments before.

'He didn't answer a bloody thing – nor will he,' said an impassioned Barclay. 'Watch this.'

'Iain,' began Barclay's long-suffering wife, but he was not for turning.

Remote in hand, he reversed the report and replayed what we had just heard. 'OK, first answer: "We are ruling nothing out." It's meaningless, don't you see? He's not ruling anything *in* either. It doesn't mean anything.' He let the interview play for a few seconds. 'Right, then he says, "I make no apology for putting every resource into this." Why on God's green earth should he apologise for that? Well, good for him, standing up to unreasonable, yet *non-existent* critics of his determination to do the right thing. Do you see?'

He was building up quite the head of steam and, after last night's tirade, I wondered if he hadn't finally cracked.

'What next? Oh yes, he's asked about this so-called Wolf of Badenoch and he clearly doesn't want to talk about that, so he just stonewalls it by saying "I'll get there," or some such – well, you can be bloody sure he won't. He is a master of the art of taking one question and answering a completely different one without anyone noticing. It's straight into "We must focus on the immediate issue" – in other words, "Let's focus on the issue *I* want to talk about, not the one *you* want to talk about."

'Then he throws in a mention of technical issues – or, in other words, "This is really something for people far cleverer than you," or, better yet, "This is too dull for you to worry yourself about; leave it to us, we'll sort it."' Barclay spoke faster and faster, becoming redder in the face. 'And of course he says – entirely reasonably – that "lessons must be learned". What he doesn't need to say, because it is implied, is that they will be learned "from an event that clearly was no fault of mine, but I'm going to fix it because that's the kind of benevolent ruler I am".

'So, you see, he's doing the classic trick of sounding engaged, clear, and helpful, when he hasn't actually committed to anything, nor has he furnished us with a single fact.' If there was a table, I am sure Barclay would have banged it. 'So, all we've really learned from this huge news story is how good the Marischal is.'

'Iain, please,' said the Colonel, who had clearly had enough.

Barclay realised everyone was waiting for him to unfreeze the picture. 'Oh, sorry,' he said lamely as the hologram sprang to life again.

The reporter was pressing the Marischal on the Wolf, which seemed to me like poking a rabid dog with a stick. What colour there was in his cheeks was draining away. I wondered if anyone else noticed the tiny shaking movements in our leader's body that presaged one of his unpredictable, violent outbreaks of rage.

'Now, with respect,' the Marischal continued, staring at the reporter as if trying to keep his fury in check, 'I need to talk to our heroic emergency services, who are working so hard in dangerous conditions . . .'

'What's the secret subtext to that then, Iain?' asked Lizzy, a devilish gleam in her eye.

'It means CBC is going to have to get another reporter,' Iain muttered after a pause.

All heads turned to him, waiting for an explanation.

He looked deflated. 'No one, least of all the Marischal, says "with respect" without actually meaning "I can't stand you and wish you were dead." Goddamn it. It's so difficult to find good reporters these days. Such a young man too, what a waste.'

With that, he turned and walked back towards the dining room, casting the briefest of longing glances at a bottle of gin on the sideboard by the door. It struck me how hard it must be for this man, once a scion of hard-hitting journalism, now little more than a mouthpiece for a tyrannical regime, reduced to railing impotently at a poor-quality holo-screen. Perhaps it was that very impotence that meant he could get away with it. Surely by now the local Mallice were aware of his outburst last night and were itching to make an example of him? It made no sense that they hadn't dragged him off into a bespoke hell unless he served a higher purpose – an example to others of their own powerlessness. I mean, if a media magnate had neither the power nor bravery to challenge the status quo, who would?

Don't get me wrong – I had no sympathy for Barclay. He'd made his bed of nails and should bloody well lie in it. Many journalists had gone to the O-Tanks for speaking out against the regime in the early days. Not him. His punishment was a lifelong sentence of deep-seated personal loathing. His execution would be a slow death, carried out through cirrhosis of the liver.

There was an uncomfortable silence in the room as Barclay stalked out. The Colonel was the first to break it.

'Well, while we're here, shall we quickly see to our Citizen Points?' she said in a bright, practical voice.

There was a general nodding of heads. It was always good to get this out of the way. Even if you approved of the Marischal, having to log in to listen to his preachings every day to build your Citizen Credit Score (and so ensure you had access to all the products and services you needed) was a daily burden. The Colonel pointed us to a small black box off to the right of the holo-screen and we dutifully stood in line, waiting to press our smart device of choice against it and register our attendance. I noticed Hildebrand watching the whole process – so mundane to us – with a mixture of fascination and horror. I enjoyed his discomfort. It helped calm me down.

Lady Anne tapped instructions into an old tablet, prompting the holo-screen to flicker back into life. The Marischal jumped up in front of us. For a moment I didn't recognise him. My God, it was the tea towel speech! This film was an early one – maybe the earliest there was.

Revolutions have started, and history has turned, on many things. But I struggle to think of another time that history has turned on a tea towel. Yes, that's right, a tea towel. But *what* a tea towel! It had inspired a nation and was now resident in a museum, surrounded by invisible lasers and the adoring faces of acolytes. Yes, it had come a long way from its humble beginnings in an old woman's kitchen, where its menial tasks included drying dishes as well as other assorted crockery. Few (if any) visitors who passed by the mid-range four-hob electric oven, upon whose door the towel so often hung, would have looked upon it and realised they were in the presence of greatness. It just quietly and resolutely went about its business until, one day, it was plucked from obscurity and called upon to rescue a nation.

So radical and so hallowed now, yet there the tea towel was on the flickering holo-screen, dangling unnoticed in the Marischal's hand. No, not the Marischal. Not yet. Just Duncan Finlay. Just another firebrand party agitator taking the stage at another tedious party conference.

God, he looked different. Handsome and debonair, his thick brown hair combed fastidiously to the side and sprinkled with just the right amount of salt and pepper. Most of those who saw Finlay back then didn't know him. Didn't care. But we all learned quickly, didn't we just? We learned he was different. We learned he wouldn't change his mind, and he certainly wouldn't change the subject. Only Finlay's large aquiline nose projected further than his self-righteous certainty. We came to know him as someone chronically tormented by the people, the beliefs, the very environment he was forced to inhabit. Indeed, he bore all the hallmarks of someone who would remain angry for some time to come. He was not a man who measured his progress against others. He alone moved as the world stood still, awaiting its orders.

I was lost in time. I was there at the party conference, watching the moment Finlay first spoke to the nation. The moment everything changed. I stood enrapt, witness to the world being set on fire. The air in the hall was still. Stale from the tedious speeches and incessant posturing. No one cared. The energy and belief brought by Scotland's independence from the United Kingdom just a few years before had disappeared. Disenchantment at the lack of change had plunged us into a new malaise.

Finlay moved to the podium. He looked somehow different to the man we now knew. What was it? Yes! The suit. It was his beautifully cut suit that caught my eye. It betrayed the hidden wealth, the change of name, the secret past, in a way he would never permit now. It was an amateur mistake, a beginner's error. Yet his *essence* was the same. His belief. His authenticity. A wise man once said, 'You shouldn't look at a man the way he is, but the way he could be.' As Finlay stood there he surveyed a nation and, unsatisfied with what he saw, determined to make it what he knew it could be.

As soon as he began to speak, those sharing the stage with him could tell something was awry. Any political apparatchik of the time could have told you this was a man who had made a virtue of vocal viciousness, a man known for his terrible temper and unwillingness to compromise. Yet his tone was measured and conciliatory. It was the gentle lilt of the Highlands, not the abrasive language of

Holyrood.* On that crisp autumn day someone – perhaps some-*thing* – different stood before the Assembled Faithful. He looked straight down the barrel of the camera, ignoring the conference hall completely. Then he spoke to the nation.

'People of Scotland! It is time for change. In the last few years you have achieved amazing things. You have had the courage and the faith to free this country, which I love so much, from hundreds of years of cultural and physical imperialism.

'You. Set. Us. Free.

'But your strength and belief has not been repaid. In a time that cried out for confidence, for a steady hand at the tiller, you have been sold out by a parcel of rogues. The same rogues I share the stage with today. This movement that has lost all momentum.'

A ripple of surprise and discontent coursed through the hall.

'You know who they are,' Finlay continued. 'They are that parcel of rogues that have wallowed in their power and offered no solutions. That parcel of rogues that offer no real ambition, just their boasts and grievances for shortcomings that they lay at the doors of others. You have watched it. You have seen it. You have suffered it. They promised so much, but have shown themselves to be bankrupt fantasists! A counterfeit administration. They have tied us up in half-truths, damned lies, and murky statistics. All to mask their failure.'

There were some desultory boos to be heard from the audience at this point, but there was also an energy in the air that had not been there before. What was going on?

'It is time for certainty,' Finlay called, now addressing both the crowd and the cameras. Warming them up. 'It is time for us, once again, to rise as a nation and claim what is ours. And to do that we must embrace everything that has made us great. This is a country that has led the world in so many ways in the past. It is time for us to face the world again – and lead.

* The location of the Scottish parliament building.

'Under this government, the collective has become all-powerful. They speak of "Scots Together" as a way of removing individual responsibility; as a way of ensuring you stay where you are and *how* you are.

'Now, my friends, is the time to change that. Now is the time to rise. Now is the time to say "Here I am! I am going to do the best for me. I am going to do the best for my family and my friends."

'Now is the time to say "I am strong; I am self-reliant." Now is the time to be proud of your success, not to be embarrassed or ashamed of it, nor to hide it under a bushel. Because our skills, our energy, our drive is what made Scotland great once and it will again, I promise you!

'We are a nation of creators, of thinkers, of inventors, of builders. Time and again we have taken on the world and left it in our wake. Time and again the peoples of this planet have looked to Scotland for inspiration. It was three hundred years ago that the French writer Voltaire proclaimed, "We look to Scotland for all our ideas of civilisation." It was true then and we can make it true now!'

The assembled crowd was stunned. Party activists gabbled into phones, searching for narratives to spin, weighing up the depth of their loyalties as they sensed the political landscape shifting beneath their feet. But they hadn't seen anything yet.

'I've got something in my hand that tells this story better than I can,' the man on the stage continued. 'What is it? It is my mother's tea towel. No, no, this is no joke. Please, my friends, hear me out. This tea towel hung in her kitchen for years. I read the message you can see here on it over and over as I grew up. If I may, I would like to read it to you. It is by a writer called Tom Anderson Cairns. It is called 'Wha's Like Us' and it goes like this:

'*The average Englishman, in the home he calls his castle, slips into his national costume, a shabby raincoat, patented by chemist Charles Macintosh from Glasgow, Scotland.*

'*En route to his office he strides along the English lane, surfaced by John Macadam of Ayr, Scotland.*

'*He drives an English car fitted with tyres invented by John Boyd Dunlop of Dreghorn, Scotland.*

'*At the train station he boards a train, the forerunner of which was a steam engine, invented by James Watt of Greenock, Scotland.*'

Was it my imagination, or did the Invereiton holo-screen grow a little brighter and stronger as Finlay's delivery began to change? As if the passion seeping into his voice could nourish our technology, so that we guests – assembled so many years later – might benefit all the more from his wisdom?

'*He then pours himself a cup of coffee from a Thermos flask, the latter invented by James Dewar, a Scotsman from Kincardine-on-Forth,*' Finlay continued unabated.

'*At the office he receives the mail, bearing adhesive stamps invented by James Chalmers of Dundee* . . . And where is that, my friends?'

'Scotland!' called back a small, but vocal, element of the crowd.

From then on the footage played out as if a missing piece had fallen into place. As if those in the room had been handed a script and were now extras in a new drama that was unfolding before their very eyes . . .

FINLAY *During the day he uses the telephone invented by Alexander Graham Bell, born in Edinburgh* . . .

[Pause for effect to allow the crowd to holler back.]
ENSEMBLE CROWD Scotland!
FINLAY *At home in the evening his daughter pedals her bicycle invented by Kirkpatrick Macmillan, blacksmith of Dumfries* . . .

[Brief pause, then thunderous response.]
ENSEMBLE CROWD Scotland!
FINLAY *He watches the news on his television, an invention of John Logie Baird of Helensburgh* . . .

ENSEMBLE CROWD Scotland!

FINLAY *And hears an item about the US Navy, founded by John Paul Jones of Kirkbean . . .*

ENSEMBLE CROWD Scotland!

FINLAY *He has by now been reminded too much of Scotland and in desperation he picks up the Bible – only to find that the first man mentioned in the good book is a Scot, King James VI, who authorised its translation.*

[‘Hallelujahs!’ resound around the hall with force enough to wake the Almighty.]

FINLAY *Nowhere can an Englishman turn to escape the ingenuity of the Scots. He could take to drink, but the Scots make the best in the world.*

[Wild cheers.]

FINLAY *He could take a rifle and end it all, but the breech-loading rifle was invented by Captain Patrick Ferguson of Pitfours, Scotland.*

CROWD MEMBER 1 Och no! Poor wee loon!*

FINLAY *If he escapes death, he might then find himself on an operating table injected with penicillin, which was discovered by Sir Alexander Fleming of Darvel, Scotland. Or given chloroform, an anaesthetic discovered by Sir James Young Simpson of Bathgate, Scotland.*

CROWD MEMBER 2 Aye, he’ll be on his feet in nae time!

FINLAY *Out of the anaesthetic, he would find no comfort in learning he was as safe as the Bank of England . . . founded by William Paterson of Dumfries, Scotland.*

[Scattered boos, prompted by the great currency debacle that followed independence, but one can’t have everything. Then, pause for quiet.]

FINLAY *Perhaps his only remaining hope would be to get a transfusion of guid Scottish blood, which would entitle him to ask, ‘Wha’s Like Us?’*

[Further pause for dramatic effect.]

* Boy.

FINLAY So I ask you, friends: Wha's like us?

[Assorted yelling and cheering, followed by raucous cheering and clapping.]

CROWD MEMBER 1 Damn few and they're a' deid!*

[Pause for calm to return.]

FINLAY Now is our time. Now is *your* time. The looks on the faces and belief in the hearts of those who stand before me today – and many more in their homes – will be the weapons that make us unbeatable.

We are a nation of heroes and warriors. Yet we have been taught to blame others for our woes. We have learned to see everyone else as our oppressors: they are our excuse for everything that has gone wrong.

Well, no more! We will shake off this doctrine of grievance that has weighed down on us like chains. We will take back Scotland's heritage! We will rejoin the march of the makers! We will each take responsibility for ourselves and we will once again be a real system of government – of the people, by the people, for the people. We will end their era of polite banality. Their right to blather is over.

You have stood calm and resolute, like a forest of ancient pines. Together. Unwavering. But, my friends, now we shall take Birnam Wood to Dunsinane, for we are the many and they are the few! Follow me. Join The Rising!

Then the picture flickered and vanished at the touch of a button from the Colonel. And that was it: a mere thousand words or so that gave birth to the creature that would soon become the Marischal. Watching it at the castle, so many years later, I had to admit it still made me tingle with a mixture of genuine awe and relentless indoctrination. Somewhere a server processed our obedience. The faint buzzing of devices around the room confirmed that our time

---

* All dead.

spent observing the Marischal's wise words was acknowledged and appreciated by a grateful nation.

'We mustn't let breakfast get any colder or Cookie will be furious,' the Colonel cut in, extending an arm to usher us back to bowls of life-affirming porridge and piles of kippers.

For a rare moment I was not fooled by her easy and authoritative charm. My dislike of the Farquharsons grew at their easy engagement with the state's propaganda so that their ill-deserved privilege might be maintained. But it was a passing thought. I had bigger things on my mind, and not even a hefty dose of the Marischal could change the fact. I left the room with a skip in my step and a warm glow in my breast. It had finally sunk in that the dam was gone. The smouldering wreck was there for all to see. No amount of propaganda or manipulation could change it. More important still, there was no one hammering angrily at the castle door. No one was invoking the Marischal's name and demanding entry; no one was forcing a black bag over my head and dragging me to oblivion. All had gone to plan. Forget the Marischal and his speeches: the Wolf of Badenoch had taken centre stage.

CHAPTER 12

Accidental Discharge

Over breakfast, the only topic of conversation was the Wolf of Badenoch. Since no one was as foolish as Barclay, I listened to the 'insurgent' being damned to hell and back again, until the tourist Hildebrand chipped in.

'Why do they call him the Wolf of Bard-o-nock?'

'One for me, I fancy,' said Alasdair, Lord Farquharson, striding into the breach, tapping his water glass with an ornate silver fork to command silence. 'It was after Elgin that the Wolf of Badenoch was born.'

'Elgin?' asked Hildebrand.

'Attack on the railway lines,' Farquharson snapped back. 'Do keep up. Where was I? Oh, yes. A journalist on some local news site looked into when there had last been a major attack on the town and found it had been a very long time ago indeed: late thirteen-hundreds, I think. You see, that was when Alexander Stewart, the first Earl of Buchan . . . Delightful family, the Buchans, by the way, have a great duck shoot—'

'Alasdair.'

'Yes, dear? Short of time, are we? Well, maybe if I wasn't interrupted . . . No, no, you're quite right. Where were we? Yes, Buchan attacked the town with a small army, a *band of wild, wykked Hieland-men*. All terribly romantic. They burned Elgin Cathedral to the ground over a dispute with some local Bible-basher. Well, God knows, Scotland has had more than its fair share of unpleasant characters throughout history. But despite seven hundred years going by, this man, Alexander Stewart, remains in the premier league. He was a tyrant's tyrant with almost unfettered power.'

The wistfulness had crept back into his voice as if he pined for the times when the peasantry accepted their own pillage and murder if they knew what was good for them.

'He ruled over much of the Highlands for his father – who, fortunately for him, was the King – systematically terrorising the area, riding out at the head of his private army from his stronghold at Lochindorb Castle – I don't know if you've seen it? It's on an island in the middle of a loch up towards Inverness; quite beautiful, really.'

Farquharson paused and lowered his voice, forcing those round the table to lean in to hear him.

'They say Stewart met his end at the hands of a mysterious man in black, to whom he lost a game of chess and his life. You'll be pleased to hear the Devil is the prime suspect.' He sat back in his chair, a pensive look on his face. Once again dreaming of the ineffable benefits of the feudal system, no doubt.

'Alasdair, the cars will be here soon.'

'Hmm, what? Oh, yes, where was I? So, this enterprising young journalist took his little historical discovery and connected it up with the nearby attacks – all of which happened within the very Badenoch area in which we are now sitting. He whacked the headline WOLF OF BADENOCH STRIKES AGAIN above his story . . . and the legend of the Wolf was born.'

I would love to claim this had been my intention, but not a bit of it. The sites we targeted early on were certainly chosen to cause maximum damage, but they were really test runs for the dam and selected in an attempt to hide my involvement, because the results were hugely inconvenient for me. In fact, I had never heard of Alexander Stewart before. The whole country knows him now, for sure. Just not Hildebrand Blunt, it seemed.

'Well, unless I'm mistaken, I hear the distant rumble of vehicles,' Lord Farquharson said, slapping both hands onto the table with a bang. 'Time for the guns to mass out front.'

I couldn't hear a damn thing and could only look aghast at my unfinished kedgeree as I shuffled out of the dining room. The castle atrium was a riot of shooting paraphernalia, all mixed up with the assorted detritus of decades. A giant warped mirror was propped up against one wall, its glass reflecting little more than indistinct shadows. Wellington boots stood variously in pairs and singles. Overcoats hung half a dozen deep from pegs. There were sticks and cartridge belts, fallen caps, and a stray hip flask. Umbrellas stood in an elephant-foot umbrella stand by the door and a pile of wooden tennis racquets poked out from a large wooden chest. Modernity held no sway here.

Amid cheery chatter, I pulled on my heavy shooting jacket and wellies, slung a cartridge bag over my shoulder, and picked up my gun case. Everything had been laid out just so. God bless Archie. Before we set off, sloe gin was administered, which did me the world of good, and we picked our pegs, which would determine where we stood on each drive. Lord Farquharson was in his element, jabbering in a lively fashion with his keeper, beaters, and other assorted members of the shooting party.

'. . . and the hammer throw, as well?' he was saying in dismay to an old gentleman, who was leaning on a shepherd's crook. 'I'm terribly sorry to hear it.'

'Aye, weel,' said the man philosophically. 'It wiz affy* wet at the Games and Angus couldnae get a decent grip oan it.'

'Ye should ha'e seen the trouble they wiz havin' wi' the cabers,' another wizened old local chipped in in support. 'Yeh couldnae toss it worth a damn in yon conditions.'

'Aye, weel,' they both concluded at once.

* Awfully, very.

'Aye, well,' said Lord Farquharson, nodding. The three stood together in silence, sharing a mutual understanding of the dire struggle humanity faces when participating in inclement Highland Games.

The growl of ancient petrol engines came to us over the cold air. Shortly after, three battered old Land Rovers crunched across the gravel and came to a halt in front of the castle. I was directed to climb into the back of one by a short, gruff old Highlander, whose flat cap was pulled down so low I couldn't see his eyes.

As I hauled myself up through the back door, cursing at the strain this put on my delicate condition, I came face to face with Hildebrand and Lizzy – sitting awfully close to one another, I noticed jealously.

'You don't seem the type to be taking to the braes* on a cold November morning,' I said to Lizzy, my breath emerging as a cloud in the crisp winter air.

'I'm not. But it's either stand in a muddy field for hours or be forced to help prepare lunch for you with the other women. Neither are attractive options, really.'

'So why—'

'Am I here? I'm here to support Hildy, of course,' she replied, taking his hand in hers.

'Hildy?' I stuttered. 'Oh, wait. *Hildy*. Seriously?'

Out shot the latter's hand to grasp mine and it struck me that, amid the confusion and impromptu tours of last night, we had not formally met, nor did I know anything about him aside from Catriona's jaundiced assessment.

'How do you do?' he said in that inexplicable accent. 'Hildebrand Blunt.'

'James Macfarlane,' I replied, taking his hand warily.

'Oh, I know who you are!' he exclaimed, as a sudden bump in

* Hillsides.

144

the farm track caught me off guard and I banged my head against the window.

Lizzy sniggered, damn her.

'In fact, you're one of the main reasons I'm here,' *Hildy* went on in a steady, businesslike voice, tinged with a childlike excitement.

I didn't like the sound of that at all.

'I run a small distilling business – moderately successful, I'm pleased to say. Gin and vodka, mainly, but I'm keen to add some whisky to my stable; distribute some proper Scotch . . .'

Well, that at least explains the appallingly dull chatter about inward investment at the dinner table last night, piped up Common Sense.

'. . . and all the civilised world knows you're the man for that.'

'And a good part of the uncivilised world,' I replied.

I suppose it's the right time to mention that I owned a highly successful whisky concern, which is the source of the fame and fortune mentioned earlier. This is why folk know who I am and why I could afford an Archie, a Wally, and a small but ambitious insurgency. It also explains why the police on the road last night were so upset for me when we discussed how the Wolf destroyed the mountain aquifer, as it cut off a major source of water for my company. There's much more to tell, but for the sake of momentum, let's keep this on a need-to-know basis. And that's all you need to know for now.

'So, I'm planning a tour of Scotland to look into a potential supplier and I'd very much like to talk about how we could be of service to each other. I'm pleased to say Lizzy is looking after me for the duration.'

'My, my, you must be doing very well for yourself if you can afford her company,' I almost said.

'She has been most accommodating . . .'

'I have no doubt about that,' I actually said. Lizzy scowled at me.

'In fact, she's the one who recommended meeting you. And it's thanks to her wily ways we got an invite here at all. I told her she didn't need to come out with me today – almost begged her to keep inside and stay warm – but she simply wouldn't listen!'

He turned and smiled at her, before giving her a playful squeeze on the arm. I'd have squeezed a lot more, but each to their own.

'So, do you think you might spend a few minutes talking business before dinner?' came the proposal. 'I promise I won't keep you long.'

'Why not,' I said, with a mind to coming away from that chat with as much classified insight as I could. As it happened, I had my eye on gin back then. Mother's Ruin had fallen out of favour over the last decade, and I felt it was ripe for a revival. I had little interest in actually doing business with Blunt. He was irritating and an unknown quantity. I had enough concerns about my current acquaintances without having any more to worry about. This prompted a curious sensation in me, which I realised was one of being in agreement with Lord Farquharson. There was another problem: an alarm bell had started ringing in the back of my mind almost as soon as Blunt had started talking and, for the life of me, I could not work out why.

That bell was left to ring as he prattled on about stills and the merits of 'steep and boil' versus 'vapour infusion'. The Land Rover was swaying alarmingly as it made its way at speed over a rutted field. I knew exactly what His Lordship was up to with these battered old vehicles. If you ever run your own shoot, send your guests out in old, badly sprung Land Rovers to the drives. Meanwhile, you mount your most sure-footed pony and make your way there. They'll think you're doing them a favour, which couldn't be further from the truth. If it all works as it should, you'll save yourself a fortune in birds as the guns will be so shaken, they won't be able to shoot straight.

I was all set to warn the driver that our chassis was about to part company from our axles – shortly followed by the breakfast from my stomach – when the Landy shuddered to a halt and we were disgorged at the bottom of a wide stubble field. It rose in a gentle incline to a wood, perhaps three hundred metres away, where the sun hung low above the trees.

Hammered into the iron-hard earth was a line of three-foot sticks – our pegs – about fifteen metres apart. Behind mine stood Archie, stamping his feet and grumbling about how it was 'all very well for yeh guns tae be late but ah'm about tae lose a toe tae frostbite and ah cannae afford tae lose anither . . .'

The usual complaints.

I crunched over the lines of hard stalks: all that was left of the grain that had covered the field in gold a few months before. Archie held out a Thermos to me and I shook my head in disgust until he brought out a hip flask. I removed a gun from its case and handed the other one to the big man, who was acting as my loader.

On the peg to my right were Hildebrand and Lizzy – dear God, she was loading for him as Archie was for me! That truly was dedication. I wondered what she was getting in return. Money? It would have to be an awful lot. Was it information? If so, what could he possibly know that she wanted so badly? The alarm bell rang a little bit louder.

A shrill blast of a whistle prompted me to fish around in my cartridge bag, before popping a couple of shells into the barrels and leaving the gun cradled in my arm. The sound of yelling and crashing floated over the windless air from far ahead of us. Beaters, hidden in the wood, were thrashing at the undergrowth to flush the pheasants out and down towards the Thin Tweed Line.

Out they came, gliding serenely to their imminent deaths. Out of old habit, I mouthed *bum-belly-beak-bang* – the mantra held sacred by my grandfather, which helped ensure I swung my barrels

147

up properly as my prey rocketed overhead. Then the guns exploded around me and the noise echoed off the hills. An acrid and invigorating smell filled the clear November air.

I bagged a brace of pheasants in the next few minutes, before having a passive-aggressive dispute over a woodcock with Hildy, after the bugger shot across my line. An amazing shot to be fair – he'd clearly done this before – but still, poor form. Or, as Archie put it while taking my empty gun and handing me the other, 'Fucken cretin.'

As the morning went on, we were ferried between drives to send lead rocketing into the sky with merry abandon. Lunch was a great feast on long tables in a large shed out in the woods. Once fortified against the growing cold by some surprisingly good red and more sloe gin, we were shipped back onto the hills to go a last couple of rounds with the birds.

It was on the final drive that everything went wrong. We were dropped off next to a thin line of pine trees as the gloom of dusk descended. We scrambled through the spindly trunks, using paths made by deer, before emerging onto a narrow track. The wood was now at our back, and about ten metres in front of us was a high bank, covered in scrubby grass, rising to twice the height of a man. To my right, at the end of the line, Hildy stood alone. It seemed Lizzy had abandoned her post now lunch was over and the threat of domestic servitude gone. To the left was someone whose name I have forgotten, while the gun beyond him was obscured by the bend of the track, which followed the slowly curving face of the bank.

This was a bloody tough drive any way you cut it. Once the whistle had blown, the beaters would walk through the kale field above and beyond us. Their calls of 'Over!' were the only warning we'd get of impending birds. The whistle blew and the pheasants duly appeared, as if out of nowhere, streaking over our heads in their last dash for the safety of the woods behind. I shot wildly into the air, worrying the birds not one whit.

After a few misses, I began to lose interest. The cold was creeping in and Archie was stamping his feet. A couple of minutes later, I had pretty much given up. My hands were stuffed in my pockets and my face buried in the collar of my jacket. I consoled myself with the thought that this was the last drive, and before long my damp toes would be steaming in front of a roaring fire. Off to my left I could still hear the occasional shout of 'Over!' and a cartridge or two being unloaded into the sky. The curtain was coming down on a good day.

I looked around, gun hanging in the crook of my arm, when I spotted a pheasant approaching from the far right, gliding silently high above, carving a route along the line of the bank. This bird was on a suicide mission: if it didn't change course, it would fly straight along the line of guns and be enfiladed.

Then something spooked the bird, making it squawk in alarm and flap its wings. It picked up speed and came rocketing towards Hildy at the end of the line, dropping lower and lower until it became clear it was not only going to come across our line, but it was going to do so directly across the face of the bank. I smiled, musing that this was a cunning tactical ploy on the part of the bird – it's not the done thing to shoot birds flying so low. This pheasant was taking the mick and I couldn't help but admire its gall.

Then I noticed Hildy had drawn a bead on it and was tracking it from right to left as it came across the line. I watched without concern, presuming he was using it for a final practice swing. Yet he continued to pan left. If he didn't stop, he would soon have both barrels pointing directly at me. He didn't stop.

A scream rang out from the trees, as Lizzy waded out of the wood. 'Hildy, stop! You're going to—'

But it was too late. He pulled the trigger.

It is often said that in the moment before the Grim Reaper casts his shadow in one's direction, one experiences a moment of calm. Whether that is driven by acceptance, resignation, or simply a sense of 'Oh, bugger', who knows? But as one who has felt the cold hand of Death upon my shoulder more than once, I can tell you there is something in this. As I stared directly down the dual steel tubes of Hildy's shotgun, I was calm. So calm, in fact, that I had a revelation of sorts.

The reason alarm bells had started ringing in the Land Rover earlier was that Lizzy was guiding Hildy in his planned tour of Scotland. That meant he couldn't be the tourist about whom there had been so much grumbling. Which begged the question: who was? And why was this mystery traveller so loathsome to Lord Farquharson?

In terms of revelations – particularly those experienced on the cusp of oblivion – I'm aware it was pretty prosaic. But there was no time for my brain to conjure up any profundity, because that's when Hildebrand Blunt shot me.

CHAPTER 13

Going Underground

As some bright spark has no doubt pointed out already, the joy of shooting depends entirely on which end of the gun you are on. I was very much on the wrong end at that moment. Lizzy's shriek had barely left her lips when Hildy's gun exploded with smoke and flame. I felt a rush of wind and a huge weight crashing into me, followed by a loud cry. I lay motionless on the cold hard ground as Archie climbed off me, feeling dazed and with a searing pain in my temple.

I lay still, and tentatively opened my eyes. Archie, being a proactive type, had used the intervening seconds and his impressive athleticism to cover the ground between Blunt's and my pegs. He was now holding the scoundrel six inches off the ground by his lapels and shaking him like a rag doll. It was unclear whether this was due to rage or whether Blunt's assault on me had been so cack-handed that it offended Archie's sense of professionalism.

My head hurt. I put fingers to my temple and, taking my hand away, saw they were covered in blood. So, the bastard had actually shot me. I remember thinking that this attack, coming so soon after the disputed woodcock, was all a bit much and that whoever this mysterious tourist really was, he or she couldn't be half as infuriating or dangerous.

More fool me.

Nonetheless I stood up, swayed a bit, and said sternly, 'Archie, please put Mr Blunt down before you damage him.'

No matter how well justified, we couldn't have the staff murdering us, could we? The next stop would be revolution and Christ alone knew what would happen with the likes of Archie in charge. Greater rewards for recreational violence, certainly.

Hildy was unceremoniously dropped in a pile, while Archie pointedly opened and emptied his gun. The single cartridge expelled revealed he'd only got one barrel off. This was a small mercy for me but not, apparently, for the neighbour to my left. Mr No Name had taken a bit of a peppering, although it appeared his heavy shooting jacket had borne the brunt of it.

'Shot, by God! I've been shot!' he was shouting, hopping about, as the rest of the shooting party congregated to see what the commotion was about.

Then Hildy was by my side, white in the face and pouring out apologies.

'My God! I'm so sorry. I was just tracking the bird and when Lizzy shouted, I got a fright and squeezed the trigger . . . Oh Jesus, are you OK?' he stammered.

Lizzy's jaw tightened at this attribution of blame. No doubt she thought she'd just saved me. But her consummate professionalism prevailed and she said nothing, thus proving the client is always right, even in cases of ballistic mishap.

'Think nothing of it,' I replied in a jocular tone that made it clear he needed to have a bloody good think about it. 'I'd go and square it with Whatsisname on the next peg if I were you.'

At that moment, Archie strode up, pushed Blunt aside and started examining my damaged noggin.

'Och, it's jist a scratch but it's bleedin' pretty badly,' came the good doctor's diagnosis. 'Push this cloth on there . . .'

'Oh, Archie, don't make such a fuss,' I replied.

This was just for appearances, as there's nothing I like more than to be made a fuss of. Archie paid no attention and busied himself yanking off my jacket. I was about to protest that I had been shot in the head, not the chest, and, point of fact, it was really bloody cold, when he growled, 'Come oan, come oan, quickly! Or the blood'll get onto yer jacket and it's hell tae get oot.'

* * *

The journey back to the castle was subdued, and you'd have thought all this would be quite enough fun for one day. But no: fate was already preparing to drag me to the floor and have its wicked way with me again.

I was given temporary respite as I got to warm my toes, which were now resting gratefully on top of a padded fireguard. The only evidence of the 'mishap' (as it was being called) was my face, which was now half-covered by a large gauze bandage. As important as the roaring fire and my steaming tootsies was the monstrously large gin and tonic in my hand. I gave the glass a shake and revelled in the sound of the ice cubes clinking together.

Hildy, for his part, was *persona non grata* and nowhere to be seen. Quite right too; you simply can't go around shooting people at such formal gatherings. Lizzy, it seemed, had gone into hiding with him, which was a shame, as the sight of her tight tweeds would have done me the power of good.

In fact, I didn't have to wait long for a viewing as Archie, in his usual sneaky fashion, had appeared at my ear and was asking if I could accompany him from the room. He was using his Serious-And-Not-To-Be-Ignored voice so, amid much protest, I dragged myself upright and followed him. I hadn't even touched my damned gin.

We walked into the hall and there, at the bottom of the stairs, was Lizzy, looking like the ultimate restorative for a person who had recently been shot. She was still in her tight tweed skirt, but had removed the jacket so her bosom was clad only in a thin white shirt. This was styled with her customary one-size-too-small-with-one-too-many-buttons-undone motif. The silk cravat around her neck fell – nay, plummeted – into the cleft of her breasts.

'Oh, Archie, you shouldn't have,' I said with genuine gratitude.

'Mr Mac—' he began, before Lizzy cut him off.

'James, I am delighted to see you up and about,' came the smouldering voice. She could have used any voice, really. I'd been shot, for God's sake, and was in need of comforting. 'Would you come with me for a few minutes?'

Well, of course I would.

Archie chimed in again, his voice insistent: 'Mr Mac, ah've got tae—'

'Not now, Archie, you have delivered me from the angels to an appointment with an angel, and you have my heartiest thanks,' I said, mesmerised by Lizzy's posterior, which was already swaying its mesmeric way up the stairs. 'Back shortly.'

Leaving Archie grinding his teeth for reasons I couldn't have cared less about, we climbed the stairs, our feet padding on the thin carpet. As soon as we rounded the corner, she pushed me against the wall, pressed herself against me and kissed me long and deep.

'And hello to you,' I managed when we came up for air.

'Oh God, I've missed you,' she purred.

I should have been suspicious at this as she rarely indulged me with such platitudes, but I wasn't thinking straight. Or even with my brain.

'Look, we haven't got long,' Lizzy continued. 'I only managed to get away from Hildy with the promise that I'd bring you up here so he could apologise again.'

'And so he bloody well should,' I rankled.

'He's decided to leave as soon as we're packed. So, we need to focus.'

I protested that I was already focused, albeit on the rise and fall of her breasts as they strained to escape her shirt. As a man of science, I couldn't help but wonder at the physics of the tailoring that bestowed the collective strength of a champion weight-lifter on its buttons.

She put a finger under my chin and raised my head so I was looking into her eyes. She had an intense look on her face that made me feel uncomfortable and disappointed.

'James, it's business time – no, stop looking at those – *concentrate*, please. I've got something to ask and you need to take this seriously. I think it will be of great interest to you.'

'I am concerned you want to talk about something dull,' I replied, my eyes returning to something – or *things*, rather – that certainly *were* of interest. 'And things are not to be taken seriously simply because they are dull.'

She gave me a playful slap on the cheek. 'Don't make me hit the other side,' she said, running a light finger over the gauze on my temple and making me wince, then leaned in very close indeed. 'Now, from the news this morning, it seems the job at the dam all went to plan, right?' she whispered close to my ear. 'And, that being the case, my intel was good?'

'It was perfect, thank you,' I replied, taking the opportunity to lean forward and enjoy another lingering kiss. 'You should be proud of what we've achieved – it's a big step forward. A proper game-changer. And none of it would have been possible without you.'

What? I hear you splutter. *She's in on this whole caper too?*

Up to her eyeballs. Do you remember me mentioning HUMINT before, or perhaps Wally asking about the 'social engineering' on our way to the dam? That little bit of real-life detail that had convinced the dam's manager to visit our spoof site? Well, here, in all her unfettered glory, was the source of that crucial detail. Lizzy Burke. Internet sensation. Agent provocateur. Courtesan. Spy. Heroine.

For months she had fed me a steady stream of information that had been crucial to our success.

Some of it she had even elicited from Thomas Loker, the head of the Mallice. Lizzy moved in high and dangerous circles and it didn't come more dangerous than Loker, Caledon's highly motivated director of state oppression. By all accounts, he was infatuated by her, no doubt because she indulged many of his more sordid desires. From what she'd told me, these often involved her applying the painful techniques on him that he so enjoyed inflicting on others. The difference was he could tell her when to stop.

I'm keen not to make light of this because it was genuinely brave work by Lizzy. (Passing on information, I mean, not beating Loker up.) They called him the Headhunter because he kept the polished skulls of his most treasured victims in a cabinet as proof of their final 'domestication'. She could beat him to death for all I cared.

Indeed, he was probably the only man who would kill her if he found she had betrayed him. Loker was singular in his life's purpose to oppress the populace, and would not care about the consequences for him if she died. He would put his very best men on the job with orders to make sure she knew she was dying.

But why on earth would she run such risks for such a reprehensible person as one James Macfarlane, Esq.? you are no doubt asking.

The answer is simple: she hated the regime and Loker in particular, although as I stood there, pinned to the wall, I didn't know why. All my previous attempts to find out were scotched with careful application of her inimitable and highly effective skill set. I was as lascivious a simpleton as any of her targets. As I've already said, she was famous – no, *notorious* – for keeping secrets, and well aware that her reputation for unshakeable discretion was crucial to staying alive. Perhaps if I had persisted and not been driven by lust and a selfish desire for gratification, everything might have turned out differently. Perhaps.

Looking back, I wonder if she loved me, in her own way, and was trying to protect me. You will no doubt say this theory is nothing more than my highly evolved ego on one of its many flights of fancy. But it was far too late in our peculiar relationship that I realised I loved her too. In an existence unencumbered, for the most part, by conscience, I feel a rare depth of guilt for what happened to her, even if there was nothing I could have done to stop it. But you can judge all that for yourself, presently. And while it is no recompense, explaining every curve of that divine form to you; telling you every detail of what she did; impressing on you how brave she was – well, that is the best tribute I can pay.

But look at me in my maudlin state! We must get on with the show, which was reaching its climax, so to speak.

'I am happy the plan was a success,' she was saying, her face still just inches from mine. 'But I need to tell you something else.'

'That's wonderful and I'd be delighted to chat in the morning, but I think we've earned a bit of R & R,' I replied. 'It's been a long twenty-four hours.'

'No. Take your hands off that . . . Seriously . . . Mmm . . . *No!* This is important. It's why I got you invited here in the first place.'

'What?' I spluttered, grabbing her shoulders and holding her at arm's length. 'What do you mean, *got me invited*?'

Her face was a picture of genuine surprise. 'Oh, come on. Did you really think, my dear James, that you are on the A-list for a day's shooting at Invereiton?'

'Of course I did, I'm Jimmy bloody Mac. Well, OK, maybe I'm not at the top of the list, but certainly a close second . . .' I tailed off, settling on a grudging acceptance that His Lordship and I were not natural bedfellows.

'Now, I'm warning you, James, you must pay attention because this is a little complicated.'

'My dear Lizzy, this is no time for *complicated*. My socks are barely dry. My gin and tonic is rapidly warming in front of the fire. In fact, I can't think of a single decent reason for—'

Her luscious frame was once again pressed against me. Yet more evidence of how unfair it was to ask me to process complicated information. This was, of course, the point.

'Have you heard of Professor Randolph Spring?' she whispered.

'Oh Lord, another person with a ridiculous name; where do we get them all from?' I sighed.

'Have you heard of him?' she insisted, pulling away to help focus my mind.

As a matter of fact, I did know the name. He had been a university dean who had, almost a year before, denounced the Marischal and then been foolish enough to begin an undercover lecture tour addressing his complaints against our despotic leader. Much to the consternation of the regime, they couldn't seem to crack the network that was spiriting him to these clandestine meetings, the content of which was being spread far and wide by word of mouth. There were widespread arrests and interrogations that proved fruitless, no matter their brutality. The regime became worried that this elusive educator might light a spark of resistance in our dispirited nation. Then, almost at the end of the tour – which I, for one, thought was nothing more than a month-long suicide note – he had disappeared. I'd presumed the Mallice had finally caught up with him.

'Why are you interested in a dead professor?' I asked, humouring Lizzy in an attempt to move things along and so get her to pay more attention to me.

'I'm not interested in a dead professor,' she replied. 'I'm interested in a professor who is very much alive. But a professor who won't be for much longer unless the Underground Railroad can get him out of the country. That's what I want to talk to you about.'

The plot was thickening – nay, congealing – in front of my eyes.

I did what I always do in these situations and tried to stall while my bewildered grey matter caught up. Without any gin in my system, it was hopeless.

'Before you ask, I have heard of the Underground Railroad,' I said, improvising like mad. 'It's an alleged secret society, dedicated to getting people out of Caledon. It's based on a nineteenth-century escape network for slaves from the southern states of America. However, like everyone else, I presumed it was a fairy tale. Apparently, I was mistaken.'

'We have gone to great lengths to keep ourselves out of the limelight,' she began.

'*We?*' I abandoned all pretence. '*We?* Who the hell is *we?*'

'Quiet!' she hissed in my ear, bringing almost every inch of her body into contact with mine.

I fell silent.

'I am not part of the Railroad, per se. I'm more of an associate member. I relay information to them, just as I do for you.'

This was quite beyond my powers of reasoning. Again, I thought of that poor gin, warming mercilessly by the fire. If only I'd done more drinking and less clinking, this would surely all make sense.

'Wait just a minute. I want to make sure I've got this right,' I stuttered, my mind again trying to assert itself. 'You give me the relevant information about the dam and then organise this dinner invitation, assuming – correctly, as it turns out – that I'd use it as an alibi when the turbines went sky-high.'

'Very good, James.'

'Which, in turn, ensured I would have to turn up so you could ensnare me in this Underground Railroad scheme – which I can only presume you are about to try to do.'

'Again, top marks.'

'But then, everything was riding on me accepting – how could you be certain I'd come?'

She moved even closer, which I had not thought possible. 'Because, my darling, you are an appalling snob and wouldn't turn this down for anything, no matter how much you rail against the *ancien régime*.'

'So, hoist with my own petard, you think?' I whispered, appalled at being her marionette.

'Certainly.'

'It seems like a lot of effort.' I struggled to gain the upper hand. 'Why not just come over for tea one afternoon and ask for my help? The result would have been the same.'

'No, it wouldn't have been the same, actually.' Lizzy smiled at me.

'Why?'

'Because he's here, obviously. Do keep up.'

And, thus, all my efforts to gain the high ground came crashing down.

'Who? The professor? Dear God, where? No, don't tell me, he'll be in some priest hole somewhere, no doubt,' I babbled. 'Why . . . How . . . I mean, what's he doing *here*, for Christ's sake?'

The plot had now thickened so much it had solidified.

'This castle is what the Railroad calls a "station" – a hiding place. There's a network of them, each anonymous to the others. To move people between them, we use people we term "agents", while the individuals who operate the stations are called "conductors".'

'This is quite the web you have woven,' I said at length, in lieu of any further insights.

'Better to think of me as being on a thread that joins two different webs, one belonging to the Underground Railroad and one to the Wolf of Badenoch,' she said brightly.

A high-wire act, more like, I thought in admiration, *performed with no net and in high winds*.

So many questions presented themselves. The list included, but was not restricted to: *Who were the conductors staffing* this *station?*

Was it really the Farquharsons? Surely they wouldn't risk this life of comfort and privilege on such a fool's errand? Perhaps it was the downstairs staff – one of those silent servants, maybe – doing it under their very noses? Could it the Helots? And just how many sides had Lizzy taken? How many other plots were there? Jesus, had she told the others about me? Could I now trust her in light of this revelation? And why, oh why, had I not drunk that goddamned gin?

'My dear, you no doubt have many questions, but there is no time,' she whispered, seeming to read my thoughts. 'But let me reassure you, the Railroad has no idea you are the Wolf, nor do they know about Archie or Wally, who, since I see them both here, I presume are in on it too.'

Best laid secret plans and all that.

'Nor will I be telling the Railroad who you are,' she continued. 'But what I *have* done is recommended you to them as a resourceful and brave man. Which means I now need you to meet them. I need you to help them get Spring out. It would mean a lot to me – and to my ability to keep giving you information.' She stared at me, letting this sink in. 'Will you help us?' Her voice was soft, gentle, and low.

When I was doing The Training, we were taught a lot about military history, and one lesson that seemed particularly pertinent at this moment was that, if you want to get something out of someone, then killing with kindness is often the most effective method. The Germans discovered this in the First World War when they found that recently captured Allied prisoners would, often unintentionally, be forthcoming with information when they were wrapped in a blanket and given a cup of tea. Lizzy's understanding of this was surely more instinctual than tutored. In her specialist field of operations, she knew there was no better time for someone to make a decision that favoured her than during the application of her highly tuned skills of seduction.

I didn't think she would sell me out if I refused, but here was the rub: I couldn't continue my own campaign without her. And she must have known it as she applied a strategically placed grind of her hips. I decided to bluster until a solution came to me.

'Well, I'm frankly appalled by the cultural appropriation. I mean, *Underground Railroad*? Seriously?'

'Cultural appropriation?' Lizzy snapped back, her seduction routine overcome by impatience. 'I have no idea what that is.'

I appraised her for a moment. All Lizzy's achievements, her intrigues and her power made me forget how young she was. Too young to remember a time when individuality was celebrated and concepts like cultural appropriation mattered. Too young to remember when that was even a thing.

She mistook my hesitation for indecision and moved closer. In fact we were now about as close as two humans could be without injuring each other.

'Now look, Lizzy. I'd love to help, but I can't,' I garbled. 'This isn't part of the plan. This will, you know, muck everything up. I'm out. That's the last word.'

'Oh, good.' *Grind.*

'The last word. I mean it.'

'Fine.' *Grind.*

'Oh, come on! This just isn't fair. I won't do it. You and your . . . arguments are not going to ensnare me in this fiasco. I mean it's, it's, well, it's just not fair.' I lapsed into sullen silence. I was beaten and she knew it.

'Thank you, my love.' Lizzy stepped back and gave me a light peck on the cheek. 'As I say, someone will be in touch.'

Pride was horrified and demanded I win back a foothold on the high ground. 'You do realise the whole seduction routine wasn't necessary? That you had me over a barrel anyway? Nice for me to wring some gratification out of you, at least.' I was charging up the hill, the high ground firmly in my sights.

162

She just smiled and put a hand on my cheek. 'Oh, James,' she said, a childish delight in her voice. 'You thought I was doing that for you? You thought the poor weak girl needed to seduce the strong man! How sweet.'

'Er, what?' I managed, aware that the ground beneath my feet was becoming treacherous.

'I know I hold all the cards. I just did that to watch the mighty James Macfarlane squirm.'

Mac fell down and broke his crown and Pride came tumbling after.

'Someone will contact you soon,' Lizzy said, turning away. 'Now let's go and see Hildebrand. He'll be wondering what's happened to us.'

As she strode off down the corridor, I was left slumped back against the wall, my mind a feral mix of fear and arousal. I had been comprehensively out-thought and outmanoeuvred.

'Wait,' I called after her. 'There's one thing I need to know. This afternoon . . . how come you emerged out of the wood just at the right time to stop me getting a barrel full of lead to the face?'

'Oh, that's a bit delicate,' she said, caught off-guard by my change of subject.

Having lost so much ground already, I stood firm and folded my arms, as Archie had done to such great effect in the turbine hall. (I never stopped learning from him, you know, right to the end.)

'It's not important,' she insisted.

Still I stood my ground. She looked at her watch and back at me, her lips pursed in frustration.

'Well, if you must know, I arrived in the other Land Rover and decided to come through the woods to meet you,' she said. 'Now, come on, before suspicions are raised about where we've got to.'

But this did not explain the delay in her arrival, nor did it explain the splash of red that was creeping over her cheeks. I stood unflinching.

'Oh, for God's sake, I had to go to the toilet. I had a dicky tummy. I did a shit in the woods. Like a bloody bear. Happy now?'

'Yes,' I replied, delighted by this smallest of victories. 'Lead on.'

We snaked our way through the corridors of the castle. The walls and ceilings changed height and width as we twisted and turned, like rings in a tree trunk marking centuries of additions and alterations to the ancient building. The further we went, the more the Railroad – and the fact I'd been railroaded into it – played on my mind. To add insult to injury, the longer we walked, the more I thought about my poor gin, now surely drowning in a sea of melted ice. By the time we reached Lizzy's room, my head was aching and I was in a foul mood.

'You might have warned me to bring a ball of string so I can find my way back,' I snapped as we stopped at her door.

Lizzy turned and looked at me. 'Why so cross? Look, I'll tell you what. Once Hildy's away, how about we slip into our haptics and spend some quality time together?'

I grimaced. The thought of squeezing into a neoprene suit for some long distance love-making in augmented reality seemed a poor consolation. Anyway, mine had mildew on it and smelled of mothballs.

'Maybe,' I replied sulkily as she opened the bedroom door and greeted dear old Hildy with a hug and kiss that made my blood boil.

I will gloss over the subsequent meeting with Blunt. It was brief and predictable, and I spent the whole time on the edge of a tantrum. He was effusive in his apologies. I made heartfelt and utterly insincere entreaties about how he should forget about the whole thing. No real harm done, and so on. I concluded amiably by wishing him the best for the rest of his tour round Caledon.

'Not a chance,' he said, an appalled look on his face. 'Can you imagine it? Wherever I go they'll point and say "That's the guy who shot Jimmy Mac!" They'd hunt me down with dogs!'

I don't flatter myself when I say that *was* a distinct possibility – partly due to my fame and partly because I'd spread the word myself, if necessary. I'd even lend people the dogs. We parted instead with a promise that we would meet two weeks hence in London and see if we couldn't do some business.

Lizzy showed me out, holding my gaze as she closed the door. 'Someone will be in touch,' she whispered before it shut.

I stood alone on the landing, trying to take stock. My brain hurt. I leaned back against the white wall of the corridor, shut my eyes, and considered the various pieces of the chessboard that were in play. I had made a great many enemies over the last twenty-four hours. This was planned and so didn't overly concern me. Much more worrying was the number of people who, quite unfairly, wanted to be my friend.

I could ignore Mr Hildebrand Blunt. He was leaving tomorrow and would surely not be able to muster the time or incompetence to make another unwitting attempt on my life. As for Lizzy, she would be gone with him in the morning and I'd learned everything I could from her, I was sure of that.

Her manoeuvrings – outmanoeuvrings, rather – filled me with feeble indignation. I considered mustering my remaining strength and frustration, dragging her from Hildy's room and giving her a bloody good spanking for taking such liberties with my time and safety. But I was forced to discount this as it would cause a scene and she'd only enjoy it.

There were a few silver linings, though. The introduction of Professor Randolph Spring meant the identity of the mysterious tourist had surely been revealed. And now I was alone, I decided I would make no plans whatsoever to get to know Spring any better and resolved to leave the castle first thing in the morning, before anyone had the chance to make formal introductions. I knew this would infuriate Lizzy, but I'd got out of tighter scrapes in the past and would work out how to square that circle later.

My rambling thoughts were interrupted as, far off, I heard a dull, deep ringing sound. Each metallic beat seemed to reverberate down the corridors, flowing past me – *through* me – and on into the depths of the castle like messengers on some urgent mission. I was no longer leaning on the uneven wall, but standing straight, alert, and focused on the noise.

Soon, the sound began to be overtaken by another: a rhythmic thump that was getting louder and louder. And it wasn't just louder; the source of this new sound was also drawing closer. Every now and again it would cease for a few seconds before starting again. After everything this day had brought, I thought it wise to take no chances and, with fists raised and a strong, wide stance, I stood prepared for whatever was coming. Ahead of me, the corridor turned to the left and out of sight. Towards that corner the noise came, relentless. Louder with every impact. It reached a crescendo as Archie came careering into view, his huge feet thudding against the deep red carpet. Travelling at speed, his unstoppable force proved more than a match for my immovable object. Despite my boxer's stance, I was unceremoniously carried back several yards in his arms. He stopped and stared at me wide-eyed. Then he placed me back on the floor.

'Ah, Mr Mac, ah've been lookin' everywhere fer yeh,' he said.

Just then Lizzy's head appeared round the door, enquiring as to what all the noise was. She saw Archie, smiled, and stepped out into the corridor in a satin chemise that would be considered inadequate as a handkerchief.

'Hello, Mr Fraser,' she said demurely.

Archie gazed at her in confusion, before taking great interest in the carpet. 'Aye, good day to yeh, Miss Burke,' he mumbled.

It's funny what frightens people, isn't it?

Lizzy nodded knowingly to me and was gone again, the door closing behind her with a brief but loud creak, before the daintiest of clicks sounded from the lock.

'As ah wiz sayin', ah've been lookin' a' over the place fer yeh,' he began, with a clear note of disapproval at my suspected indiscretions with Lizzy.

Being a petty, small-minded man, I wasn't having this. It seemed a good time to regain some of the high ground that Archie had taken from me of late.

'Is there something wrong, Archie?' I asked pleasantly. 'Only your cheeks seem a bit red. You aren't coming down with something, are you?'

He scowled and said nothing. But he didn't have to, for it was then I noticed he had transformed from shooting apparel and was standing immaculate in full livery of bow tie and tails. My heart sank. I turned again to the clangorous noise still echoing down the corridor and recognised the dinner gong. I looked down at my dirty tweeds.

'Mr Mac, it's the dinner gong. Yer gonnae be—'

'Late. Yes, I know,' I sighed.

My high ground once again reduced to the status of a molehill, I tramped after Archie in the direction of my room, no longer in any doubt for whom the bell tolled.

CHAPTER 14

To Sleep, Perchance to Dream

In the end, the Farquharsons forgave the latest in my growing list of timekeeping indiscretions. This was largely down to Archie who, bless him, having borne me to and from the shower, was clever enough to replace the white gauze on my face with an even bigger bandage.

Thus attired, I appeared in the drawing room in my tails, looking like a phantom from an opera. The guests were directed through to dinner and a gaggle of sympathetic well-wishers encircled me, enquiring after my health and damning Hildy for his downright *Englishness* in shooting me. Even His Lordship seemed unwilling to put his well-heeled boot into me on this occasion. Instead, he contented himself with a stiff nod in my direction, which was probably his equivalent of summoning everyone together for a group hug.

The lights had come back on, powered by a diesel generator somewhere. From their frames on the walls, Their Lordships of Days of Yore stared benevolently upon me. Dinner passed without incident. I don't remember any of the conversation, nor what we ate. I took the opportunity to go drink-for-drink with Iain Barclay, which probably explains the memory lapse. Hildy and Lizzy didn't make an appearance. All was well. I felt relaxed. I felt safe.

As the festivities drew to a close, I climbed the stairs, replete with wine and port (I never did get that gin). Archie led the way, picking me up whenever I tripped, while I laid out the plan for the morning. 'Archie, at the crack of dawn we will be flying this crenellated chicken coop, so please make everything ready. A 7 a.m. kick-off should be sufficient, although I'm sad to say it means I will miss out on the kedgeree.'

Archie did not appear to hear my orders, so I jabbed him in the back with an authoritative finger. He turned with a look that dared me to do it again.

'Now look, Archie,' I slurred, 'I want to be absolutely clear on something: in the last twenty-four hours I have been haunted, shot, seduced, blackmailed and, worst of all, made late to multiple social engagements.

'Once I am in bed, preferably with a large eighteen-year-old malt, I am not to be disturbed for anything until daybreak. Do I make myself clear? If there is a key in the door, it will be locked. If there is a bolt, it will be drawn. If there is a heavy piece of furniture on hand, it will be dragged in front of the door to form an effective barrier. In fact, please try to source several pieces of wood and some nails so I can hammer them in a crooked fashion across the threshold. Put bluntly, I will sleep well tonight and shall rise for no man.'

Archie stared at me. Was he even paying attention? There was something going on behind those big eyes. Levers were moving. Gears were engaging. I could almost hear the rattle. Yes, thoughts were definitely being processed, but I dismissed them as none of my concern, fool that I was.

'Aye, sir,' he said absently.

'Are you OK, Archie?'

'Och, never you mind, sir.'

This in itself should have set hares racing – unlike Wally, he never, ever called me 'sir'. And now he'd just done it twice. Even the well-practised tap on the nose that always accompanied the latter response seemed half-hearted.

The sense that he wasn't all there remained as I watched Archie busy himself about the bedroom, packing my case and preparing for tomorrow's extraction. But soon he was gone and a mixture of tiredness and booze pushed all concerns from my mind. I was tucked up in bed, Scotch in hand, a heavy armoire pushed against the door. I had everything a man could need. Wild horses couldn't keep the zzzs away. And so sleep visited your weary narrator. But sleep was an ill-mannered guest, for despite the rapturous welcome it received, it chose not to stay.

* * *

Night-time. The room was as black as pitch. Not one sliver of moonlight could penetrate the heavy velvet curtains covering the small windows.

I was awake, listening intently. The synapses have always been quick to fire when I wake up. My mind engages long before I can connect it to my physical person. A cynic would say this is a manifestation of the spirit being willing but the flesh being weak.

And there it was. I couldn't believe it at first. In fact, I might even have giggled at the absurdity of it. Yet . . .

Rat-a-tat-tat.

Well, I'm not having this! roared Pride, first onto the scene and filled with moral outrage. *Enough is e-bloody-nough.*

Woah, hold on, tiger. Common Sense staggered in, half-dressed. *You're still drunk, let's think this through for a moment.*

I don't care what it is. Pride was fuelled by anger and wine. And port. And a drop or two of whisky. *Be it a drummer boy or any other member of his ghastly ensemble, it is high time we put a stop to this nonsense.*

Oh, Jesus, you're not going to listen to any sensible advice, are you? came the beleaguered moan from Common Sense. *Well, OK, you're going to need me, so wait a second while I get my slippers on . . .*

I lurched upright, full of booze and self-righteousness, and padded towards the door in the exaggerated fashion that proclaims a drunk who is set upon adventure. A heavy maroon dressing gown with tasteful black trim had been hung on the back of the door to shield the ill-prepared guest from the rigours of Scotland in November. I pulled it around me and tied the cord. As a precaution, I took my ever-faithful china sheep back off the mantle and holstered it into the cord around my waist. I laid my hands on the armoire barricade, preparing to exert myself.

Rat-a-tat-tat.

'OK, OK, give me a minute! Damned ghosts,' I muttered. 'You'd think the dead would have more patience.'

Now, even with the demon drink coursing through my veins, you might think this quite the volte-face from my previous dealings with the ghoulish percussionist (which were less than heroic). I'd reply that firstly, it's much easier to be brave in the safety of a well-appointed bedroom than in a pitch-black dungeon. Secondly, when there's a thick oak door between you and an apparition that seems content to knock but not enter, this sense of security is amplified many times over. Thirdly, I was now certain this was some terrible trick and, having already cheated death once today, was in no mood to be trifled with.

Rat-a-tat-tat.

And so it was thus, clad in a cloak of maroon towelling and deepest sanctimony, I dragged the armoire from its defensive position in front of the door. This was not a quiet process: its wheels squeaked to high heaven and made me wince. However, this didn't seem to bother the drummer boy. He kept his paradiddle coming with a calm constancy.

But then the rattle started to fade, as if it was moving away down the hall. If I was to put an end to this, it was now or never. Muscles tensed, I opened the door, crouched low, and crept into the dark corridor, ready to draw Sheepy at a moment's notice.

I moved with a light tread born of many years' experience sneaking about in places I shouldn't have been. First, I snaked through the upper floor of the castle, then dropped down some stairs. I moved as fast as I dared, lest I lose track of the ever-constant *rat-a-tat-tat*. The fug of booze was clearing and I became perplexed at my inability to pinpoint the source of the noise. While its direction was clear, one minute it sounded as if it was coming from the ceiling, then from one wall, then from another. Sometimes the tapping seemed to be on both: a perfectly synchronised spectral drum corps.

Nonetheless, it carried on relentlessly. Never altering time. Never stopping.

Rat-a-tat-tat.

The house was dark, the hallways empty and dim, save where they were shot through with beams of silvery moonlight. I must have been ten feet from the source of the noise as I tracked it, although it was difficult to tell. Then it seemed to fade and I quickened my pace, reaching the end of the latest corridor and finding a wide set of stairs on my left that wound downwards into the dark. It was into that inky blackness that the drummer was apparently descending.

Common Sense was desperately trying to reassert himself; telling me that going into that shadowy maw was the act of an imbecile and that he would simply stop offering advice from now on, if I kept up this sort of thing. Step after silken step I descended. But his wise counsel prevailed and I slowed to a stop, alone and hidden in a place resembling the service entrance to Dante's inferno. I waited as the drumming sound became fainter, then I started to sneak backwards up the stairs. Back, back to the safety of my room. Away from the imagined terrors below.

Of course, that only made things worse.

Having reached the top of the stairs, I hugged the wall and listened. Nothing. Pure silence. Then I heard it. Ahead of me, the corridor leading back to my room turned sharply right, and from round that dark corner now came the noise of footsteps and rasping breaths. The hairs on the back of my neck stood up and my skin became clammy. A soft moaning sound came floating towards me: a deep, unearthly sound that seemed to seep out of the very walls. Sobriety was being forced upon me in the most appalling manner. Common Sense was wailing in despair, and Pride was nowhere to be seen.

The legend of the boiled sheriff returned to me: the tortured man, forever cursed to stalk the corridors looking for revenge, his death rattle heralding his approach. I whimpered at the ghastliness of it all. No, damn it! Armed with the last vestiges of my self-righteousness, Sheepy now drawn and the safety catch off, I dashed round the corner to catch the culprit.

But the corridor was empty. The hallway ahead disappeared into darkness, its wood-panelled walls unbroken by bedroom doors. The perpetrator had vanished into thin air. Everything was silent.

Bewildered, I stumbled back towards the stairs where, deep in the darkness, I could hear the merciless *rat-a-tat-tat*. Was it louder now? I couldn't tell.

Then the hellish footsteps came at me again from behind, out of sight, around the corner. The agonised breathing. The weak groaning of a soul in torment. Then an almighty crash, which was quite enough for me. I fled down the curving stairs with a despairing sob, running headlong into the darkness, china sheep to the fore, my only defence against the denizens of the dead. I bounded down at least one floor before coming to a halt and flattening myself against the wall. My breathing was ragged and I forced myself, against all my basest instincts, to recalibrate the fight-or-flight mechanism in favour of fight.

Here the stairwell was bathed in pale-grey moonlight from a small window above my head. The steps now beneath my feet

173

were different to the others. These were bare grey stones, worn into uneven shapes by centuries of use. The walls were sheathed in a rough white loam. I realised they must be access stairs for the great horde of servants that once served the household, allowing minions to come and go while minimising the indignity to guests of having to see or hear them.

Down we went, the drummer boy, the sheep and I. I counted three complete spirals, although the dim light and treacherous steps made the descent disorientating. Suddenly, the steps ended and we emerged into a large open kitchen. My feet stepped on large, cold flagstones. I cursed myself for ignoring Common Sense's earlier plea for slippers.

Rat-a-tat-tat.

The kitchen must have been ten square metres, awash with moonlight that was pouring in silvery streams through imposing lead-cased windows located opposite the doorway through which I had just emerged. Two long wooden preparation tables stood in parallel in the middle of the room. Great cabinets leaned on the walls, stocked with crockery and glassware. An immense fireplace, blackened from centuries of use, yawned at me from across the room. Above it hung immaculately burnished brass pots and pans that glinted in the moonlight.

To all intents and purposes, that stairwell might have been a time machine that had transported me back centuries to a time of great feasts and wassailing. The only thing ruining the medieval illusion was the old black oven with heavy cast-iron doors and great stone hotplates, without which no self-respecting country house is complete.

I moved over to it and was pleased to find that it was one of those that remained on all the time. I pressed my hands, then feet, against the warm front, stalling for time – steeling myself for the inevitable showdown with my ghoulish nemesis. I had by now – as you no doubt have long since done, astute reader – unravelled the mystery of where the drummer was taking me.

The warmth of the oven failed to remove a chill that had come over me, caused by something ghastlier than mere cold air. The drumming was growing louder, as if the drummer boy was angered by my lack of movement. The noise was beginning to echo on the whitewashed walls, as if frustrated at my refusal to go on the final leg of the journey. The synchronicity of before was now being replaced with a mad free-for-all. One *rat-a-tat-tat* started overlapping with another as the racket bounced around the room. I shrank down into the shadow of the warm oven, feeling besieged by the hellish noise and remonstrating with that idiot, Pride, who had crept out from whichever sofa he had been hiding behind and was now demanding, over the din, that I see this fool's errand through.

Then, all of a sudden, the terrible *rat-a-tat-tat* was gone. Silence lay thick across the kitchen. I stayed crouched and sweating, listening for the slightest noise. I sent Sheepy out to peer around the corner of the nearby table, but she came back with nothing to report. All was still. Was it over? Had the drummer boy fulfilled his quota of fear and loathing? Could he rest easy, if not for eternity, then at least until some new guests arrived? I listened. I strained every sinew until there was nothing left to be wrung from them.

Yes . . . No . . . Wait . . . *Oh God, please, no* . . . I willed the room to be silent.

But it wasn't.

The *rat-a-tat-tat* was still there. It wasn't gone but was instead very faint. It was now coming from behind the rough wooden door I had gone through on last night's jaunt to the dungeons. I felt like weeping.

I crawled across the floor, holding Sheepy before me as a china shield. My last hope was that the door would be locked. I placed Sheepy on the ground and, whimpering, tested the cold metal handle. With tedious inevitability, it opened with the smallest tug, even giving an obligatory, sweat-inducing creak as it gave way. I hoped that somehow the sight that would greet me as it swung wide would be different to the appalling tunnel to the dungeon; a place where a man and his tiny sheep might live in peace. A place of happy-ever-afters. But the walls and ceiling beyond were still that same bare and rough, cold and clammy consistency.

Yet something *had* changed. What was it? Looking ahead into deep gloom, I realised I was not facing the same impenetrable darkness of the previous evening. This time there was a dim glow, flickering off the claustrophobia-inducing walls.

As I stared into the abyss, the *rat-a-tat-tat* stopped. At first, I refused to believe it – it seemed too much to hope for. I was rooted to the spot. Waiting. Listening. But it was gone, no doubt about it. Whatever the source of the glow, it was clearly intended to be my guide. I sidled a few metres down the corridor before realising – horror of horrors – that I had left Sheepy, my sole protector, on the floor in the kitchen. I turned back to get her, only to see the heavy door to the kitchen close behind me. Running to it, I shook the handle and pulled. Someone – or something – held it fast. I hammered upon the door with a strength born of cowardice and despair. I called out to Sheepy. Begged for help in my hour of need. But there was no reply.

'Et tu, Sheepé?' I murmured forlornly.

Bereft, I slid down onto the floor, my back against the door. I was lost and cold and unsure how things had got quite so far out of hand. I mean, Jesus, I could blow up major infrastructure with unerring accuracy, but I somehow couldn't navigate basic social engagements? The absurdity of it had a strange calming effect. The longer I sat, the more the sense of being tested – tricked – came back to me. The ghost could have had its wicked way with me whenever it wanted. Why here? Why now? None of it made sense. The only certainty was, with the door firmly closed, there was only one way to go. To the light.

I inched down that thin corridor, no place to hide, feeling hemmed in and exposed at the same time. On the plus side, with all my current travails, at least I was less concerned about being raped than on my previous visit. Silver linings and all that. The further I moved along the corridor, the stronger the dancing light became and the darker the shadows appeared as they flickered upon the walls. As if they were slowly coalescing into the wraith that had brought me here. Still, the source of the light eluded me.

I emerged into the small, vaulted atrium. A heavy door that I had not noticed before blocked the way to the dungeon. Then the true horror of the scene revealed itself. Turning to my right, I gazed upon a single candle, standing upright in a pool of its own melted body. Above it was the entrance to that medieval masterpiece of engineering: Farquharson's Bottle. Except this time there was no board blocking the way.

It was wide open.

Awaiting my arrival.

CHAPTER 15

Out, Out, Brief Candle

I was past despair now. A sort of mania took hold. Pride was yelling incoherent threats into the pit. I set my jaw and stared unflinchingly into the darkness.

'Bring it on, Drummer Boy,' I whispered, with a relish that was entirely unfelt and unjustified.

Picking up the candle, I thrust it into that godawful hole, but the tunnel curved sharply to the left, meaning I couldn't see anything. I poked my head in. That was no better. I leaned a little further, being careful not to over-balance and ride the flume into the abyss. Still nothing. I bent my whole torso into the tunnel. Now there was just my arse left hanging out in the proverbial breeze.

With my head still deep in the hole, I came up with a plan. It was not a *good* plan, but a plan nonetheless. I would use the rough-hewn sides of the tunnel as footholds and inch my way down, ready to put my close-quarter skills to good use, if necessary.

Poorly laid plans and all that . . .

I was about to pull myself out of the tunnel to begin my descent proper, when a fresh terror hit me. Last night's worst fears about unwanted access to my nether regions materialised as large, rough hands placed themselves on my well-toned buttocks.

I began to protest when the words were lost in my throat as – *oh Jesus!* – they began to push.

I clamped my hands desperately on both sides of the tunnel, dropping the candle, which briefly lit the pitch-black drop before extinguishing and clattering away into the abyss. Despite my best efforts, I followed it shortly after with a despairing yell.

I flew downwards, headfirst and screaming blue murder. Faster and faster I slid, cold, damp air rushing against my face. I cut my hands on the rough sides as I tried to stop, or at least slow, my descent. The chute began to level out and the darkness gave way to a dim glow. As I sailed helplessly towards it, the glow turned into a bright square of light, shining ahead in the blackness.

Stay away from the light! cried Common Sense, but it was far too late for that. Into the light I went and I tumbled down, down . . . A dirty stone floor rushed up at me and I reached out my hands to cushion the landing that would surely break my arms. I closed my eyes and gritted my teeth, ready for impact.

And then . . . Well, nothing. No crash. No splintering of bone. No agony. I relaxed. Maybe I had fallen on my head. Maybe I had broken my neck. *Maybe I had died.* That was a nice thought. Peaceful. I liked it.

When I opened my eyes, I seemed to be floating, upside down, a couple of feet off the ground. Looking down, I could see the grimy surface of the dungeon. Stretching out my arms, which were hanging loosely below me, I ran my fingertips over the cold stone. Most strange.

Raising my head, I was confronted by a pair of hairy knees, inches from my nose.

Uh-oh, said Common Sense.

Pride said nothing. He was hiding somewhere, wallowing in shame.

Then I registered the thick arms wrapped around my thighs, holding me, still upside down, off the floor. My eyes followed the knees to the thick wool of a kilt, criss-crossed with the blue, green, and red of the Farquharson tartan.

A new horror hit me: I was in the 69 position with a septuagenarian aristocrat. In a dungeon.

Surely this whole ruse wasn't just to induct me into some disgraceful sex club? The hands on my arse at the top of the slide, my current inverted position . . . The evidence didn't look good. Moreover, whoever the members of this sex cult were, they could have just asked. I might well have been game. But they didn't. Why not? Dear Lord, did they mean this to be burglary? Now, I am a liberal person – indeed, a libertarian and libertine – but in my book, you've got to ask permission first. It's good manners.

'Put me down! You beast! You wrong 'un!' I bawled.

He dropped me on my head. Now on my back on the cold stones, I wondered if I should just lie there and let him get on with it. Then I could go back to bed, with the minimum of fuss. God, but it's exhausting visiting these ancestral piles. Then a voice bored into my dazed bonce. It was high, clear, and authoritative. More significantly, it was admonishing my captor.

'Alasdair, what did you do that for?' Lady Anne said. 'Get him up. No, I don't want to hear it!'

Another face appeared, gazing down at me. The last person I expected to see: Allen Fletcher, Laird of Belleville. This was reassuring as it meant the threat of an involuntary rogering was receding. His gentleman's code wouldn't allow it. I mean, this wasn't boarding school.

'Are you OK, James?' Fletcher asked.

'Yes, Allen,' I replied. 'Are you part of this club too, then?'

'Club?'

'Oh, never mind,' I muttered. 'Would you help me up?'

He pulled me to my feet and made an embarrassed move to retie my dressing gown, which was hanging open. How I wished I had worn pyjamas. For the first time, I took in my surroundings. If you'd put a troupe of tumbling dwarves in there, I'd have hardly been more surprised. This was supposed to be the infamous Farquharson's Bottle. Yet it looked more like a homely, albeit sparsely decorated, studio apartment. There was a bed in one corner, a table and chairs, and various kitchen implements – even a small gas stove. A couple of rugs lined the floor and light was coming from lamps placed around the room. Room? I meant dungeon.

'I like what you've done with the place,' was all I could think to say.

Lady Anne bustled round me, brushing off dust and retying my dressing gown with matronly authority. Yet the Colonel was in no mood for small talk. 'I am sorry to have done this to you,' she said, 'but you know who we are and what we are doing – and the urgency of the task.'

I was about to say I had absolutely no idea who they were or what they were up to, but she forged ahead.

'As members of the Underground Railroad, we had hoped to enlist your help, but then we got word you were planning to leave *without* a meeting.'

Her eyes narrowed at this. The accusation was like a blow. Pride shrank from her in shame.

'We didn't think we'd get another chance to talk to you until, well, until it would be too late.' Her voice was even, but cold. 'So, we had to . . . expedite matters.'

I couldn't think of anything to say, so I stood as straight, noble, and unruffled as I could – people like her despise weakness, you know – and simply raised an eyebrow.

She appraised me for a second, then continued. 'We have been assured you are a man of courage and dedication. A man who could help us in this dark hour.' She took a step closer. 'Will you help us, James Macfarlane?'

Don't you just love how powerful women speak? It positively gives me the shivers. Her tone was soft and insistent, leaving me with no doubt that if I did not bow to her will, this would become a personal duel. She would give no quarter and would grind me into the turf without pity. I resolved, then and there, never to play golf with her.

Questions were coming to me thick and fast. The bang on the head must have stimulated something somewhere. One: did she know Lizzy had spoken to me? I had to presume yes, as she was taking my knowledge of their activities for granted. Two: did she know Lizzy had leverage over me, or what that leverage was? I decided this was unlikely as the strumpet was, as a rule, true to her word. Three: could I still talk my way out of whatever harebrained scheme they were cooking up? And four: if I did manage to do so, how on earth would I explain my backsliding to Lizzy? I couldn't risk losing her invaluable services; the Wolf would be finished. The only definitive answer was that I was truly in the soup. Wryly, I reflected that this must have been how the ancient sheriff felt when he realised he was about to become the hors d'oeuvre for those ancient lords.

If you ever find yourself in a similar situation, take it from me, all you can do is stand up straight and look interested, until such time as an exit strategy presents itself.

'James? *James!*' came the urgent entreaty from the Colonel, cutting through my ruminations.

'I, I'm sorry, Your Ladyship,' I babbled, playing for time. 'This bump on my head . . . I was a little dizzy for a second there.'

'Are you recovered?'

'Er, yes, I suppose so.'

'Well, there's someone I want you to meet.' Her voice had changed. There was a warmth there now. An excitement.

I sighed and braced myself to meet Professor Randolph Spring.

'May I introduce you to our honoured guest?' A regal arm swept out, revealing a figure slouched in a high-backed armchair pushed up against the far wall.

I say 'slouched', but 'slumped' would be a better word for it. My

God, he looked terrible. If he were a boxer between rounds, I'd have suggested his team throw in the towel. He was painfully thin, and an old tweed jacket hung off his shoulders like a shroud. He was all nose and forehead, as academics so often are; and bald, but for tufts of grey hair that spiralled out from the sides of his head. His hollow cheeks were covered in short white stubble, and he was peering at me intently from behind thick-rimmed black spectacles. The one exception to this decrepit mess before me was the eyes, which were bright, sharp, and enquiring.

He grasped the arms of the chair and pulled himself upright, revealing himself to be much taller than I expected. He seemed to roll up and out of the seat, like a hose uncoiling. Or a snake.

He strode towards me with unexpected energy and purpose. With each step he appraised me, as if I were a specimen ripe for academic study. I loathed him instantly.

'Professor Spring,' His Lordship addressed him, straightening perceptibly as he did so and betraying that he too was in awe of the man. No, not in awe of the man – this was the tourist he despised – rather, in awe of the woman in awe of the man. 'May I have the honour of introducing James Macfarlane?'

Spring stopped in front of me, but didn't say a word. I had foolishly extended my hand. He didn't extend his. I let mine fall lamely to my side, hating him a little more. Spring's eyes narrowed as he assessed me.

'Are you aware of the importance of the task at hand?' he said, in the voice a lecturer reserves for an irredeemably hopeless student. He lifted his chin high so he could look up at me, while simultaneously peering down his nose.

Quite a trick, I thought, *I must try that on Archie.*

'Do you know how important I am to helping set us free from the yoke we labour under? This tyranny?'

'I'm sure you are about to enlighten me.'

'*Sic semper evello mortem tyrannis!*'* he declared, shaking a fist.

Baffled by this pompous creature, I gawped, no doubt affirming his suspicions about my mental ineptitude. But the Colonel was smart enough to see this introduction was in danger of collapse and moved to put a firm hand on one of my arms.

'The Underground Railroad has done what it can to get people out of this terrible country,' she said. 'But the cost has been tremendous: so many good agents have been lost and so many escape routes discovered . . . But we cannot give up, not now. Here, in Professor Spring, we have a chance to strike a blow at the heart of the establishment. He is worth as much as all of the poor souls we've helped put together.'

I couldn't see how, but wasn't kept in suspense for long.

'He has the education, the intelligence, the vision to change everything,' she continued, impassioned. 'Imagine him – a world-renowned scholar – taking our story to governments, heads of state, the UN . . . *everywhere*! He has seen it all. He has suffered. Been hunted. And he has the wounds and the words to tell our story.'

I wasn't convinced this would be as fruitful as the Colonel might think. Rarely had I met anyone I'd disliked in so short a time. I think I even preferred Hildy – and he had shot me.

'Can you do it?' the bag of bones cut in with acid tones.

'Yes, of course he can,' the Colonel said. 'Can't you?'

I've already explained how she was one of those bloody awful people from whom one feels compelled to seek approval. That natural authority and charm, allied with a powerful position in society, stirs a primeval urge to serve. Still, having such a person in your debt is no bad thing.

'Yes, I can do it,' I said simply.

And it was true. In fact, almost as soon as Lizzy tried to trap me into this madcap scheme, the solution had come to me, ready-made

* Thus always I bring death to tyrants.

184

and boasting all the crucial tenets of any successful MacPlan: namely that it would demand little effort (from me), be cheap (for me), and offer as little risk (to me) as possible. I would use the Shetland Bus. I just had to hope the damn thing actually existed.

'All I will need is some funds to ease the passage,' I added, smiling at Spring.

The professor's eyes bulged, as I had hoped they would, and he turned to the Farquharsons. 'Ha! *Caveat emptor!** Or, better still, *Paucis carior est fides quam pecunia!*** he spluttered. 'He is nothing more than a mercenary. He is entirely unsuitable! Surely there is someone else who actually believes in this cause? In my importance?'

He paused for breath and then was off again, railing about how he had been judged a criminal, but was proud of his crimes and other such nonsense. At least it was in English. Lord Farquharson scowled at Spring, but the Colonel was quick to reassure the professor that he had misunderstood me, that I was a noble fellow and true, and all sorts of other bilge.

'Professor,' I barked, interrupting them with my well-honed Voice of Command. '*Excreta tauri cerebrum vincit.* You know it and I know it. So, let's cut the crap, shall we?'

Magnificent classical wordplay, you'll agree, and the only Latin phrase I knew. It translates roughly as 'bullshit baffles brains', but was enough to stop Spring in his tracks. Faced with this barbarian whom he couldn't impress, confuse, or confound into submission, he lapsed into a sullen silence. Lord Farquharson, meanwhile, regarded me with something approaching respect.

'As I was saying, Randolph . . .' I began.

'How dare you address me like that?' The professor's veins bulged on his temples at the affront. 'I would ask you to show some respect. You may call me Professor—'

---

* Let the buyer beware.

** Few do not set a higher value on money than on good faith.

'*Randolph*,' I interrupted, 'the money is not for me. It is to pay the boatman.'

From the look on the professor's knitted brow, his classically educated brain was going twenty to the dozen, trying and failing to find the answer to this cryptic allusion to Charon's ferry service. It was nothing more than a simple play on words, so he was wasting his time. (Although comparing my plan to a trip to Hades across a river of death was actually pretty close to the mark.)

'Lord and Lady Farquharson.' I turned and addressed them in formal tones befitting a heroic lead. 'I cannot tell you any more as it wouldn't be safe for you [*subtext: safe for me*]. But I give you my word that the limited funds I'll need are crucial for the success of the journey. I would pay them myself, but my bank and my firm are riddled with spies from the Mallice. I am closely watched, being so . . . *high profile.*'

This was nonsense, of course. I could move whatever money I liked, whenever I liked, and did so all the time. But I was buggered if I was going to pay for this little adventure. Have you noticed how people with fanatical gleams in their eyes – as exhibited by the professor and Lady Farquharson – are always keen to throw someone else into the deep end? Why should those of us floundering about have to pay for the privilege as well?

As it turned out, there was no need to convince them to hand over the cash, as they were all for it. I'm sure the castle walls must have been stuffed with untaxed wodges of dough, just waiting to be employed in so noble a venture.

'How do we proceed from here?' Spring was clever enough to know when the battle had been lost and keen to regain his own piece of the high ground.

Ignoring him, I told the Farquharsons what I needed. I stressed the importance of secrecy, protecting my sources, and so on. I spoke a lot and told them nothing. In a matter of minutes, all was settled.

From some dark corner of the dungeon, His Lordship conjured up a bottle of Scotch – one of mine, the scheming bastard – a twelve-year-old Sherry Cask number (classic, light-bodied, subtle notes of dark chocolate, orange and dried fruit on the nose). When everyone had their drams, they raised a toast. That's when I saw the peculiar arcing motion for the second time and the penny dropped.

'The King over the Water, eh?' I said to Farquharson, my eyebrow raised.

'Ah ha! Well spotted, Macfarlane,' he replied jovially, the sickening, dangerous nature of our scheme seemingly lost on him. 'The secret greeting of the Underground, don't you know? Will you join me in the Loyal Toast? All in it together, what?'

'*Supped in a broo* you mean, surely?'

Then it was all brave smiles, firm handshakes, 'fare thee well's and 'speed bonnie boat's. Allen, Laird of Belleville, even did a little clap of excitement, patted me on the back and praised me for being 'a noble fellow'. As I said before: lovely guy, but a terrible judge of character. Spring, for his part, had crumpled back into the depths of his chair and was eyeing me like a malevolent stick insect.

'Before we go, I have two questions, if I may,' I said.

'Fire away,' said Lord Farquharson, looking less wary of me now. The layer of permafrost that coated him whenever he confronted me had started to thaw. Maybe he was just delighted to be rid of Spring.

'Firstly, the dungeon,' I began. 'Now, I imagine this whole set-up wasn't achieved by dropping furniture down that horrible chute? So, can I assume you somehow unsealed the path from the cellars that you mentioned before?'

'Spot on!' exclaimed His Lordship, more meltwater becoming apparent. 'That'll teach the health-and-safety blighters, what?'

'Then, here's what's bothering me,' I said slowly. 'The drummer boy. That weird percussion that I couldn't seem to place. And the footsteps? The breathing? The moans? All of it. How did you do all that?'

'Never you mind,' said the Colonel, putting a conspiratorial finger to her nose.

'I'm sorry, what did you just say?' I said, my eyes wide.

'I'm pleased we old dogs still have some tricks up our sleeves!' His Lordship interrupted jauntily, the permafrost now dissolving at such a rate as to threaten environmental disaster. 'It's an old trick we've been using on tourists for generations. Ha! Doesn't have to be the drummer boy, of course. We've all sorts of disembodied creatures to keep folk entertained. Never fails, you see. All you need is—'

That's as far as he got. A dull rumbling above our heads stopped him in his tracks. We all looked up in unison at the black hole in the chamber roof. My worst fears of betrayal were confirmed. Perhaps it was the anguish of that that rooted me to the spot, as the rumbling resolved into a disgraceful stream of Glaswegian blasphemy, and seventeen stone of flailing fury came crashing down on top of me.

'Hello, Archie,' I croaked.

CHAPTER 16

Aces High

I was furious with Archie when I woke the next morning. Being safe and sound in my own bed did nothing to ease my cold and ineffective rage. It wasn't because of his part in the drummer boy plot. He admitted that the Colonel had enlisted him the previous day – with precious little effort on her behalf, I might add. I pressed him on this and didn't let his customary 'never you mind' pass muster, nor his attempts to make light of the whole thing by classifying it as 'a' baws'.

'Yeh cannae say nae tae the Quality, no' in a place like this, can yeh? No' when we're all oan the same side anyways.'

I begrudgingly accepted that was all I was getting, but I still wasn't happy. Archie being a terrible snob (in his own way) was a truth I could stomach; more difficult was the niggling suspicion that he had thought me a coward for backing out of an opportunity for danger and unpleasantness, and had taken it upon himself to force bravery upon me. I masked these uncomfortable suspicions by focusing on the revelation that it had been Archie who had propelled me, *per anum*, down the chute. This was tantamount to revolution.

'Och, ah'm affy sorry aboot that, Mr Mac,' he said, as I glared at him with my glariest glare. 'Ah thought yeh wiz no' gonnae go through wi' it, yeh see? Ah thought yeh wiz climbing back oot o' the hole tae go back tae bed.'

I explained the true reason I was getting back out – to shimmy down with dignity – when he started laughing.

'May I ask what's so damned funny?'

'Ah wiz tryin' tae dae the same thing!' he guffawed.

Yes, actually *guffawed*. Not many people can carry off a good guffaw. Unless you have a body mass index of at least thirty, then I wouldn't even try it.

'That's so funny, inn't it?' Archie went on. 'In went ma big feet, but there wisnae anywhere tae hang on tae an' the slide wiz so steep ah jist hurt ma hands.'

'You could have bloody killed me!'

'Aye, but ah didnae, did ah?' *A's weel that ends weel* in Archie's world.

I tentatively prodded the lump on top of my head, which marked where Farquharson had dropped me in the wee hours and upon which this Glaswegian behemoth had tumbled shortly after.

Archie took considerable delight in explaining the plotting and scheming that had gone on behind my back. It seemed I had been inadvertently caught in a pincer movement, surrounded and outmanoeuvred by the buffalo horns of the impis, commanded by the Colonel and Lizzy respectively. Being equal in their capacity as arch-strategists and manipulators, they had separately lit on the idea of enlisting me to do their dirty work; one (who didn't know me very well) by appealing to my sense of virtue, righteousness, and honour, the other (who did know me) by getting me aroused and then threatening me.

'Aye, they're affy guid at the schemin', thon lassies,' Archie said wistfully. 'When ah found yeh drinkin' yer G&T, ah'd come tae bring yeh tae Her Ladyship so she could get yeh oan board wi' the Undergroond Railroad plot. Oan board, eh? Heh heh.'

'Archie, concentrate.'

'Aye, OK. Well, we wiz aff tae speak tae Her Ladyship when Miss Burke came doon the stairs, swayin' in that funny way she does, yeh ken?'

'Yes, I ken.' All too well, dammit. If I had ignored that enticement and faced the Colonel instead, I fancy I would have found a way to turn Her Ladyship down. With time pressing, who knows when or if Lizzy would have been able to use her wiles and her leverage to entrap me in this scheme. There's a lesson there that revolves around ignoring nice bottoms clad in tight dresses, but I'm sure I shall never learn it.

'Archie?' I said warily.

'Aye?' he said boldly.

'I have one more question.'

'Aye?'

'The ghostly beat of the drummer boy: how did they do it?'

'Oh, aye,' he said, looking thoughtful. 'That wiz affy clever. First, they thought, seein' as you'd heard the Prof drummin' oan the walls the night before – he's quite good, yeh know, he wiz in a pipe band at school—'

'Archie, please focus.'

'Aye, well, since ye'd been a' fearty* . . .'

'What did you say?'

'Oh, ah mean, taken by surprise, like, eh?' he corrected himself as my disgrace burned inside me. 'Well, tae yer credit, they figured ye'd no' let yersel' be feart . . . ah mean, *surprised*, agin an' would want tae sort oot this wee drummer bairn.** Yeh know, gi'e him a bit o' laldie.***

'Quite,' I said.

'So, the plan was tae get yeh to the Prof before yeh ran awa' in the mornin'—'

'I'm warning you, Archie.'

'Aye, sorry, ah meant before we left nice an' early, like . . .

---

* Scared.

** Child.

*** Give him a hard time or a beating.

191

Anyway, it wiz easy. We each had a stage o' the hoose to cover an' oor drumsticks . . . Noo, apparently, this hoose is affy old, see?'

'So I'm told.'

'And it's been built in lots o' different bits in lots o' different ways, eh? Noo, there are certain bits where the ceilin's and floors – even the bluidy walls – are hollow or just filled wi' auld ash for insulation. Can yeh credit it? Ash, like frae the fireplace? Affy clever, yon auld builder men—'

'Archie!'

'Oh, aye, sorry. So, when yeh bang oan them, wi' drumsticks or the like, the sound bounces all o'er the place, just like a wee ghostie! They've been doin' it tae the visitors for years and years, so they've got it doon tae an art. Can lead yeh a merry dance almost anywhere in the castle. Clever bastards, yon aristos, eh?'

I lay back again on the pillow and shut my eyes. The bed was warm and soft and safe. But I couldn't help but wonder how soon fate would once again grab me by the arse and pitch me into oblivion. On the current schedule, around lunchtime seemed likely.

'I think it's time to go home,' I said. 'Can you prepare our belongings?'

'Already done it.'

'*All* of them?' My eyes narrowed.

'Aye. The biggest piece of baggage didnae half complain when ah told him he wiz goin' in the boot wi' the rest o' the clobber.'

'Does he have air?'

'Enough.'

'Is he comfortable?'

'Ah shouldnae think so.'

'Oh, *good*. I feel better already. Perhaps we can stay a little longer, then. What's for breakfast?'

* * *

Standing in the cold winter air outside the castle, I bade the assembled company 'cheery-bye!' with a jaunty, carefree air that I hoped would confuse and unnerve them. If I'd known the circumstances in which I'd see some of them next time – and how I'd never see others again – well, I might have lingered longer. Might have shown them more respect. But it's always easy to say that with hindsight.

The drive back home started badly. I had presumed Wally, now sat in the passenger seat, had spent his time in the castle holed up somewhere doing his day job. You know, monitoring security at the distillery, stopping cyber attacks, catching thirsty still staff unconscious at their stations, that sort of thing. But this was not wholly true, a fact that came to light almost as soon as we set off, when he dissolved into another of his asthmatic coughing fits.

'Will you get that looked at, for God's sake?' I said. Then I stopped. And listened. Listened to his heavy breathing; laboured breathing of the kind you might hear in the dead of night while being pursued by, say, an irritated ghost with the flesh hanging *aff his banes*. 'Archie, stop the car. And, Wally, you stop breathing. Don't start again until I say so.'

We pulled onto the verge at the side of the road and I saw the two of them exchange glances. Then it all came tumbling out: how Wally had been in on the act, hiding in one of the priest holes until I passed, then sneaking out. I should have bloody guessed from all the asthmatic wheezing.

'Aye, an' then yeh nearly bluidy ruined it, yeh careless bawbag,'* Archie sniffed.

'So, yeah, er, I tripped climbing back into the hole the second time and fell on my head.' A sheepish tone crept into Wally's voice. 'Made a bit of a noise.'

'I should have bloody guessed; no self-respecting creature of the

---

* Scrotum.

night would be so slapdash in his haunting,' I snapped. 'You almost gave me a heart attack.'

'Thank you, sir,' he said, pride all over his face at a job well done.

'Don't call me sir.'

'Sorry, Mr Mac.'

'And, both of you, don't ever, ever, *ever* do anything like that again. Now, for God's sake, take me home.'

Outside, the heather-clad hills drifted past, magnificent, bleak, and beautiful. Earth as hard as iron. Water like a stone. The bare winter countryside was peaceful under the overcast sky, brimming with unrealised dangers. All was at peace, save the cacophonic efforts of our visiting lecturer, Professor Randolph Spring (MA, MSc, PhD), who evidently didn't like his digs under a tarpaulin sheet in the boot. Of course, this hiding place would only have stood up to the most cursory of glances, but I hadn't been worried about that – not to start with, anyway. We'd been stopped countless times in the past and all I'd had to do was flash a winning smile, extend a generous hand, and absorb the cries of 'Gawd! It's Jimmy Mac! How are you, sir? Big fan, of course' as they shook it. (As such, the search we'd endured on the road to the dam was extremely rare.) But I'd never tried this with furious Latin oaths pouring from the rear. The banging and yelling was unrelenting, the arrogance unfathomable. If we had been pulled over, the game would have been up. But that seemed to matter less to the professor than the lack of respect being shown to him.

Soon the three of us were of one mind: would it really be so bad if the poor professor *accidentally* shot himself with one of the guns in the boot? Indeed, that was the charitable option. Archie was a keen proponent of 'blood loss after accidental castration' being the cause of death. We ended up pulling over so he could explain this to the professor in his own dulcet way, then resumed our journey in blissful silence. There were checkpoints, of course, but we sailed through them without even slowing. Hulking great ostentatious cars are a terrific way of being inconspicuous.

The countryside was more open now as we approached our final destination, leaving the unforgiving peaks of heather and scree of the Cairngorms. To the north and east the low, undulating hills were covered in a patchwork of fields, gradually falling away as we approached the coast. We turned off the road and crossed the small river marking the entrance to my home. The driveway ploughed through a short, thick wood, originally planted to make the house invisible from the road. The trees gave way to lawns as we drove up the gentle slope to the top of the hill, coming to a halt on a gravel turning circle in front of the house.

Welcome to Glenlairig, pronounced 'Glenlarrich'. Built over the course of nearly five hundred years, it had originally been a castle. But unlike Invereiton, Glenlairig's previous owners showed no yearnings for the past. In time it had become a fortified house, before being remodelled as a Georgian mansion in the late eighteenth century. This evolution left a mixture of open, airy rooms and corridors with high ceilings at the front, leading into a warren of narrow corridors with low doorways and dark little rooms at the back: relics of its ancient past. Three rows of windows crossed the whitewashed frontage, aligned with the gabled roofs in perfect Georgian symmetry. It was a big house; I had never actually counted the bedrooms.

The surrounding hills never failed to inspire me and on a normal day I would have soaked up the spectacular view as I approached the house. But today was not a normal day. A large black car parked on the gravel was seriously marring the whole vista. Next to it stood an enormous Mallice officer, hands clasped capably in front of his black suit.

'Whit the hell is goin' on here?' Archie appraised the scene with a professional eye. 'Why's a goddamn pig standin' in front o' the hoose?'

195

Even though we'd recently destroyed a vital piece of national infrastructure, Archie was correct: this didn't feel right. The Mallice were not in the habit of making polite house calls to those suspected of, well, anything. They just didn't do polite.

'Right, Mr Mac, if ah pull up quick, ah can be oot an' banjo* him. Three seconds tops, ah reckon,' said Archie with military precision.

'Questions first, violence later,' I replied. 'Let's see what he wants.'

Archie grunted his acceptance but, with one hand on the wheel, flicked open a compartment by his knee, removed the small automatic from inside, and lodged it in the door beside him.

'Easy now,' I said, scanning from left to right to gauge whether there were any more visitors playing hide and seek in the bushes. 'Wally, put that away.'

Wally had pulled out his tablet and was in the act of unrolling it. 'But I was—'

'—going to do nothing at all. If they wanted trouble, they'd be all over us by now. If anything, they're waiting for us to make a mistake. Just take it easy. Archie, you drop me off and then take Wally and the cargo over to the gun room. Just like we've done a thousand times before. Nice and easy.'

We pulled up behind the car and Archie dutifully tramped round to open my door. The air was cold and heavy with menace. I took a deep breath as my foot crunched down on the gravel, affecting to study the steel-grey sky, as if the weather was my greatest concern. The Mallice man didn't move, his stare hidden behind the regulation sunglasses that said *I may be looking at you, I may not. Wait and see.*

'Good morning, officer,' I began, stopping when an almighty ruckus broke out behind me. Muffled howls and banging emanated

* Beat up.

from the boot of the car. My face must have drained of colour. The Mallice officer stepped forward to investigate.

Without missing a beat, Archie strode to the rear of the car and banged on the boot. 'Quiet in there, you horrible creature, or I'll leave yeh in the hands of this nice Mallice gentleman!' he yelled, hammering on the panelling. The noise stopped. He turned back, a look of contrition on his face, arms spread wide. 'Sorry, Mr Mac, but yeh know how the gun dog gets when he can smell hame. Ah'll deal wi' him over at the strong room, if that's OK?'

'Yes, Archie,' I replied, shock giving way to anger. 'And don't spare the rod, eh? Can't have that happening when the birds are coming over, can we?'

'O' course no', Mr Mac. Ah'll be oan ma way then.'

'Very good. Oh, and Archie?'

'Aye?'

'When you're done in the gun room, come back and join us, would you? Just in case our visitor – or perhaps it's visitors – need refreshment? And bring a decent assortment of your goodies, eh?'

'Aye, Mr Mac. Understood.'

I turned back to the Mallice man as Archie fired up the car. The wheels spun on the gravel and he was off. Peace returned to Glenlairig.

'I'm sorry about that, officer. Now, what can I do for you?'

He said nothing but stuck out an arm, ushering me into my own home, the cheeky bastard. I stepped warily over the threshold, expecting nothing less than the rush of feet, a black hood over my head, and then cries in the darkness. With the hairs on my neck standing on end, I took another step forward and braced for impact. Nothing happened. In fact, nothing moved at all. Staff who should have been bustling around, seeing to my every need, were absent. The officer directed me to the sitting room off to the left of the entrance hall. On my exquisite blue antique sofa sat a man, bent low over a small table.

'I hope you don't mind; I asked the staff to set up a card table while I waited for you,' said the man in a light, easy voice. He didn't look up. 'Then I dismissed them so we wouldn't be disturbed.'

I bloody well did mind and was about to say so when he flicked over a playing card with his long, thin fingers, placing it neatly on a pile on the green tabletop. He was playing solitaire.

'Oh, come, come,' said the man, 'sit down.'

He looked up and the breath caught in my throat. We had never met face to face before but I knew him, just like everyone in Caledon knew him. Thomas Loker, head of the Mallice, the most dangerous man in Caledon. The man with the dead fish eye and cupboard full of heads. He made dogs bark and children cry.

Loker must have been in his late forties, slender, with closely cropped brown hair. His face was waxen and colourless; one eye grey and misty. I have no idea why, nor whether he could see from it. The other was a piercing blue. 'Unnerving' didn't begin to cover it. Perhaps that was the whole point.

I followed his order without thinking and sat down opposite.

Loker turned the deck over one card at a time, placing each one onto the baize. 'I like solitaire,' he said, studying the table. 'It's all about creating order out of chaos. About the excitement of asserting order and control, imposing one's will on the random acts of chance inherent in the turn of the cards. Ha, look! An ace. You must always play your aces immediately, wherever you can. Did you know that?'

I had no idea what to say.

He looked up in feigned surprise. 'Come now, Mr Macfarlane. Why so coy? Surely I have not caused offence by making myself at home? Is it not the Highlander's duty to offer shelter to passing visitors?'

At some point I must have closed my mouth, which had been hanging open in disbelief at this deeply distressing scene. Why was the Headhunter in my sitting room? Silence hung heavily as he appraised me with a little smile on his tight-skinned face.

'I must admit, I am disappointed. Before me stands one of the most verbose men in Caledon, does he not? Do we, the loving people, not long for your next adventure? Do we not hang on Jimmy Mac's every word?'

There was a good chance my life might hang on my next words. My mind raced. The smouldering wreck of the dam flashed before my eyes. Down by my side my fingers shook. I clenched them tight and prayed Loker had not noticed. How should I respond? What would an innocent man do? No, wait! That was the wrong question. What would Jimmy Mac do?

'My hospitality can quickly be exhausted if my guests prove themselves unwelcome,' I said, doing my best impression of being in control. 'Why are you here? Don't you have skulls to polish or innocent people to terrorise?'

If Loker was caught unawares by this, he did not show it. Instead, he placed the pack of cards down and paused before he spoke.

'These do not sound like the words of a Good Citizen, Mr Macfarlane. You are a Good Citizen, are you not?'

'I am a Good Citizen.' It came out without me thinking and I hated myself for it.

'I am being civilised with you, Mr Macfarlane, and I would appreciate it if you extended me the same courtesy.'

'Civilised?' Jimmy Mac barked back. 'You've marched in here, dismissed my staff, ordered me to sit and are threatening me with half-baked card play metaphors. I won't have it. Not in my own home.'

He nodded. Not in agreement, more like he was trying to figure something out. Figure me out. 'If that's your preferred approach, then let's get down to business, *Jimmy*. May I call you Jimmy?'

'No.'

Loker's face registered no surprise. He just kept staring, that horrible smile playing around the edges of his mouth. I felt like a specimen being prepared for dissection. He reached his long fingers into a breast pocket and, in that same slow, fluid way he had put down the cards, removed a small cube. At some invisible command it snapped open and lay flat in his palm, revealing a compact, glowing screen.

'James Macfarlane,' he read without looking up from the display. 'Forty-six years old, six foot one, blond hair, forty-two-inch chest, eye colour: blue.'

'Two blue eyes,' I said, pointedly staring at the revolting fish eye. A childish jibe, I'll admit, but the best I could think of.

'Leading whisky manufacturer, charitable concerns,' Loker went on, like he was reading an instruction manual. 'Interesting past, I see. Single child. Orphaned at a young age. Brought up by grand-parents. Psych profile says such isolation is likely to drive a tendency for individualism and reinvention.'

'Don't forget a propensity for vengeance,' I added, the familiar surroundings and growing amount of time without physical assault emboldening me.

The Headhunter cocked his head to one side and studied me. 'Am I supposed to offer you sympathy for this tragedy?' he asked, in a tone that betrayed not concern, but a detached professional interest.

'Not at all,' I replied. 'As my dear granny used to say, "Five words, James: Just. Get. On. With. It."'

'Wise advice,' Loker said. 'So, let's see: quoted as saying you "come from a long line of smugglers, reprobates, and other business-men". Ha, ha. Yes. Very good. Four years in the Caledon Defence Force. Interesting. Black ops. Lots of redactions . . .' He looked up, and when he spoke there was, for the first time, a note of – what? Anger? No – frustration in his voice. 'Operative 2811?'

'Yes, Mr Loker?'

The deep voice behind made me start. I was so focused on Loker's weird pantomime that I'd forgotten the bastard was there.

'Make sure the next time I look at this profile all redactions and restrictions are removed.'

'Yes, Mr Loker.'

I wondered how much more he knew. And when would 'the next time' be? A gnawing fear began to grow in my stomach. Did he know about the Wolf? Was this just a game? Even if he didn't, once he had those restrictions lifted, would my private life and military record reveal all the predilections, behavioural patterns, and skills his algorithms would need to reach one inescapable conclusion?

'Macfarlane!'

Loker's voice sliced through my panic.

'I'm sorry, what were you saying?' I said, projecting a detached calm for all I was worth.

Loker's jaw tightened. He sat forwards and clasped his hands on the table, looking at me intently. 'Where were you last night?'

'Invereiton Castle.'

'Doing what?'

'Getting shot.'

He frowned, trying to discern a hidden meaning. Then he registered the scabs forming on my recently mutilated face. 'How unfortunate.'

'Quite.'

'What do you know about the attack on Pitlochry Dam?'

'They say it was the work of the Wolf of Badenoch.'

'A friend of yours?'

'Certainly not. He blew up the aquifer that serves my distillery.'

'He?'

Loker almost got me there. My heart banged against my ribcage. 'I presume it was a he; bombers do tend to be, don't they?' I replied,

201

perhaps a second too late. 'But you're right, gender neutrality is the watchword. I apologise if I have offended you. As soon as you leave, I shall instigate a full programme of diversity training, firm-wide, to make sure we stamp out this insidious habit.'

'Must be very inconvenient for you.'

'Diversity training? No, I think it's very important that—'

'Don't play games, Macfarlane. The aquifer. Most inconvenient.'

'I should say so. Terrible nuisance.'

'But you found another source?'

'Yes.'

'Very convenient.'

'Not really. The fluctuations in weather mean several back-ups are essential.' This was true, thank God, or he would have had me.

Loker sat back, tapping a finger on his lips.

This was no time for full-blown uncomfortable silence; Lord knows where that would end. 'Are we done now?' I snapped, trying to regain the high ground, all bluster and feigned indignation.

But he refused to play my game and we sat in silence; him studying me, me thinking happy thoughts to bring my nerves back down from DEFCON 1 or 5 – whichever the really bad one is.

'I wonder,' he mused, that slight smile once again playing at the edge of his thin mouth.

'You wonder what?'

'Would you die for what you believe in, Mr Macfarlane?'

I was at a loss, but it seemed an answer wasn't required as the Headhunter pressed on.

'Perhaps you are one of that rare breed who would go further. Perhaps you are someone who would give up more than themselves. Tell me: are you that person? Are you someone who would give up *everything*?'

I've already given my thoughts on this matter, but at that very moment they were hardly so well considered. At that moment I was reeling; trying to stop the sweat from breaking out on my forehead, betraying my guilt and sealing my doom. Pride and Common Sense raged within, demanding I pull myself together. They made clear in no uncertain terms that the slightest slip would mean ruin.

'You come across as impetuous, perhaps even brave, but I wonder what you would say if I had Operative 2811 break a couple of your larger bones. Would you still be so fearless?'

Strangely, this question was something of a lifeline. It gave me a chance to play my own ace. An ace with clubs.

'Probably not,' I snapped back. 'But by the time your officer got to the second bone my butler Archie would have torn his spine out and begun forcing you to eat it, so it's all moot really.'

Loker stared at me, eyes narrowing as if he was grasping for some vital insight that was just out of reach. 'Do you know, the longer we talk, the more intrigued I become?' he asked, knitting his fingers together and peering over them like a demented psychologist. 'Until now I had wondered if you were putting up a front, or if you were really a man of courage; a choice that I perceive now to be a false dichotomy. No. It is not bravery or cowardice. It is something else.' Loker paused then spoke slowly, choosing his words with care, as if one slip might rob him of a long-sought prize. 'I perceive that you think of yourself as untouchable. You think you are safe from the laws that bind everyone else and keep order in this storm of chaos. Yes . . . You have piqued my interest. Please indulge me for a second.'

I had no intention of indulging him. Jimmy Mac swung into action. 'Mr Loker, I am a busy man. As much as I'd love to keep exchanging pleasantries and thinly veiled threats with you, there's work to do—'

He cut in before I could finish. 'Just one more enquiry then, if I may.'

'One more,' I said, with feeling.

'Do you believe yourself immune to The Question?'

'I'm sorry, what on earth are you talking about?'

'Interesting. Already you prove my point. The very idea of being put to The Question fills most people with terror. You, on the other hand, don't even register it. The notion is alien to you.'

'You are making no sense whatsoever.'

'Being put to The Question, surely you—'

'Oh, hang on a minute. I see. The Question. Yes, I understand. And yet no matter how you dress it up, you're still talking about torture, aren't you?'

Loker beamed. 'And still you show no signs of fear.'

Clearly, he was mistaking my reddened cheeks for indignation, not the horror they actually reflected. My insides felt like they'd been put in a blender, just at the moment when survival depended on guts of steel. Loker's change in demeanour had brought home just how different he was to the Marischal. Our leader had a rawness – a deadly honesty – that was single-minded. Yes, it was unhinged and potentially lethal, but it came from a belief in a purpose. Loker was a different creature altogether, a creature of honed malevolence that would inflict misery for nothing more than its own sake. He knew where the bodies were, and where they would be. The Marischal wanted to save souls. Loker wanted to own them.

'I have a theory,' Loker continued, 'that people of your category are more difficult to control for two reasons. The first is a natural arrogance born of a life of safety and privilege. This makes it difficult to conceive of the kind of consequences that others take for granted. Are you following me?'

I nodded without thinking.

'The second reason is an extension of the first, in that it is the measures we are sometimes forced to inflict—'

'Forced?'

'Oh, I won't lie and say I don't take pleasure in people's . . .

rehabilitation. It is an art. *My* art. You must weigh each specimen's tolerance for fear, humiliation, pain, and desolation. Perhaps mathematics is a better allusion than art? You see, it is a delicately balanced equation: a problem to be solved. But when these factors are weighed in perfect proportions, the transformation is joyous. You unleash a symphony of despair that marks the moment of your victory.'

'You're mad. Quite mad.'

'Aha!' Loker sprang to his feet and lunged forward to grasp my shoulder. 'You have made my point for me, don't you see? You have turned a theory of mine – a supposition – into hard fact.'

I recoiled as he bent over me, his good eye shining and the dead fish eye blank.

'Do you know the old phrase *the hangman's whip holds more immediate terrors than the fear of hell*? No? Most would never insult me – not to my face, certainly. They would hardly dare to do it in private. They know I am everywhere. But you? You have an innate belief that you are immune from the consequences. You are outraged by the very notion that they lie in wait for you! Because of who you are – *what* you are – you have not made a contract with me in the way most others have by their mere acceptance of the established order; by their acknowledgement that certain actions demand certain consequences. No, you do not for one moment truly believe you could ever be put to The Question!'

I started as Loker began shaking my hand vigorously, as if he were having some Road to Damascus moment.

'I cannot thank you enough, Mr Macfarlane! It is rare I can have such a frank conversation with a man of your position. Rare that I can put these ideas to the test in such an unpolluted environment!' His good eye glinted with a devilish light. A manic excitement had taken hold. 'Don't you see? Once I have your sort at my leisure in the Tolbooth and they realise their folly, it is too late for both of us.

Yes, I can stop them from transgressing again – I can break them and I can rebuild them – but I cannot undo their previous disobedience, can I? It is too late by then. Already I have failed them. But if I can recognise the symptoms, characterise and categorise the likely offender, then I can predict defiance . . . perhaps before it has even begun coalescing in their own minds. I can tear it out at the roots long before it can bloom, and then we find ourselves in a different position altogether, do we not? Yes. If I can do that, then I can save them from themselves.'

He tailed off into silence, my hand still grasped in his. Loker's eyes dropped and he stared at the floor, nodding, as if deep in thought. Suddenly, his face snapped back up and I was met with that horrible grey, watery eye.

'Thank you, Mr Macfarlane, I have made unexpected progress here.' He jerked his head towards the card table. 'Please feel free to finish my game.'

He released my hand, turned on his heel and – just like that – was gone, Operative 2811 in his wake. I still hadn't moved when the sound of crunching gravel drive drifted through the big windows as the car pulled away. I stared at where it had been and thought about Loker. About *the next time.*

'Whit the fuck wiz that aboot?' said a voice behind me.

I almost soiled myself. 'Jesus H. Christ, Archie! Stop sneaking up on me like that.'

'Sorry, Mr Mac. He's a total daftie, that one, eh?'

'I'm not so sure. I'm going to need a drink, Archie. A really big one. And I know it's early, but gin just ain't going to cut it. We need whis—'

'All ready for you,' the big man replied, pointing me towards a silver platter, laid out with two large glasses of Scotch and a couple of teacakes.

'How? When?'

206

'Never you mind, Mr Mac.'

And I didn't. There had been quite enough intrigue for one day. I sniffed the glass and closed my eyes as the notes of chewy sultanas and morello cherry, dried herbs, and cooked fruit filled my head. The xxv Glenlairig from the sherry casks. One of our finest. God bless Archie. He was always ready with the right prescription for the patient. As I drank the life-giving whisky, the clock chimed 10 a.m. There are days when rules are made to be broken.

CHAPTER 17

Whisky Galore

The end was coming. The old man knew it. He could feel it in the air and in his bones. He could hear it on the wind, in the rustling of the trees and the whisper of the barley, all calling him back to the earth he had dug and cut and shaped. He was not scared. He never had been. He was a hard man, hewn from violence and struggle and hope. He never would have survived otherwise.

'Fergus!' the old man called from the bath chair, his large, scarred hands resting lightly on the steering handle.

'Aye, Mr Macfarlane,' came the response as the heavy-set servant hurried into the room.

'Take me over to the window, please.'

'Of course, Mr Macfarlane.'

The old man looked out of the large round window and surveyed the land, timeless and beautiful. No, he wasn't scared, just sad. He was sad that time had passed so quickly. Sad that the land spreading out in front of him was so ordered, so tamed; so clear in its declaration that his work here was done. He was sad that his legs had abandoned him. They had been thick and powerful once. They had carried him to this place from far away – mile after mile after mile. His arms, now barely able to lift a glass, had hefted the axes and spades that had forged his fortune. They had lifted sacks of grain so heavy it took two normal men to carry them. Thousands of those rough sacks; day after day, year after year. He took a deep breath; it was all so long ago and yet the time had fled so fast. At least his memories were clear. Age, it seemed, could not take them.

The old man's eyes ranged across the hills beyond the glass. So different now from the day, decades before, when he had wandered into this glorious valley. The heather had been thick under his feet and the damp air had filled his nostrils with rich, peaty scents. The young man had sat down and scrabbled around in his sack for the penny whistle that lay somewhere in its filthy innards. He'd looked at the instrument thoughtfully before putting the tin to his lips. It was the last relic of a miserable childhood – of a life to which he would never return. He blew softly and the bright notes hung in the air before they were carried off by the wind. He might have been nothing more than another hairy, dirty smuggler drawn by the promise of the landscape, but his senses were honed by experience and hardship, and they told him he was home.

And so he was.

As the young man toiled, Mother Nature revealed what he already knew in his soul: the climate was perfect, the altitude and cooler temperatures ideal for whisky creation and ageing. He laughed with delight as the pure, freezing water of the springs bubbled out of the dark earth and over his calloused hands. He relished the inhospitable terrain, the splendid isolation that made it perfect for an illicit distiller with no intention of sacrificing a single penny to the obscene tax system. Hidden away, he crafted his whisky for as long as he dared in his sma* stills, running rings round rivals who shipped their filthy firewater up from the Lowlands. It was a heavenly match: Robbie Macfarlane and this place with no name. He would give it one in time.

The old man shifted in his chair as the stiffness in his bones reminded him of the toll that life had taken. That lifetime. He raised his eyes to the braes and his long, thick beard was split by a rare smile as he surveyed the ingenious system of pits, dug long

* Small.

ago to store his whisky over the winter and to keep it safe from the prying eyes of the gadgers.* He had never had time for religion, but even now he marvelled at the sense of destiny he had felt upon discovering that the pits also offered perfect conditions for maturing his product. How he had given thanks, laughing long and loud into the cold, still air!

The dour, bent figure in the bath chair almost laughed aloud again, all these years later, as he thought of the time he had tried to float a whisky still into the middle of a loch, so he could tip the evidence into the peat-black water at a moment's notice if the men of the revenue hunted him down. He had almost drowned that day when the rickety vessel tipped and swayed and sank without trace. It was funny to think of the old contraption lying in the gloomy depths even now, safe from prying eyes.

Then the wide smile retreated as the old man pictured this fragment of his existence resting alone and unremembered in the darkness, long after he was gone. If, in days to come, strange people with strange clothes, contrivances, and conversations pulled it up, would they marvel at the queer apparatus that appeared, rusted and bent, from the bottom of the loch? Would they conjure up pictures of a wild young man in ancient times and guess of his adventures? Would they wonder at his hardships, his triumphs? Or would his existence be relegated to a raised eyebrow – a passing curiosity – as if he had never really been there at all?

Enough of these troubling thoughts and creeping fears. They were unbecoming to a man of his stature. He was not scared. He never had been.

The old man turned, reaching out to grasp a picture frame on the writing desk next to him with a shaking hand. He read aloud the letter it contained, written by the long-dead Duke of Gordon. *Dear Robbie . . .* He still felt a powerful sense of pride that a duke had

* Tax collectors.

known his name all that time ago. Plenty did now, of course. He felt pride that they'd fought together and won, the letter proclaiming joyously that parliament was slashing duty on whisky. Proud that he had changed the world. On that day in 1823 – so long ago! – the ancient art of illicit distilling and smuggling had been dealt a deathblow, although many would fight to the last to keep it alive.

The old man closed his eyes and swept his memories for the final batch of illicit grain he had soaked in the burn; a eulogy for the end of an era. But it was not there. It had been a monumental act in its own way, but also a mundane task he had performed hundreds of times before.

'We rarely see these historic moments for what they are at the time,' he murmured to himself, causing his servant to turn in expectation of command. 'Only too late do we realise they are to be nurtured and dwelt upon, but try convincing the youth of that!'

'Aye, Mr Macfarlane.'

'Our achievements are to be celebrated. We must treasure auld lang syne,* must we not, Fergus?'

'Aye, Mr Macfarlane.'

For a moment the rose-tinted veil lifted and the old man remembered the battle for survival that had begun. It was dirty and mean. The weak fled or they died. Rivals fought and stole and murdered. Yet he was still here. His hair-trigger pistols had not been fired in fear or anger for almost fifty years. Now look at them! James, his son, had caged them in glass. He had turned tools of killing into a museum piece that celebrated the false romance of a life of villainy, where no quarter was asked or given.

Oh, how life had changed. Now all their battles were with lawyers as they fought to protect Glenlairig, a name the old man had chosen to honour the Lairig Ghru hill-pass, where he had once smuggled his spirits south. How he hated the lawyers, with their

* Days gone by.

clever words and their endless entreaties, documents, and demands. There was honesty in a pistol. But that time and his world were gone forever.

The sun was setting outside the window, turning the countryside a deep gold. The air in the room was cooling. The night would soon be here, and the old man turned quickly from the past to stare down the ages to come. He saw his son James fighting those damned lawyers and winning. He smiled at the sight of the high-collared, clean-shaven, industrious man – the son of an outlaw – so proper and polite as he built an empire.

He saw his grandson and namesake Robbie dragged from the trenches of the Great War, shell-shocked and broken, bringing the distillery to the edge of ruin with his drinking, gambling, and speculation. He saw the green marble floor of Glenlairig's great hall – his one act of decadence that had caused him no end of embarrassment – torn up to pay off debts. He watched the man, whom he knew now as his playful, carefree wee grandson, as he wept and drank and yelled out in his sleep.

But there was redemption to come. The old man saw Robbie's daughter and her husband rebuilding the Glenlairig fortune as they cleverly shifted between malts and blends, reading markets and people with an intuition that rivalled his own. He saw them raise a grandson out of tragedy and prepare him for the great adventure ahead. Glenlairig was safe, for now.

It was enough.

The sun was almost below the horizon. The hills were lit a blazing gold. A hundred years had passed before his eyes and all was well. The old man knew his time was well spent and he would be weel kent.*

It was enough.

He looked around, surprised at the sudden cold in the room. He

---

* Well known.

turned in the chair, ready to remonstrate with the servant who had failed to light the fire. Instead he was amazed to see it was roaring in the grate.

A shiver passed through him, the like of which the old man had never felt before – not even as he had crouched in his meagre stone cottage years ago, wrapped in furs, carving a slice from his block of porridge with shaking hands as the wind blew swirling snow through the cracks, making him wonder if he would survive another winter.

No, this was an unfamiliar sort of cold. Sheltering behind those dry stone walls, so long ago, young Robbie Macfarlane had known deep in his marrow that his time had not yet come. Now, in the palace he had built, safe from the terrible elements and with a rich meal in his belly, icy fingers of a different kind were beckoning the old man home.

'Fergus,' he called.

'Aye, Mr Macfarlane.'

'Please take me to my bed.'

'So early, Mr Macfarlane?'

'Aye. And Fergus?'

'Aye?'

'One for the road, I think.'

'Of course, Mr Macfarlane. Is it tae be yer usual?'

'I think so.'

'Very good, Mr Macfarlane.'

'Oh, Fergus?'

'Aye?'

'And one more.'

The servant smiled. 'Anither fae the road, eh?'

Robbie Macfarlane looked back out at the hills, but the sun had now set and the hills were gone.

'No, Fergus,' the old man said quietly, his eyes alive with hills that had once shone gold in the setting sun. 'Not for the road, no. For *auld lang syne*.'

* * *

The story that began it all ends there. The story of how a smuggler and an outlaw set about building a legacy and bestowing a fortune on me; a story I've told a thousand times to tourists, dignitaries, despots, and other animals. But it is at that point my story really begins – the story that all those others will never hear (please tip your guide on the way out). The story that made my name around the world and gave birth to a Wolf.

As I look back on that version of me, sitting at his great-grandfather's desk and looking out of the great round window over the same golden hills Robbie Mac had gazed upon over a century before, I flatter myself that I've had a hand in turning the great man's mound of cash into a mountain of riches. Perhaps another time I'll tell you about how a drunken incident involving a bottle of our limited edition Wyckeham Collection (*Colour:* deep amber. *Nose:* rich aromas of treacle, raisins and homemade apricot jam. *Palate:* soft fruits, sweet treacle, and juicy orange. *Finish:* long, smooth, hint of dryness) and a hair-trigger pistol led to us rebuilding Robbie Macfarlane's whisky pits. (At least, we said they were on the same sites and of the same dimensions as the originals, although we had no evidence for it. But there was no evidence they'd been anywhere else either, to be fair.) Then how we triumphed by calling our whisky 'mountain matured', which meant nothing because we controlled the conditions very carefully. But they weren't *not* mountain matured – and who else could say that?

While we're on the subject, let's stray into how a bottle of Glenlairig Stillmaster's Special – part of our Golden Age of Travel range (*Colour:* deep amber. *Nose:* warm, fruity, with hints of spice.

Palate: Dundee marmalade, vanilla, ginger. *Finish:* long and spicy) – combined with my selfish quest for immortality to create Jimmy Mac, the hearty, plainspoken Scottish soldier (who has already saved my skin a couple of times in this story and will do so again). How the rugged man o' the hills that stares out from our labels created an international brand.

Like all good ideas it was simple and just waiting for someone to stumble upon it. The Scottish soldier had always had a barbaric magnetism that invoked a primitive and feral lust for the mists and the glens. He fitted perfectly with the symbols and beliefs, prejudices and delusions that drove both the image of whisky and the stream of jingoistic nonsense we were being fed every day. As I sat in my office, looking for inspiration at the bottom of the Stillmaster's Special and appraising the old portraits of my forebears, my gaze fell on a framed photo of me in my army dress uniform, all kilts, buckles, and badges. I was saluting the photographer, a sardonic smile on my face. The man in the picture looked proud and honest, but he was also self-aware and cheeky. He was at your service. It was the kind of image that could build a brand – and a cult of personality.

I dashed out the office waving the photograph and demanding at the top of my voice that the image be henceforth on every bottle. In that moment I gave birth to Jimmy. And, by God, didn't the country yell back, 'Jimmy Mac, we salute *you!*'

Since I've promised to be honest in this account, I admit I can't lay sole claim to my monstrous success. Kudos must also go to the Marischal. In a country oppressed by international sanctions, the industry I had ill-deservedly landed in was a key strategic asset and given all the help the regime could muster. Again, I'll just point out this tactical importance wasn't a new thing. There are well-documented tales of Scotch being stockpiled as an economic hedge rather than gold. During World War Two, Winston Churchill even recognised how invaluable an export it was, ordering that the Ministry of Food should 'on no account reduce the amount of barley for whisky'. Wise man that; I don't care what the revisionists say. They should put all his statues back up for that insight alone.

But I gloss over all these things because what I really want to do is tell you a love story, which has all the violence and misery you'd expect from my involvement with these sorts of things. You see, apart from myself, I have loved precious few people in my life. My grandparents were two of those people. They raised me and taught me and made sure I wanted for nothing. I owed them everything. Then I betrayed them.

My dear grandfather died first, aged eighty-four: the victim of a disease that took him before we could even work out what was wrong. My grandmother, meanwhile, was already ill by that time. For my ailing granny, it seemed my grandfather's death would be another nail in a coffin that already seemed close to being hermetically sealed. But she had the heart of an ox and lived on for another ten years, despite numerous renditions of the last rites (during one of which, she actually opened an eye and winked at me).

Ultimately, it was the enemy within that did for her. Being a sweet and trusting woman, she was neither prepared, nor had the constitution, to withstand the most perilous of foes: a family already counting its inheritance. During that final decade the vultures never ceased circling, pecking away at her, one fleshy chunk of cash at a time. Aunties, uncles, cousins, long-standing friends, and well-wishers from hard-up charities appeared from the woodwork, before promptly disappearing with their pockets lined. That indomitable creature took to referring to herself as the 'old woman', as if preparing for obsolescence and demise.

It appalled me and I tried to reason with her, but the response was always that 'it's nice to be able to help the family'. It made me angry; it filled me with hatred for these unconscionable beasts. This was soon replaced by self-loathing, as I couldn't find a way to stop it. How do you tell a dying woman that the loved ones gathering around her are only there because of their love for her wealth?

And so, I did the worst thing I could when confronted by this onslaught: I abandoned her. I ran away to join the circus. Or rather, the CDF – the Caledon Defence Force – which was pretty similar to a circus, what with its penchant for funny outfits, training in foreign climes, and death-defying antics without safety nets. I couldn't even call it a military in good conscience. It's more of a consultancy than an army. History has shown that invading Caledon is a pointless and frustrating exercise, and no one has shown the remotest interest in doing so for a long time. Even the Americans have left us alone, what with the oil all but gone. Which means there's not much to keep restless soldiers entertained at home. Even if there had been, the Mallice have got internal security pretty much sewn up, being the capable fellows they are. So, more often than not, our specialist regiments are simply contracted out to project manage the building of militias for regimes that any self-respecting armed forces wouldn't touch.

But, still, it was to the CDF I fled, overwhelmed by a sea of troubles that felt fearsome, haphazard, indiscriminate. It was there I hid and left dear Granny to her fate, finding solace in the regimented, predictable discipline of army life. I sailed through The Training, eventually ending up in a unit that dares not speak its wicked name. You may have heard of that famous Victorian soldier, Sir Garnet Wolseley, who said the only way for a young man to get ahead in the army was 'to try to get killed in every way he possibly can'. I followed this philosophy to the letter and earned quite the reputation for reckless bravery. All a sham, of course, because there was nothing heroic in driving myself to the limits of physical endurance and wantonly endangering myself. It was simply penance for my cowardice: sackcloth and ashes in camouflage. I didn't even manage to get properly injured in the line of duty. A scar above my right eyebrow that still itches when it's damp is all I have to show for any of it (the result of a night exercise, faulty night-vision goggles and a low branch, I'm horrified to say).

Granny died while I was stationed with some despot friend of the Marischal, training his bloodthirsty militia in darkest Africa. Sitting in the cool of his vast, air-conditioned library I gazed in wonder upon works by, and about, *personae non gratae* in Caledon. Works long since sent to the bonfires back home. Names like Wolseley and Churchill, Shelley and Tennyson, Sassoon and Wilde, Bonfiglioli and Wodehouse transported me far away, even as I breathed the warm, sweet air that breezed in through the latticed shutters, carrying with it an exotic cacophony from the dark, chaotic alleys of the old town below. All these historic writers made me far better educated than I had any right to be. They filled me with a zeal and a passion I'd never felt before. (Although I'll admit I never got to the end of that massive book by Victor Hugo, but I presume it worked out for all of them – they're such romantics, the French.)

I was sitting in that very library when I learned of her death. The news of her passing was relayed to me a full week after it happened by my dear family, and I was refused leave for the funeral due to the short notice. I never got to say goodbye.

Her last will and testament preyed on my mind. Not because I wanted the money – I was certain I didn't deserve it. Rather, I didn't want it to go to all those work-shy hangers-on I was forced to call family, who deserved it even less. I would have made a bonfire of it if I could. To my surprise and shame, I was bequeathed the distillery and the house along with it. Not long after, and at the first opportunity, I cashed in my military chips and headed back, Archie and Wally in tow.

Standing in front of Glenlairig House on the beautiful summer's day that I returned was just plain horrid. I required grey clouds and a steady rainfall to match my disposition. Instead I was cursed with that rarest of things: a fabulous day in the Highlands. This meteorological phenomenon is unusual (and will be spoken about in hushed tones for years to come), but when it does sneak up on you un awares, the sky seems clearer and the air somehow less obstructive to your progress. The light feels brighter and cleaner, as if a filter has been placed over your eyes to intensify the colours. But on that glorious day I felt like a ghost who had not yet realised he was dead. I stood in front of the house and watched, waiting for my childhood self to come barrelling out of the great front door, laughing. I would be pursued by my grandfather, growling and pretending to be some beast o' the moors, or by my granny, berating me for putting my fingers in the jam or playing naked in the flowerbeds. Instead, all was silent.

I walked up to the house and placed a hand against the stone, maybe hoping to channel a last drop of that spirit out of the old place. The huge bricks were warm from the sun and I stepped back, looked up, and appraised the old girl. I knew these walls had seen generations of happiness and heartbreak. They had welcomed generations of Macfarlanes as they were carried over the threshold wrapped in blankets. They had said goodbye when those same bodies were carried out in boxes. They would wait patiently and faithfully, long after I was gone, to offer another generation shelter. A safe haven from the storm.

I wandered alone down the long corridors, the air becoming cool and musty as I ventured deeper into my stronghold. Eventually, I came to a room and stopped at the open door. It was a door I knew from my first memories. A door little James had so often charged through to leap on the bed, taking its unsuspecting occupants by surprise at some unholy hour of the morning. It was a room where stories had been told, snuggled deep in blankets as the Scottish weather beat at the windows. Where advice was offered and lessons were learned. It had been my grandparents' room. Then just my granny's. Now it was empty.

I stepped inside and found it almost untouched. The bed was made, the ornaments and photographs on the dresser, just so. The only anomaly was the wardrobe doors thrown wide open. The clothes were untouched but the meticulously labelled jewellery drawers were empty. In their rush to clear them, the family vultures hadn't even bothered to shut the drawers before moving on in search of other treasures. All that was left, cast aside on a dresser, was a dull bangle, so tarnished it looked like old copper. Clearly only I knew it for what it was: one of Granny's most prized possessions. Underneath the grime was brilliant 18-carat gold, inscribed with each of her children and grandchildren's names, each tiny letter engraved with infinite patience and care. I slid it onto my wrist and left the room.

And so I went to work at the distillery and, through some fault of my own, slowly built an empire. I had money, fame, and influence to add to my skills in the fields of violence, subversion, and survival. It made me a lot of friends and it made me a lot of enemies. (One of Lizzy's sites had the gall to call me 'the greatest combination of power, resources, and hubris in the country today'.) People came to me from all over the world – princes and paupers alike – at all times of day and night. They came to make time pass faster, slower, or sometimes disappear altogether. But for all that success, I could not forget and I could not forgive. I tried to purge Glenlairig of any evidence of my family's existence, but still I knew they were out there living their lives of undeserved ease – the aunts parading the jewellery, the uncles vying with me to build dynasties of their own with their ill-gotten gains.

Yes, they were there, and all too often, without warning, some trigger – maybe a stray phrase, an unusual smell, or a long-forgotten song – would bring their taunting, sneering, lupine faces rushing back. And whenever it happened my hand would stray to that bangle – once again a glorious gold – and shame would burn within me. Then I would mouth the names carved into my butcher's bill, swearing revenge on the whole bloody pack of them.

CHAPTER 18

A Walking Shadow

After the Loker incident I could see nothing else for it but to throw myself into a hard day's work, to cleanse body and soul, and satisfy the army of radio waves, drones, spy satellites, and other forms of surveillance that would surely be all over me for a day or two after the Headhunter's visit. Fortunately, this Presbyterian mood passed quickly and instead I drank at least half of the bottle of xxv with Archie. Then I went for a nap where I was plagued with terrible dreams of Loker coming at me, dressed as the Red Queen from *Alice in Wonderland*, yelling 'Off with his trousers!', whereupon a Mallice officer clad in the garb of Alice approached with sparking electric cables attached to a car battery, all the while repeating 'I don't see how he can ever finish, if he doesn't begin.' I woke up feeling grotty and drank some more. After that, I ran out of excuses and there was nothing for it but to go to work.

It was a short walk from the house to the distillery at the bottom of the hillside opposite. This was a simple building: long, low, and painted white, with *Glenlairig* emblazoned in big black letters along the side. Within those walls sat the stills and visitor centre. Behind it, forming a courtyard, were the old barrel stores that were superseded by the pits we'd dug further back on the hillside. I gazed around, breathing the air that was heavy with malted barley, and feeling a sense of relaxation for the first time in days. The whole thing needed a lick of paint.

My eyes followed the line of the hills that rose gently up behind the distillery, starting as fields before the ascent steepened to thick, dark pine trees, which covered the peak like a blanket. To the left of the distillery was my personal field of cows. The weather was fine and the cows were all standing, blissfully chewing the cud. It promised to be a fine day. It was good to be home.

When night came, I took a long time to find sleep. Where was Loker? What did he know? When would he come for me? How sharp were the knives and how hot the tongs? Before I knew it, it was 10 a.m. and Archie was pulling the curtains open. (Yes, I know that's early, but I had a business to run, you know.)

A wide tray on little silver legs was placed on the bed before me and I launched into traditional Caledon fayre: bacon, Lorne sausage, Cumberland sausage, tattie scone, black pudding, fried egg. Half a tomato for health. I savoured then devoured it in turns. I hadn't had such delicacies for months while we were in training for the Pitlochry job. I turned to Archie, who was looking immaculate in his suit. I knew he'd rather have been wearing his butler's tails, which he saw as crucial to his place as first amongst equals downstairs, but I'd vetoed this. If we found ourselves in need of a quick escape, I didn't want to be gallivanting around the countryside with a six-and-a-half-foot penguin. Wally appeared, late as usual, and managed to bash into Archie as he did.

'Watch it, yeh wee daftie.'

Wally said nothing and concentrated on looking dishevelled.

'What's burning up the internet superhighway, Archie?'

'Och, normal shite.'

'Anything that might impinge on our happy marriage of malted barley, water, and yeast?'

'Yeh mean makin' the whisky, aye?'

'Yes.'

'No.'

'Anything more about that *terrible* explosion at the dam?' (The walls have ears.)

'Well, actually, the wee man,' Archie began, referring to Wally, 'he wiz just sayin' he'd seen rather a lot of it.'

'And this godawful Wolf person? Is he being held responsible?' (Play up; play the game.)

'Yes, they're giving him both barrels,' said Wally. 'They've set up a whole public safety campaign. They're calling it *How to keep the Wolf from the door.*'

'That's surprisingly imaginative.'

'Miss Burke's going to front it, apparently. Thought you'd want to know.'

'Lizzy? Well, that's, er, nice. Why are you looking at me like that? Anyway, well done to all of them. We should make sure we do our bit. Up security at the distillery. Can't have wolves at doors, can we?'

'Aye, that'd be a howler.'

'Touché, Archie, touché.'

'You might be interested in the branding for the campaign,' said Wally.

'No, I don't think—'

'Oh, please. Go on, Archie, show us on your tablet.'

The big man grimaced like an embarrassed but doting elder sibling and reached for his pocket. Then his face changed to a look of confusion.

'Wait a minute, mah tablet, it's no' there. It wiz definitely in ma pocket. I can't ha'e dropped it.' Archie prided himself on his organisation and that tablet was also deeply incriminating if it fell into the wrong hands. He was caught between shame and worry, patting every pocket in his suit.

'This tablet, you mean?' Wally said, holding it up.

'Where did yeh get that?' said a mystified Archie.

'Out your pocket, of course.'

'Whit? How? Why?'

'I spent last night knocking about some other countries' internets and came across a fascinating film about pickpockets,' Wally announced, his eyes alight. 'You see, the best time to pick a pocket is when you and your mark are moving or in contact somehow – that's why busy railway stations and going up staircases are so handy. The victim expects to be touched and what you're carrying is naturally moving about, so it's easier to mistake a hand in your pocket for natural movement. Thought I'd give it a go when I came in just then.'

'Ach, yeh wee—'

'OK, kids,' I said, keen to avoid a war. 'Take it somewhere else.'

After they had left, bickering in their usual fashion, I lay back and digested this news – and it was big news. Stories of our first two attacks had gone viral after the Wolf had been christened by that enterprising journalist, but the government's annoyingly reliable censorship algorithms had swiftly shut that chat down. This new torrent of coverage seemed to mark a very different approach by the regime. I needed to understand why the authorities were letting so much information through. Why were they, in effect, encouraging the people to talk about it? No doubt Wally would collect terabytes of SIGINT. I took a bite of black pudding.

'Archie!'

He reappeared with terrifying haste.

'The cows. You forgot the cows.'

He walked over to the window and looked across the glen, focusing on the field next to the distillery. 'Ah'd say ninety-five per cent standing.'

'Oh, good!'

In case you inexplicably do not have a field of cattle to do your bidding, I shall explain why my days often started with a bovine report. You see, cows are quite reliable meteorologists. Big, hairy, methane-belching barometers. They tend to lie down when it is cold and stand up when it is hot. Often before it rains the temperature drops and so cows lie down, effectively making them bovine weather forecasters. I liked to use them as both a meteorological and a metaphorical indicator of how the day ahead was likely to pan out.

You might find it odd that I had a field of cows to tell me the weather. It defies any explanation beyond 'because I can'. And, frankly, no other explanation is necessary if you are rich.

At some point I must have got up. I won't bore you with the prosaic comings and goings of an internationally respected man of commerce, except to tell you about a call I made to a very private person from a very private room. All half-decent country houses have secret rooms, as Invereiton had shown to my detriment. Since mine was as great a house as any in these parts, it had several too. There were a couple of priest holes knocking about, as well as a panel in a downstairs corridor, behind which lay a small tunnel that led to nowhere other than a deep hole, whose origins and purpose were lost in the mists of time. There were almost certainly other secret nooks and crannies lying undiscovered.

Then there was the hidden gem, whose existence was known only to the favoured few; a secret passed down from generation to generation. A birthright of sorts. It lay under a decrepit bathroom at the back of the house. The room itself was a disgrace. Unkempt, damp, and festooned with spiderwebs that were home to the surliest arachnids. Who knew what crouched, waiting, around the U-bend?

However, if you were to go in and stamp hard on the thick wooden floorboards, you might just notice a hollow sound reverberating under the timber. For underneath lay a small, dark room and, beyond that, a long, dark tunnel that led out onto the hillside. Here lay Robbie Macfarlane's original escape route if death came knocking and his pistols were out of reach. The boards in the bathroom – immovable at first glance – held the secret to an ingenious puzzle. This puzzle was solved by sliding one board through a concealed hole under the skirting board, followed, in specific order, by the others. This created a hole big enough for a man to slip through; he could then replace the planks from underneath. With practice, you could be below and completely concealed within thirty seconds.

Arriving at the inhospitable commode, I found I was out of practice and it took me a couple of minutes, faffing about, trying to remember the order. However, once safely ensconced below ground with floorboards back in place, I waved on the single light in the ceiling, retrieved a set of aug-specs from behind a loose brick, and settled into a small chair. The air smelled damp and the old stone floor was flecked with mud from previous excursions onto the braes. The electric light hanging from the boards above penetrated only a short way into the long tunnel before being beaten back. A slight draft came and went, carrying fleeting scents, damp and rich, from the hills that lay beyond the darkness. I turned the chair to face it, lest any supernatural beings tried to sneak up on me again.

Pushing the aug-specs up my nose, it took a few seconds for the scanners to calibrate the movement of my retinas. Before long, I was diving deep into the blackest recesses of the Dark Net, using a search engine that Wally assured me did lots of clever bouncing-signals-around-the-world stuff, thus making me untraceable.

The chat room I was looking for soon appeared, hidden amongst those established for people interested in drugs, bestiality, paedophilia, and other hideous detritus. (I'll admit, I was a little intrigued by the cannibal chat room, where one participant had begun a mouth-watering chain entitled 'If I'm alive in the morning, maybe we could eat my balls.')

As I struggled through the digital morass, there was only one place to turn: Jesus. Or, more accurately, a sub-group of a particularly aggressive Christian network that went by the name of *God's Motherfuckers*. I sent out an invitation and spoke the passcode. It was a long one this month: 'We will not fear, though the earth give way and the mountains fall into the heart of the sea.'

Minutes passed. No reply.

I tried again.

'We will not fear, though the earth give way and the mountains fall into the heart of the sea.'

A cold sweat broke out on my neck. No answer meant big trouble for Jimmy Mac. I tried again. This time, a scratchy voice responded.

'Hold on, I'm cummin'. For God's sake. Right, what is it again? Ah yes: Though its waters roar and foam and the mountains quake with their surging.' A pause. 'What do you want, Macfarlane?'

Where there had been nothing but a black space before my eyes, a fuzzy hologram now floated in front of me. It was the head and shoulders of a man, perhaps in his late fifties. The deep-set eyes were almost completely lost in shadow and adorned with heavy grey eyebrows. Long grey hair fell about the oval face, with its leathery cheeks and long, straight nose. I took a deep, steadying breath, as I always did when confronted with the best smuggler in the Highlands, perhaps one of the greatest that has ever lived (quite a claim in a place that has, over the centuries, turned smuggling into an art form). His fearsome reputation didn't stop there. I had heard on good authority he once partially skinned a Mallice informant alive. In the wilds of the Highlands – where the Reverend held sway – you had a terrible choice to make when it came to picking sides.

'Good afternoon, Reverend,' I said brightly. 'How's the import-export business these days?'

'It bides,' came the curt response. 'We're due a shipment the day after tomorrow, are we not?'

'All bagged up and ready to go,' I replied.

Barley was the bedrock of our relationship. I was the chief source of the grain he needed to run his extensive illegal whisky operation. The supply of grain being highly regulated made it difficult for him to run illicit stills at a sensible price. This was frustrating, because there was huge demand for illegal Scotch. Most of the legal product was sent abroad at eye-watering prices to prop up the country's creaking treasury. Meanwhile, I was sitting on mountains of the stuff and it was just a swipe of Wally's keyboard to make a small amount disappear. A happy marriage of convenience this, since the Reverend was a supplier of pretty much anything from essentials to luxuries. Those essentials extended as far as, for example, tools to carry out night-time incursions to a hydro-electric dam via a salmon ladder. Should you be so inclined.

'Don't go telling me there's a problem, Macfarlane,' the face growled, a frown casting deep lines in the skin. 'I don't like problems. People who cause me problems usually find themselves with problems.'

'We are indeed due a shipment and all is indeed well,' I said with exaggerated jauntiness.

I refused to be intimidated by folk like the Reverend. Rather, I refused to *look* as if I was being intimidated. I was simply not brave enough to risk showing someone like the Reverend that I was afraid.

'Here's the thing,' I continued, 'I need to talk to you about an extra, er, *consignment*, bound for the continent.'

'How many crates?'

'Well, just one, I suppose.'

'How heavy?'

'I'd guess about eleven stone with his shoes on.'

A moment of silence. 'How hot?'

'Scalding.'

More silence. The face stared intently at me, before the eyes were cast down to look at something out of shot. Risks were no doubt being assessed: dangers weighed up; load factors measured; health and safety forms completed. After a short time, he looked up again.

'So, you'll be wanting the Shetland Bus then, eh?'

'Yes,' I replied uncertainly.

The Shetland Bus was a quasi-mythical service that transported people – those willing to risk it all – out of Caledon. My whole plan relied on it being more quasi than mythical. The Reverend smiled a thin smile.

'You sure you want the Shetland Bus?'

'Yes, goddamn it!' I blurted out. 'And just so we're clear, you're saying it exists then?'

'Aye it does,' came the response. 'But it'll cost yeh.'

He gave me a price. It was less than I'd taken from the Farquharsons, but I beat him down by another ten per cent, because he wouldn't have expected anything less.

'I'll need the money now, as usual.'

'Oh, come on, I'm a very good customer . . .'

'Now,' said the face, flickering slightly in the holographic rays.

'Oh, all right, but I'm tempted to write to customer services and complain.'

'I'll give you one minute to deliver the cash,' said the face, eyes narrowed.

'OK, OK.'

His image sank into the background as my retinas danced across the lenses of the aug-specs, whisking me off to a secret off-shore bank account. Soon after, the grim-faced hologram was back in front of me.

'Done,' I said, as an icon popped up, confirming the money had made it safely down the internet superhighway and parked itself in a secure lock-up known only to the favoured few.

'You'll need to be on the lugger at nine, latest.'

'You mean *the cargo* will, obviously?'

'Mr Macfarlane, I do not waste words. I mean exactly what I say.'

'I'm not getting on any bloody boat!'

The dark eyes closed and he sighed wearily.

'Don't you sigh at me!' I protested. 'I'm paying good money for this.' (OK, it was mediocre money – and someone else's to boot – but you take my point.)

'You're new to people-smuggling, aren't you, Mr Macfarlane?'

'I am *not* a people-smuggler,' I said, affronted.

'Aye, call it whatever you like,' said the face, with the tired patience of someone tutoring a small child. 'I had a fella call me and introduce himself as a relocation specialist the other day. What a load o' guff.' The face lifted slightly and the clear, unblinking eyes bored into mine. 'Let's be very clear, *Jimmy Mac*, this is not the usual kind of free trading. Moving people – especially scalding ones – is a death sentence if they catch you. No trial, no O-Tank, just a bullet and straight over the side of the boat into the brine.'

This news thrust the fear of God into me. My desperation was palpable as I fought to keep my feet on dry land. I spluttered a half-baked story about being allergic to seawater, before explaining how I'd once had a nasty run-in with a haddock. But it was all to no avail.

'I do not know who you are exporting, nor do I wish to,' the Reverend said, speaking over me slowly, quietly, and with utmost certainty. 'However, I am damn sure that they won't do anything to endanger a single tugman, lingtowman, or anything else that impacts on my interests. And so, Mr Macfarlane, you will be there to shepherd, goad, nanny, encourage, and berate, as necessary, to make sure this consignment does what he's bloody well told, when he's bloody well told.'

I couldn't help wondering whether there could be a worse cargo in such circumstances than Professor Spring.

'That's the rules,' the Reverend said with finality. 'Take 'em or leave 'em.'

I mulled the offer over. Leaving 'em seemed far more attractive, but I'd spent the money and I doubted the Reverend offered refunds. Also, what the hell else was I going to do with Spring?

And there were bigger considerations: I'd put a lot of effort into building my reputation with this leading light in Caledon's criminal fraternity, and couldn't risk putting that in jeopardy. Folks like the Reverend did not tolerate weakness and the repercussions could be, well, painful.

'Can I bring Archie?'

'I said *you*, didn't I? I have no room for extras, especially ones as big as that.'

'But he'll be so disappointed; he loves sailing.'

Actually, Archie hates the sea. Claims he's worried about swallowing fish piss.

'Until tomorrow, Macfarlane, aye?' the gnarled face said.

'Aye,' I replied in a resigned kind of way.

With a half-smile, the face vanished, to be replaced in mid-air by a banner that declared 'Conversation ended.' This was followed by an enticing offer to join the testicle banquet in the cannibal room. I took off the aug-specs and, leaning over, slid them back into the hole in the wall. Then I sat back in my chair, exhaled so loudly that it could not be mistaken for anything but a cry for help, and wondered at the folly of best laid plans.

Pride piped up, keen to put a positive spin on things. *Another big win for the Wolf in the offing, eh? Couldn't have said that a few days ago, could we? And the odds are as good as we could hope for. Agreed, we wouldn't put the Reverend high on our list of people to have over for tea, but let's remember that strict code of honour of his. OK, so he's immovable and unforgiving and generally terrifying, but he's probably the only honest person we'll encounter in this whole saga. Last but not least, think of that paternal warmth we detected when he encountered us last, eh? An angry, dangerous, volatile paternal warmth, I grant you, but it means he's got to be on our side, right? And how often can we say that of someone?*

Common Sense was not to be left out, unfortunately. *I don't want to put a downer on things, but can we take a moment to recognise the terrible dread we feel when we think of taking to Caledon's black seas? Out there, in the dark, is the Marischal's fleet of gunboats. It's not for nothing the sailors call them the Beasties. They're lurking. Waiting to send us to a crushing, suffocating death . . .*

'Enough!' I yelled, my voice echoing down the tunnel towards the braes.

I felt positively ill. I retrieved the aug-specs from behind the brick and went looking for a medicinal solution. Soon surprisingly busty nurses in surprisingly scanty uniforms were tending to patients in front of my weary, jaded eyes. The patients seemed very grateful for these ministrations, despite their carers' perverse approach to treatment.

When I finally crawled back out of my subterranean space, heavy with self-loathing, I made my way upstairs and bumped into Archie. I started to explain the plan to get rid of Spring (whom Archie assured me he had been feeding, although I wasn't so sure).

'Here's the thing,' I said pensively. 'The Rev wants me to take him by myself.'

'Whit?' Archie snorted, eyes wide. 'That's no' happenin', Mr Mac.'

'Do calm down. It's only on the boat,' I reassured him. 'You can chaperone me all the way there. But he wants me to take the bugger out on the high seas, all the way to the handover, to make sure things don't get screwed up.'

'Oh, that's OK then,' the big man replied, happier in the knowledge that he would be more likely to be able to help me if there was trouble and less likely to miss out on any passing violence.

'I could see if there was space on the boat for you,' I said, arching my eyebrows.

'Ach, weel, ah dinnae want tae cause any trouble . . .'

As expected, Archie's loyalty and desire for brutishness did not extend to helping those in peril on the sea. Nonetheless, he was clearly uncomfortable with leaving me to face the briny deep alone and stood in front of me, shifting his weight from foot to foot. I wasn't going to give up this rare foray to the higher ground, so I let the silence settle in the gloom.

'The fishies, yeh know, they pish in it . . .' he mumbled at last.

CHAPTER 19

For Those in Peril

The next morning, I woke at a horrible hour. A dull light shuffled without enthusiasm through the windows of my bedroom. I tossed and turned, my mind haunted by visions of towering black waves and other nameless sea perils. Some time later, Archie appeared with breakfast: bacon, two sausages, black pudding, and fried bread. He'd left off the tomato in a lovely act of solidarity. This was no time to go on a health kick.

We discussed the news of the day in the normal fashion. There was still a worrying number of Wolf stories doing the rounds. I could only think that the regime was trying to stir up the nation against him (against *me*). Yet it seemed a dangerous strategy that could spectacularly backfire if it gave the beast an edge in the battle for hearts and minds.

'. . . And the cows?' I asked hopefully.

Archie walked over to the window and peered out into the gloom for what seemed like a long time. 'It's a wee bitty misty today, Mr Mac, so it's difficult to see.'

'Archie, please, there's no need to sugar-coat it.'

'Ah'd say aboot seventy per cent.'

'Standing?'

'No.'

'Ah.'

My morning shower went on longer than usual as I mulled over this portent. Yes, it was a bad start to the metaphorical and meteorological day, but, I reasoned optimistically, if my bovine oracles were predicting rain, this could be to our advantage. A spot of bad weather would limit the visibility of the authorities, whether on the ground, from drones or satellite in the air, or through radar. Combined with the Reverend's men – the best in the business – and more than ten thousand miles of Caledon coastline rutted with cliffs, coves, creeks, and caves, the chance of getting caught seemed virtually nil.

'Yes, a little bad weather will suit us just fine,' I told myself as the hot water eased away the tension.

* * *

Around eleven hours later, my comforting shower long forgotten, I was cursing the Farquharsons, Lizzy, Spring, the Reverend, and even the cows. Rain lashed down on our truck as it wound its way in the dark, carrying our cargo of grain and academia ever farther north. Worst of all, I was in the back behind a concealed panel with Professor Randolph bloody Spring. I had to suffer the discomfort because it would never do for me to be found delivering grain. If we were stopped, eyebrows would be raised, shortly followed by electric shock batons.

This mission to save the Professor – odious though he was – had felt like it would be a huge victory for the Wolf of Badenoch; a huge blow against a regime that was powerless to stop this noble bringer of freedom. But sitting in that lorry, being buffeted by a furious wind, and thrown around by crevasses masquerading as potholes, it felt like we were going to our doom.

The fact we had nothing to defend ourselves with made the situation even worse. I had decided that the only thing more incriminating than me delivering grain was me delivering grain while carrying a machine pistol. Wally had heard this news and come bumbling down with a handful of devices, which he went through in turn and I turned down likewise. In a desperate final attempt to arm me, he forced a small electromagnetic pulse device of his own design into my hand.

'It's a highly concentrated, unidirectional EMP,' he said breathlessly. 'It'll take out any electronics in—'

'Wally, I can't take it,' I said, looking at the small, tubular device. 'Look, I'm sorry, I know it must have taken you ages.'

'No it didn't, it's quite easy really. You just need a capacitor, tact switches, and—'

'Wally, I can't take it.'

He took it back, looking distraught. And then, as God's my witness, he threw himself on me and gave me a hug. Wally never did this kind of thing.

'Dinnae fash yersel',* wee man,' said Archie tenderly as he peeled Wally off me. 'We'll be back in no time.'

Wally smiled wanly, while I stared at nothing in particular. All of a sudden the mission felt very real and very scary.

Archie was driving the truck, which was no small mercy and gave us a half-decent chance of arriving in one piece. It was touch and go, though; the vehicle shook as the wind hammered on the canvas sides, roaring to be let in like a drunk who had lost his keys. At least the noise cushioned my ears from the ramblings of Spring, who complained incessantly about both his current lodgings and the many perceived indignities being heaped upon him.

As we rolled northwards through the storm the relentless swaying continued, but at least Spring started to run out of steam. He moaned one last classical reference, which has stuck with me as it seemed appropriate. (Wrong, of course, but still appropriate.)

'*Forsan miseros meliora sequentur*,' Spring muttered as I stared

* Don't be concerned.

blankly back in my usual fashion. 'It's Virgil: For those in misery, perhaps better things will follow.'

The professor sighed and lapsed into silence, his head to one side, eyes narrowed. I could tell that mighty synapses were firing in that monstrous brain. It was an unnerving experience, as we sat almost knee to knee on sacks of grain in that dark, cramped space. Just as with Loker, I had the uncomfortable feeling of a specimen being studied. Being prepared for mounting, a nail through my chest.

'I try not to think, really I do,' he murmured, barely audible over the elements. 'Whenever I do, I can't help but reach the same conclusion: that none of it is worth it.'

'Look,' I began, before the truck hit a rut in the road and I was hurled against the false panel.

Spring didn't appear to notice. He was lost in reverie. 'Yes, yes; I bow to our friend Schopenhauer. It was he who said, "The world is the product of a blind, insatiable, and malignant will." Did you know that?'

I gave the smallest shake of my head.

'Blind, insatiable, and malignant. A constant fight for procreation, status, and power. If it wasn't the Marischal, it would be someone else, wouldn't it?'

I didn't answer. The truck gave another violent lurch as it was buffeted by the wind. Archie, hidden away up front, was struggling to keep us on the road.

'Wherever I am going, am I not just venturing from one circus to another?' Spring went on in that weariest of tones. 'Am I not just swapping one big top for a different one? It is the same glitter and flashing lights that cover up the superficial tawdriness of the whole enterprise, is it not? The same shows, and farces; the same rehearsed, contrived spectacles that dictate day-to-day life from now to the last syllable of recorded time?'

He stared at me expectantly. Lord knows what he was hoping for in response.

'Do you know *Macbeth*, Mr Macfarlane?'

'Of course.'

'Well, then you will know that all our yesterdays – every single one to *this* very moment in *this* godforsaken box on *this* interminable journey – have done nothing more than lighted fools – yes, you and I and everyone else! – the way to dusty death.'

He sighed and leant his head back on the taut, canvas-covered frame of the lorry and stared upwards. Then, to lift our spirits, he began reciting the famous words of Macbeth.

> 'Tomorrow, and tomorrow, and tomorrow
> Creeps in this petty pace from day to day,
> To the last syllable of recorded time;
> And all our yesterdays have lighted fools
> The way to dusty death. Out, out, brief candle!
> Life's but a walking shadow, a poor player
> That struts and frets his hour upon the stage,
> And then is heard no more. It is a tale
> Told by an idiot, full of sound and fury . . .'

Here he paused for a long time, his eyes shut and his tired face betraying a moment of inner peace.

'*A tale, told by an idiot, full of sound and fury . . .*'

Spring lowered his head and leaned towards me.

'. . . *Signifying nothing,*' he whispered, inches from my face. Then he sat back again, staring at me; or perhaps at nothing.

I had the briefest pang of sympathy for his predicament. It was easy to forget this was a brave man brought to the edge of exhaustion. In some ways he was no different from me; he was fighting the same fight, just in a different way. But he was also a pompous, patronising, loquacious prick, and I haven't lost any sleep over what happened to him. I imagine he's not such a big fan of mine either.

He was right about one thing: the interminable nature of this journey. We must have been travelling for two vomit-inducing hours before we left the main road and bumped along a short track, blessedly coming to a stop. God only knew where we were. Archie was to have received satellite coordinates en route. No names. No places. All I could tell was that we were a good way north.

The noise of wind and rain was undiminished as three knocks sounded on the false panel separating us from the piles of grain sacks in the back of the truck. These knocks were then followed by two more raps on the plywood. I slid back the bolts and groaned as I staggered up out of our hole, stretched my aching legs, and promptly tripped over a sack of grain onto my face.

I lay there for a moment, before the slabs of meat that passed for Archie's hands hoisted me effortlessly upright.

'Yeh stay right where yeh are,' he said, pointing at Spring.

I pulled my coat tight around me, turned the collar up, and peered around the loosened tarpaulin at the back. It whipped from side to side, trying to tear itself from its moorings. God, but it was dreich.* Somewhere far off to our right, lost behind a wall of fog and rain and rumbling darkness, were the majestic north-west Highlands. To our left rose banks of thick gorse, pointing accusingly at everyone and no one with their sharp thorns. Thin paths snaked into those black bushes, before disappearing.

I vaulted over the tailgate and landed on the soft sandy ground, swaying as the wind buffeted me. Through the gloom and sheets of rain I could see three more trucks like ours parked a little way off. They'd be for the lingtowmen; the ones charged with bringing the Reverend's contraband ashore and getting it far from here to the old man's distribution centres.

* Dreary or bleak.

And then, like ghostly porters bidden from the bowels of the earth, they appeared, large black silhouettes on the small sandy paths, marching out of the tempest. They tramped in single file through the gorse, which grasped and scratched impotently at their heavy waterproofs. Each was laden with boxes and crates of God knows what. They were heavy loads that I wouldn't have even tried to lift. But these were hard men, bearded and grim, betraying only the occasional grunt as they laid down their burdens.

Having shed their wares onto the trucks, they marched back from whence they came, a heavy curtain of wind and rain coming down behind them, encircling and embracing them in the tumult. I stood and watched the Devil's Logistics Corps come and go half a dozen times before they shed their final load and, without a word, turned in unison and made for our truck like robots. *Evil* robots, I thought; the kind of robots that don't care one jot for Asimov's First Law.

With a roar to match that of the wind, an unseen driver started his truck and manoeuvred it next to ours. Displaying well-practised ease, the men whipped back the tarpaulin, formed a chain, and hefted the bags of grain along it, from one lorry to another. I was pleased to note that those who caught my eye couldn't help but betray surprise at their companion, the famous Jimmy Mac. I fancy one even gave me the briefest of smiles from somewhere behind that beforested face.

The task was done in a matter of minutes and then they were gone, swallowed once again by the gorse and the storm. Archie and I climbed back into the empty truck and waited in the semi-darkness. Suddenly, the tarp was pulled back and an evil-looking face with piggy eyes scowled at us from under a red sou'wester and copious facial hair.

'Fa's cummin'?'* the troll-like creature enquired in Doric, the

* Who's coming?

strain of Scots spoken in the north-east, his malignant gaze sweeping back and forth across us.

'That'd be me,' I said.

He threw a set of thick waterproof clothes to me without a second glance. 'Fa's the ither one?'

I got up, walked to the other end of the truck and peered into the hidey-hole. 'Time to go.'

Spring climbed out and followed me, before stopping in his tracks as a set of waterproofs flew into the truck and hit him square in the chest. This seemed to flick a switch, waking him from his maudlin state. He gave full vent to his frustrations.

'Don't you dare throw these rags at me!' he exploded. 'I mean, look at you! You look like you've crawled out of a bloody bog.'

This wouldn't do.

'Professor,' I began, before noticing a raised eyebrow briefly alter the landscape of the hairy face.

Idiot. Idiot. Idiot. I silently scolded myself for using his title; the last thing I wanted was to reveal that our passenger was weel kent. I was about to remonstrate with Spring when the troll cut in.

'Put it a' oan, noo,' the little mouth spat out. 'Yeh'll be oot oan the caul* soon enough.' Then the tarp fell back down and he was gone.

I turned on Spring. 'Look, you fool, you need to stop this madness now! This is your last chance to get out of here alive. They could find us at any minute. Do you understand? If you mess this up with your arrogance and stupidity, it's game over for you – and more importantly, for me. Now, for God's sake, be quiet and get bloody dressed.'

He shot me a venomous look, then turned away and began pulling on the heavy garments. Sitting on a bag of grain, the wind banging the canvas cover of the truck against my back, I repeated

* Out in the cold.

the routine. The outfit consisted of dungarees, a thick jacket, gloves, wellies, and sou'wester hat, all in glorious yellow technicolour.

I gave Archie a little twirl. 'How do I look?'

'Like a great big bluidy lemon.'

'It'll have to do.'

'Aye, there's nae point in bein' bitter.'

He started giggling at this comedy masterstroke. It was a horrible sound, like a chuckle being dragged over a cheese grater. I started giggling too and soon we couldn't contain ourselves. Spring looked at us as if we were mad. But then he had no idea what was coming up, did he? Ignorance can be bliss.

Again, the tarp cover at the back of the truck was torn aside and the wind charged into the truck, buffeting us.

The troll was peering at us once more, looking from person to person. 'Oot,' it growled. 'The noo. Come wi' me.'

We climbed down and I shook Archie's hand.

'You know the drill if this goes wrong?' I said, as quietly as I could while still trying to be heard in the howling wind.

'If it goes *sour*?' he said, his face a picture of delight at this extravaganza of citrus puns. What a night he was having.

'Exactly,' I said, humouring him.

'Aye.'

'Good.'

'*Sour*, eh? Heh heh.'

'Archie!'

'Sorry.'

'You'll wait here?'

'Aye.'

'Shouldn't be long.'

'No, Mr Mac.'

'A cup to the dead already, eh?'

'Aye, and hooray for . . . och, but yeh'll be OK.' The uncertainty in Archie's voice was clear and he turned quickly to Spring and put out a giant hand: 'Good luck tae yeh, Prof.'

Spring looked at it with thinly veiled contempt and reluctantly took it, saying nothing. Then he winced as Archie repaid the disrespect. Fond farewells completed, we followed the Reverend's man into the gorse, the strains of 'Bitter . . . Sour . . . Heh heh! Bluidy brilliant!' soon lost in the wind behind us.

The sand paths were thin and my imagination turned the tiny spikes of the gorse into wizened, greedy claws. No doubt a naturalist would look on it and proclaim it bleak and beautiful. To me it was just plain horrible. My wellies were far too big and I stumbled several times in them, not helped by the buffeting wind that threatened to impale us on the sharp bushes. Our footing was made even less sure by the sand dunes we were now clambering up and skidding down. A growing sense of unease was coming over me that had nothing to do with the weather, nor with the uneven, inhospitable terrain. Then my breath was taken away.

Cresting the last of the dunes, a vast silvery beach spread out before us. Beyond it, the sea churned and the waves leapt and fell in the storm. The whole black mass was in uproar; writhing and twisting, as if trying to tear itself apart. It was awe-inspiring and utterly horrifying. Then the wind changed and the full noise of the meteorological orchestra hit us. It was a rhapsody played with all the stops out. The howling wind soared and fell, overlaid with the rhythmic crash of the waves as they beat out time on the shingle.

Up on the sand, lolling on one side of its hull, was a white skiff with a little outboard motor. It looked awfully small. This couldn't be the Shetland Bus, surely? 'Minibus' was too grand for this little toy boat. It was the maritime equivalent of a piggyback. Two men huddled close together by the bow. One was short and round and dressed in the same yellow garb as us, his face hidden under a large waterproof hat. The other was a tall, thin man clothed entirely in black, standing with his back to us. His hands were stuffed deep in the pockets of a long coat, which was being whipped by the wind.

The Reverend stood tall and unmoving in the maelstrom, his long grey hair blowing against his face. He couldn't possibly have heard us coming in the uproar yet he broke off his conversation with the other man and turned around, extending a hand.

'Jimmy,' he called across the howl, an amused smile playing across his craggy face.

'Reverend,' I bawled, without enthusiasm. He wasn't about to take to the waves in a gravy boat, after all. 'Lovely spot you've chosen.'

'Cromarty,' he replied.

'Cro-what?'

'Cromarty,' he repeated over the gale. 'Average wave height: 2.1 metres. Maximum wave height: 13.3 metres. Average wind speed: 16.9 knots. Maximum wind speed: 75 knots. Probably the coldest, windiest place in these isles. And one of the best places to avoid detection if you're smuggling the worst kind of contraband.'

'Ah, it's the name of a sea area,' I said, catching up. 'How on earth do you know all that?'

'It's what I do,' he answered without any hint of arrogance, before turning back to look out at the sea.

We stood in silence as the elements bellowed in our faces. I wasn't sure what to do next, but the Reverend was good enough to pick up the reins.

'I've been told yer cargo's a bit of a talker,' he said, casting a leery eye over Spring, who was hunched in his yellow waterproofs, looking as if he might be blown out to sea at any moment. Then he turned back to me. Some people look at you; the Reverend's stare felt more like a scan. 'Are we going to have trouble, Mr Macfarlane?'

'Nothing to worry about,' I lied, out of respect for his terrible reputation.

He leaned closer. 'Have you heard of micro-expressions?' he

asked, in a quiet voice that carried even across the raging storm.

I shook my head.

'They are uncontrollable, fleeting facial expressions; the missing link between thoughts and words. They reflect your true feelings, no matter what may be coming out of your mouth.' The Reverend cocked his head to one side. 'Fascinating little things. Almost impossible to control. More often than not, it's those fleeting expressions that give one what is known as a *gut feeling*. The feeling that something isn't right. Most people don't know why they have that feeling, because they miss the cues. But I don't. I never miss the cues.' He paused, his face now stern, deep lines resembling the crests of foam on the water ahead of us. 'So, I ask again: do we have a troublemaker on our hands?'

'On any other night, yes, but right now I'd wager he's too far out of his depth,' I replied, honesty streaming out of every pore.

The Reverend leaned back, seemingly satisfied.

'He'd better no' be a' ower the back,'* came a shout from the man in sailing garb, who had been listening in. 'Ah'm no' wantin' any stamagasters.'**

'Captain Larssen, I assure you your passengers will do exactly as requested.' The Reverend turned back to me. 'You wouldnae have me break an oath now, would you, Jimmy?'

And that was that.

'I see yeh've paid yer sixpence fae the wind,' said the Captain, more friendly now. 'Would yeh do me the honour o' boardin', while Bessie's still on oor side?'

He marched off towards the waves and I turned to the Reverend. 'What did he mean *sixpence for the wind*? And who the hell is Bessie?'

'Bessie Miller. Old witch on Orkney. Long time ago. Sailors paid her sixpence to call up a favourable wind.'

* Out of control.

** Unpleasant surprises.

246

'You call this a favourable wind?'

'They're a superstitious bunch but they know their business better than anyone.' He stared hard at me. 'If they tell you to get out the way, you skidaddle. If they tell you to do something, then you do it without question. If they laugh, you laugh. And if they pray, then, goddamn it, you pray.'

I nodded mutely.

'Time for you to go.' He nodded. 'Good luck to you, Jimmy.'

'What are you going to do?' I asked. 'Will you be counting us back in?'

There was a hint of desperation in my voice that I couldn't quite control and I gritted my teeth, embarrassed by my need for some kind of validation from him. The Reverend glanced at me sidelong, the storm still whipping the long hair about his face.

'Them that asks no questions isn't told a lie,' he smiled, leaning close. 'Watch the wall, my darling, while the gentlemen go by.'

There are easier ways to tell someone to mind their own business than quoting Kipling, but such understated showmanship was just one of the building blocks of his fearsome mystique.

'Good luck, Jimmy,' he said, thrusting an arm in my direction.

'Thanks,' I replied, taking the dry, cold hand in mine. 'Cheery-bye, then.'

'Aye. You take care not to damage my boat, eh?'

With that, he strode over to the captain for one last confab, the details of which were lost to me in the roar of the wind and the crash of the waves on the sand. Then he stomped up the beach without a single glance back, hands still pushed firmly into his pockets.

'Intae the boat, gen'lemen!' yelled the captain, mere metres away but struggling to make himself heard.

The professor was muttering – prayers, I think – as we boarded the skiff. The small outboard motor roared into life and we bounced over the dark waves, out towards a lone light that seemed to be hanging in the air, far out to sea. It swung from side to side above the swell, like a drunken glow-worm that had taken a fatal wrong turn out of the pub.

As we closed in on the light, a fishing boat revealed itself out of the rain and fog, before being lost again behind a giant swell. The weather was just as bad, if not worse, out here than it had been on land. The vessel heaved from side to side as the water bulged beneath us. The trawler must have been eighty foot or so, and behind the cabin stretched a long deck that ended in various poles and cables that stood upright around an A-frame of thick steel beams. Whether any of this was operational and the boat actually did any fishing, or if it was just a smugglers' ruse, was impossible to say.

As we closed on the trawler, we rose and we fell on the dark waves. It seemed with every lurch our vessels would be pounded together, with no one offering odds on the bigger boat. Several times we came close and sheered away in well-organised panic, our captain helpfully muttering about 'no' wantin' tae be turned intae kindling'. But our seamen were clearly able, and soon we were tethered alongside, with – for all I knew – lines lashed amidships, mainbraces spliced, and crows safely in their nests. All that remained was to come aboard, which, God help us, merely required climbing a bloody rope ladder up the side of the hull.

I stepped on the first rung, the skiff rolling beneath me and the vast black sea throwing up tendrils of spray that, in my fevered mind, wanted nothing more than to drag me into its freezing depths. I made slow work of it, clinging to the wooden rungs as if my life depended on it. Which, of course, it did. The wind battered me and I swung from side to side, the air forced out of me with every dull smack against the metal hull.

I treated myself to a rare indulgence then: I prayed. When I unscrewed my eyes and looked up into the driving rain and dark mire of a sky above, I saw no suggestion of divine intervention.

(Quite right too: if I were Him, I wouldn't help such a godless back-slider either.) But He works in mysterious ways – for giant golden hands descended from above and the celestial choir sang unto me: 'Come oan, m'freen.* Up yeh come.'

I was still calling out blessings when the golden arms revealed themselves to be attached to a giant of a man clad in the same yellow sou'wester as I. He grasped me by one arm and one shoulder, lifted me over the rail and placed me onto the deck. I found myself saluting and asking 'permission to come aboard'.

'Yer a weird one, Jimmy,' the oversized seraph replied, bright eyes shining from deep within a heavily lined, weather-beaten face.

Of course he knew me, as these horny-handed sons of the sea always did. My face was plastered all over their breakfast-, lunch-, and suppertime tipple, after all. I spluttered my thanks at my saviour, but he was already back at the rail, yelling something over the edge.

Spring, I soon gathered, was making heavy work of his climb. I peered over the rail into the heaving black morass below. It made me feel positively ill. But it pays to appear brave and stoic in such circumstances. So I yelled words of encouragement at Spring; words that were lost in the storm as soon as they left my mouth. I even leaned as far as I dared over the edge, arm extended in a token effort to reach him.

Spring was slowly putting hand over hand and foot over foot, eyes alternately wide in terror and clenched shut. Then, halfway up and just out of reach, the professor froze. He clung to the rungs, eyes screwed shut. The ladder swung from side to side, despite the desperate efforts of the skiff's captain to steady it.

'Climb, yeh baldie-heidit bawbag!'** yelled the giant sailor beside me furiously.

* Come on, my friend.
** Climb, you bald-headed fool.

Down in the boat, the captain was mouthing bloody murder up at Spring, but an impenetrable wall of sound separated us. It's odd watching someone screaming and not being able to hear them. Every now and then the swirling wind carried a couple of stray words up to me, including reassuring bon mots such as 'smashed' and 'smithereens'.

Then a big swell rolled under the boat, sending me – extended over the rail as I was, cheering Spring on – toppling over the edge and plunging down towards the terrifying brine. I threw out a hand and, by sheer luck, found it fastened round a rung of the ladder next to Spring's knee. The only thought in my mind was regaining the safety of the deck and so I pulled myself upwards with the super-human might reserved solely for panicking cowards. With Spring above me, my shoulder engaged squarely with his bony buttocks and I hefted him off his feet and up into golden hands. The sailor dragged the professor over the edge and, in a jiffy, reappeared to grasp my hand and pull me aboard.

I was shaking from adrenaline (which is just another way of saying, 'I was shit scared,' let's be honest), but when I regarded the big man from my seat on the deck, I saw a look of awe on his face.

'That wiz amazin' . . .'

I clambered to my feet and we enjoyed an odd moment, the two of us standing mute in the hurricane, being lashed with wind and rain. Him in silent admiration. Me wondering whether I was suffering from post-traumatic stress disorder.

'Alec!' he yelled to a man on the other side of the boat.

Alec wandered over, another huge vision of yellow in a world of black and grey, apparently immune to the inclement weather. 'Fit's goin' oan, Davey?'

'Did yeh see that, Alec? Yeh wouldnae believe it! Jimmy bluidy Mac jist dived o'er the side and hefted that bugger o'er there up the ladder afore the cap'n wiz sunken!'

Davey inclined a contemptuous head towards Spring, who was on his hands and knees on the deck, looking wretched. Then the sailor's monstrous arm was around me, pulling me to his side and prodding me in the chest with a digit the size of a frankfurter.

'See here, Alec! Ah've nivver seen anythin' like it! He really is the hero frae the bottle! Oan ma boat! Fucken legend!'

So, that was it: he thought I'd swung over the side like some demented gymnast to free Spring from his rigor mortis grasp and so save the captain. An idiotic conclusion, you'll agree, but there we are. All you can do in such circumstances is be bluff, manly and understated. And no one was more amazed than I when I discovered my night of desperate, undeserved heroism had only just begun.

CHAPTER 20

Here be Beasties

After a poor start, Spring made things worse by blaspheming liberally as he clung to the deck.

'Cauld airn!' went up the call from Davey, who grabbed the nearest piece of iron (all of it was cold, of course), followed by all the other crew within earshot. I did the same – I have no problem with a little superstition when the odds aren't in my favour.

Having countered the ill-luck that would surely come from Spring taking the Lord's name in vain, Davey manhandled the hapless professor towards the back of the boat. The latter looked as if he was going to be fool enough to complain at this treatment until Davey growled 'Haud yer wheesht'* at him. I doubt Spring understood the words, but the meaning was clear enough.

I followed as nonchalantly and heroically as I could while we were led to a large metal cover that Davey lifted, revealing stairs descending into the pitch-blackness of the hold. Davey guided me out of the turmoil and down into the space below, where he flicked a switch, illuminating a strip of lights that ran the length of the hold. They revealed an echoing cavern of steel and bolts and rust.

I climbed down and settled onto a wooden pallet covered in thick fabric. Outside I could hear the muted sound of the storm clamouring to get in like an unwanted guest, but the solid iron walls stood firm. For a brief moment I felt a sensation that approached peace. But it didn't last, as the question of whether they did any

* Be quiet.

fishing on this boat was answered in spades. It took just one deep, calming breath on my part for the stench of fish to attack us. Yes: attack us. It didn't creep across the air and languidly float into our nostrils, it actually attacked us. It was vile. It stung the eyes. It felt as if the air was forcing its way into every pore and infecting my bloodstream. It was like being rogered in the nose by an invisible assailant.

I yelled up to Davey, who was climbing back up and into the storm. 'At least this answers the question of whether you actually do any fishing in this boat!'

'Fit d'yeh mean?' Davey shouted back, momentarily silhouetted by a flash of lightning that turned the churning grey sky to blinding white.

'I said, at least I now know that you actually catch fish!'

'Fit?' he bellowed back in confusion, the tempest roaring above his head. 'Ah've nivver caught a fish in mah life!'

Well, that had me stumped – Davey too, until the look on his craggy mug brightened.

'Oh, yeh mean the smell! That's just fae the seagulls.'

'The seagulls?'

'Aye, the Beasties are quick tae catch the smugglers when there are nae seagulls following the boat. Nae fish smell means nae seagulls. Nae seagulls flyin' behind yeh makes them wonder fit yer carryin'. Makes them want tae take a closer look. So, we drop a load o' guts doon there every week, so the birdies stick wi' us. Well then, see yeh later, Jimmy.'

As he climbed out into the night and slammed the metal cover down, the storm was blotted out, being swiftly replaced by another noise: Spring being sick. Over and over again. How I wasn't sick is still beyond me. And just when I thought things couldn't get worse, a further assault on the senses began as the engines roared into life. They say an empty vessel echoes the loudest, which in metaphorical terms may or may not be true. However, I can tell you that in the hull of a trawler, it's right on the money.

We sailed on in that iron tomb for around two hours, maybe more. (To avoid being tracked I had left everything electronic at home, so that's just a guess.) I filled the time productively by comprehensively cursing Lizzy, the Farquharsons, and all the other buggers who had led me down into this stinking, swaying nightmare. On we went, numb from cold, deafened by the engines, and sullied by the ferocious violation of our nasal passages. On to God knows where.

At last the engines were reduced to a dull snarl and the hatch was dragged open. There was a rush of air – sweet, blessed sea air! – and Alec's big head appeared above us.

'A' hands oan deck,' he announced before disappearing again.

We dutifully stumbled up the stairs like drunkards, both of us unable to walk straight due to the swaying of the boat. It was still pretty foul in the open, but a considerable improvement on the conditions we had endured when we'd first set sail. The sea remained a vast and terrifying undulating black carpet, and the wind still buffeted us, but the rain had reduced to a mere squall. Fog hung thick around us, restricting visibility to about twenty metres. Aside from the billowing wind and the groaning of the hull, there was no sound at all. When the wind dropped, as it did every now and again, an unearthly silence settled on us. The single light still swung from the mast, but its steady glow offered no comfort. The crew, of whom I counted about half a dozen, were all lined up along one rail, staring left and right, trying to see through the curtain of grey. What could they possibly be looking for out there in the middle of the North Sea? Thoughts of what might come tearing through that shifting shroud made me whimper. We waited.

Then the wind eased once more and the sound of a ringing bell echoed across the water, strong and clear, before becoming muffled and swept away by the rising gale. This brought the men at the rail to life and they began busying themselves about the deck. I marvelled at their well-drilled manoeuvres. A minute later another trawler slid from the gloom like a ghost. Again, there was no panic; the crew just went about doing whatever it is smugglers do in such circumstances. The other vessel was brought alongside, perhaps ten metres away, so our ships rose and fell in time, next to each other. It was only then that it dawned on me, cold and bedraggled as I was, that this was a handover.

On the deck of the other vessel, men were moving as swiftly and surely as on ours. Then the clanking and whining of machinery being coaxed into life filled the air, and Spring and I were hustled up to the wheelhouse at the front of the boat. Davey grabbed hold of the professor and started fitting him into some kind of harness, quite oblivious to his protests.

A long metal arm had swung up and out from amongst the tangle of lines and poles that made up the trawling machinery at the back of the boat. Down from it came a thick wire, looped at the end. Davey reached up and hooked it out of the sky with a long pole. Then, with one giant, calloused hand, he fastened it to a carabiner. Spring's eyes widened in terror as the big fisherman yanked him forwards and clipped said carabiner onto his harness. Davey eyed the quaking man curiously.

'Yer lookin' affy peely wally.* Hey, Alec! Is he no' lookin' affy peely wally?'

Alec looked over. 'It's the weather, it gets yeh doon,' he yelled philosophically through the tumult as Davey secured the clips.

'No. Wait. Stop,' the professor garbled. 'Please! I don't want—'

But Davey had no patience left, and muttered, 'Och, shut up, yeh nickum.'**

* Unwell or off-colour.
** A mischievous person.

255

As if to make a point, Davey gave a mighty tug on the wire, making Spring swallow his words and stagger forward along the deck. 'Package secured,' he announced to the cabin, before turning back to Spring. 'Send us a postcard, eh?'

With that Davey thrust an arm into the air and waved a pointed finger around in small circles.

I looked Spring in the eye and, trying to be helpful, said, 'Think of Virgil, eh? You know, the miserable people, better times . . . What was it? Forsum miserus something something, eh?'

He looked at me with pure venom and was no doubt all set to lecture me on the subject of Latin conjugation. Instead, all he could do was yelp – for on Davey's signal there was a whirr, a screech, and a bump, and the melee of trawling machinery came to life. The wire, which had been hanging limp off the harness, went taut and Spring was dragged away from me, first forward along the deck and then up into the dark grey sky, yelling in terrified protest as he went. A bolt of lightning flashed, searing his black silhouette onto my eyes.

The metal arm from which he was dangling then swung out and away from the boat, leaving the professor suspended over the black waves, swaying back and forth in the wind. It was mesmeric watching him: a human metronome measuring the ebb and flow of the swell.

The ships roared back into life as the captains tried to bring them closer together, so Spring could be lowered onto the other deck. It seemed a hugely dicey manoeuvre, what with God-knows-how-many tonnes of steel ready to smash together and Spring's eminently squashable torso swinging wildly in the wind.

There was no doubt about it: the gale was picking up again. Despite the best efforts of the captains, our boats shifted from being too far away to being terrifyingly close – but never finding a happy medium.

I grasped my way round the wheelhouse to the cabin door and, stepping up and over the seal, stood next to Captain Larssen. He was staring intently at Spring and operating two small joysticks. I thought it best not to say anything. He broke the silence, his gaze still fixed on the airborne academic, who was swinging in an ever-greater arc.

'What dae yeh want?' he said, adding absently, 'Bluidy wind.'

'Er, well, I was wondering why all the trouble,' I stammered. 'Why don't you just scoot him over in the skiff?'

'Simple,' he replied. 'Presumin' we didnae sink in the first place, which would be very likely in this weather, then if one o' the Beasties comes along, we'd be high an' dry. So tae speak. This way we can swing him back and be gone intae the fog before they can get a bead oan us.'

Just then, as if waiting for the line to be delivered, a siren screamed out in the darkness, accompanied by the roar of an engine and the raking arc of a powerful lamp, scanning from left to right, somewhere out in the heavy fog.

'Beastie!' yelled Larssen, leaning out of the cabin door. The crew began moving in their well-drilled way around the ship with a new urgency. The captain replaced his hand on the joystick and the arm began moving back.

'No!' I snapped. 'We can't bring him back.'

'We most certainly can,' said the captain, as if we were in polite conversation. 'There's a gunboat somewhere oot there and the waves are gettin' tae big. If that bugger wisnae oot there in the dark we'd find calmer waters, but we've got tae bring yer boy back an' get oot o' here.'

'We can't! If we make it back to land, he's got nowhere to go, and if we're caught with him out here, I promise you, it's game over.'

He stopped and looked at me, an unflappable look on his face. The kind of look worn by a captain who goes down with his ship with little more than a grimace, merrily whistling 'The Skye Boat Song' as he sinks.

'What dae yeh suggest?' he said, cocking an inquisitive eye at me while the other boat began to sheer away from us, accompanied by a burst of Viking-sounding expletives from the radio.

'What do *I* suggest?' I squealed back. 'What do *you* bloody suggest?'

'It's yer gig, Mr Macfarlane,' he said. 'It seems ah'm jist learnin' the words.'

My brain was working furiously. Only one answer came. 'Cut the line.'

'Drown the bugger, yeh mean?' he mused, still infuriatingly calm. 'What if they find the body in the sea? No, wait, they widnae, he'd go down like a stone wi' that wire attached . . .' His expression was one of simple calculation, his eyebrows rising and falling as he contemplated his options. 'But whit if he gets the carabiner aff an' they pick him oot o' the sea alive? Then he could finger the lot o' us . . .'

You'll note there was no concern for the professor's actual well-being. I began to like the man, despite everything.

'Aye, it's a toughie,' he concluded.

Then a wave of inspiration hit me. 'Well, don't drop him, then. Throw him.'

The captain looked at me quizzically.

'You must be able to cut the line. When he's swinging over the other boat, cut the line and let's hope he hits the deck.'

'Aye, ah suppose. But, weel, they'd have to be quick in grabbin' him or the wire would pull him o'er the edge, an' wi' that kind o' impact an' then the weight an' momentum, he'd be richt doon* tae see Davey Jones, true enough.'

'Well, then, problem bloody solved then,' I said, my voice rising

* Right down.

to match the increasing noise of the siren and the engine. 'Do you have a better option?'

'Yeh'll have tae dee it.' He looked at me steadily.

'Me? Why me?' I replied, panic rising once more.

'Ah'm no' gettin' the reputation o' dumpin' cargo – 'specially no' human cargo – at the first sign o' trouble,' he said, his voice still as calm as the doldrums.

I stared at him, appalled.

'Yer choice.' He shrugged his shoulders. 'But make it quick; they'll find us soon enough. We've the usual countermeasures, of course – wouldnae leave home wi'oot them – and the weather'll throw their radar aff, but only fer so long.' He turned and tapped his finger on a large round radar screen that glowed green. 'Aye, as soon as yeh see her here, yeh can be sure she'll see you. Yer choice.'

It was no choice at all really. I took the joystick in my hand.

'Tell the other boat to stand still . . . Hold fast . . . Park . . . Oh, I don't know the right words – just ask it to bloody well stay where it is.'

The captain picked up his radio and mumbled the same gobbledygook into it that we'd just heard and replaced the handset in the cradle. There was a moment of silence, followed by a flurry of indignant noises from the speaker and then more silence. But it seemed the other boat was no longer moving away. I stumbled as our boat heaved to one side.

'What do I do?' I asked urgently.

'Just push that button there when yer ready tae let fly,' the captain said, taking a polite step back and pointing to his right.

The release button was under a clear plastic cover. It was large and flat and round. Just the kind of button you'd want to hit in an emergency.

'This one?' I asked, jabbing my finger towards it, just to be sure.

'That one.'

I lifted the plastic cover and watched the yellow figure of Spring swinging in the air. Backwards and forwards he went, like an autumn leaf tossed by the wind. I gave the joystick a jerk and he swung more wildly still, lashed by the rain. The sudden movement must have triggered something in Spring. His wide eyes were fixed on a point. That point was me. It was as if he had divined what was about to happen. The look of fury bored through the glass into the cabin, taking me quite by surprise. All I could think to do was smile back. It was very awkward. Then the siren from the Beastie sounded again, much louder this time. The searchlight seemed to be scything an ever-clearer beam through the thick air.

The captain tapped the face of his watch with his finger. 'Tick tock, Mr Macfarlane. She's cummin'.'

Spring was now mouthing something at me, but I blocked him out, as well as everything else. I waited for my moment, but it wouldn't come. Each time Spring sailed towards the other boat, he came just short of the arc I needed him to achieve to land him squarely on the deck. All the time the professor's eyes were locked on me in undisguised hatred. A wall of water crashed over the boat.

By my side the captain was muttering something: 'Prepare a harbour before me in the homeland of eternity . . .' Oh God, he was bloody praying.

Again, the siren sounded, nearer still. It was now or never.

'Fuck, fuckety, FUCK!' I cried eloquently, hitting the button as Spring almost reached the edge of his swing.

There was no noise to announce what I'd done. In fact, I don't remember any noise at all. Just the cable breaking and Spring sailing onwards into the night. To my utter amazement he crashed down onto the opposite deck. His momentum took him across the ship and he slammed into the railings on the other side. Still his trials were not over, for the ship lurched on the waves and the weight of that long, thick wire was now dragging him back across the deck. Like a sea serpent making a break for freedom, the end of it plunged into the churning water, pulling Spring with it to his doom. Towards us he slid, with a terrible, inevitable pace, before hitting the nearside railings and slipping underneath them. I watched with a horrified curiosity as his thin arms reached out and, with the strength of despair, gripped the rail for a split second before they were wrenched free.

That split second was all that saved the professor from the crushing fathoms that the inch-thick wire had been preparing for him. It gave the other crew time to swarm onto him. In a heartbeat, the wire was released. It whipped out of sight into the waves and was gone. The crew cradled him and lowered his limp body slowly to the deck. He didn't move.

I stared out of the window of the wheelhouse, feeling strangely empty. No excitement, no fear, no nothing. Just emptiness. Then the siren called again, closer now than ever, and our engines roared back into life. The other boat slipped away into the rain, fog, and darkness, complete with its precious cargo. A fragile cargo. Which I'd dropped. God only knew how many pieces it was in now.

That was the last I saw of Professor Randolph Spring. I should probably wonder how he is and where he is. If he *is* at all, that is. Perhaps he *was*? But I don't. I did what I could, and he made it damned difficult. So, no, I don't think about him. I wonder if he thinks of me?

My musings were interrupted by an earsplitting noise as the siren sounded again and a dark-grey vessel came leaping out of the storm. It crested a wave and an arc of light came flying at us. I recognised the tracers as soon as I saw them. One crew member did not. His body shook like a rag doll as the bullets tore into him, turning the yellow red as I watched, lying prostrate on the deck.

Not a word was spoken by our crew. I alone screamed 'Beastie!' and pointed uselessly at the gunboat spewing steel off our starboard bow. They moved as they had before, with careful deliberation. Alec pulled a cloth off a pile of what looked like metal tubes and quickly assembled them into what looked awfully like an M2 .50-calibre machine gun. Davey appeared with a large box, which he wrenched open, then took out an enormous ammo belt and began feeding it into the weapon. Alec dropped into a sitting position behind the gun, now ready and waiting on its tripod, pulled back the cocking mechanism with one giant arm and returned fire.

The bullets were black-tipped incendiaries and they tore into the Beastie, punching holes in its hull. One body was flung off the deck, as if swatted by a giant hand. Another exploded in a red mist that was quickly swept away in the storm. Alec raked the hull again, opening up a large hole that the angry sea rushed into. The boat began listing quickly. Safely hidden once more behind the cabin, I fancied I heard the screams of the terrified and the damned, but that must have been wishful thinking.

When I peered round the corner, the Beastie was gone. Alec was still surveying the empty scene, while Davey checked the steaming gun over. I sat back against my side of the cabin, freezing water running down my face. I stared out into the darkness and found solace in its emptiness. Then the second Beastie appeared right in front of me.

I sat open-mouthed, incapable of speech. A yell from Alec was the first the crew knew of the new threat as a bullet hit him and spun him round. He crumpled to the deck before Davey dragged him away as bullets smashed the machine gun to pieces. I crawled round to the door of the cabin and launched myself inside.

'What do we do?' I yelled at Larssen, who was staring steely-eyed at his scanners, radars, and God knows what else.

'Nothin' we can dae,' he said calmly.

'What do you mean, nothing we can do?' I yelled back.

'They've taken oot the gun.'

'Where are the other guns?'

'Whit ither guns?'

'Oh, Jesus.'

Bullets hammered into metal and smashed glass all around us. Larssen leaned out of the cabin and, calm as you like, began issuing orders.

'Alright boys, as many as yeh can intae the skiff. Injured crew first. I'll lead them awa'.'

I grabbed his arm. 'What about me?'

'Whit aboot you?'

'Where do I go?'

'Ah guess yer cummin' wi' me.'

'Wi' you? I mean, with you?'

'Nae room in the skiff, ah'm afraid.'

'But I'm a paying passenger, I—'

'Nae room in the skiff, ah'm afraid.'

For a moment I thought of battling my way past the injured and the prone to get on the little boat, but realised the likes of Davey would pull my arms off if I tried. In despair I slumped down on the floor and gave a small cry as something sharp dug into my hip. I looked down, expecting to see a red stain growing on my leg, but there was nothing. I patted my thigh and there was something there. It just wasn't a bullet wound. It took me a while to find the offending item under all that yellow garb, but when I did I positively whooped in delight. Larssen looked down at me, wondering if I had lost my mind.

'Oh, Wally, you beautiful, disobedient little bastard,' I said, holding up the little homemade EMP that he must have secreted in my pocket when he hugged me. God bless his new-found pick-pocketing skills.

'Larssen,' I said. 'We've got one chance. This is an EMP. It'll disable the Beastie; let us get away.'

'How does it work?'

'It . . . well . . . oh, bugger.'

I had no idea. Wally hadn't told me. I looked at it. It was little more than a small black cylinder. There was a button in the middle, which demanded pushing, but I distinctly remembered Wally saying it was unidirectional. Oh God, there was nothing to say which way to point the damn thing. If I pointed it the wrong way I would disable our own ship.

'I don't know which way to point it,' I said in despair.

'Fifty-fifty chance then,' said Larssen philosophically. 'Best get oan wi' it. The boys will be o'er the side soon and I dinnae fancy their chances much more than oors.'

I stared at him. He gestured with one hand – now bloody from flying shards of glass – at the door.

'After you, Mr Macfarlane.'

There was nothing left for it. I plunged out of the door and onto the deck. My arrival must have surprised the gunners as they stopped firing. I looked at the EMP and, out of options, spun it in the air, just as Archie had done with his screwdriver back at the dam.

'To the dead already,' I whispered as I caught the little tube, pointed it at the Beastie and pressed the button. Nothing happened. I pressed it again. And again. I dashed it down on the deck and let out a roar of frustration. Then the Beastie exploded.

Wally later explained that the little device had generated some kind of current surge in the semiconductors (or something like that), but all I knew was that I was lying on the deck, thrown back by the force of the explosion.

'Hooray for the next to die,' I whispered as I lay there, the rain and lightning and thunder and general misery momentarily forgotten.

A hand was resting on my shoulder and I looked up to see Larssen smiling at me.

'That went well, eh?' he said, helping me up off the deck. I had the presence of mind to ask after Alec who, I was assured, only had a scratch and would be back on his feet in no time. Then the captain turned back to the cabin and the engine roared as we smashed our way into the waves, raising great plumes of spray that crashed over the boat.

I walked with the gait of a traumatised landlubber to the rails. My hands grasped the unforgiving steel and I just stood there, oblivious to the walls of rain that hit me over and over.

The engine churned up great lines of foam behind us, leaving a white highway stretching out on the rolling waves. But our escape route was soon distorted and broken by the swell, and then lost in darkness. There were no more sweeping lights, nor klaxons. The monsters had given up the hunt.

The clamour of the wind grew as we headed back into the heart of the storm. Then there came a voice from my left that was filled with wonder, and a huge arm encircled my shoulders.

'D'ye see that, Alec?' the voice said. 'Swung the bastard o'er tae the ither boat, he did! What did ah tell yeh? Then he blew up the Beastie wi' that wee twig thingy! Fucken legend!'

I stared at him. Then I started to laugh. Great peals of laughter that made my shoulders shake. Davey joined in. He couldn't possibly have seen the salt water of the sea mingling with the salt tears from my eyes. Relief surged through me with the force of one of the mighty waves that were crashing over the bows.

Much, much later, I came staggering out of the gorse, having gained my sea legs at just the wrong moment. I was now struggling terribly with the machinations of the unshifting dunes.

'Jesus, look at the state o' yeh,' Archie rumbled as I vomited on his shoes. He looked down at them, then at me, a philosophical expression on his face. 'Och, that's a lot o' fish piss tae come oot o' one man.'

To impress him further, I was sick again. When I stood up, wiping liquid misery from my cheeks, my long-suffering heart got another shock. As if by magic, the Reverend had appeared.

'I hear you did well out there, Jimmy,' he said.

I hoped the darkness and the rain were hiding the red that was spreading across my pallid cheeks. 'Thanks,' I mumbled. A small part of me wanted him to ruffle my hair. Both of them smiled at me. I smiled back. And, just for a moment, I forgot the burning in my throat and the exhaustion and the confusion and the fear. Spring (or what was left of him) was on his way to God knows where; Lizzy, the Farquharsons, and all those whom I didn't know and might never meet, were out there somewhere, behind that curtain of rain, fighting their own private battles against tyranny. For one moment, as we all stood together in the storm, it felt like we were winning. Like we had a chance.

Then the Reverend looked to his pocket and retrieved his tablet. 'I see the Wolf of Badenoch is already taking credit for getting Professor Spring out of the country,' he said. A laughing wolf's head was beaming out from the screen. Clearly Wally was working overtime.

'That's a bit much when we know it was you who did it, James,' he went on, looking at me steadily.

'Well, quite,' I said.

'You'd best set him right one of these days, whoever he is.'

'If I see him, I'll definitely be having a word.'

The Reverend smiled the thinnest of smiles and turned to shake Archie's hand, the big man nodding his head in respect. 'I'll be seeing you then,' the Reverend said, gripping my hand in turn. 'Let's try to make it a little more low key next time, eh?'

Before I had time to respond he turned and walked off into the storm. There was no car I could see. He just walked, his long coat dancing in the wind until the rain swallowed him up.

'We'd better be goin' oorselves,' Archie said, taking my arm. 'We're aff tae London the morra, Goad help us. Aff tae see bluidy Hildebrand Blunt. Yeh remember him, aye? The man who shot yeh in the face?'

He stopped and shook his head, staring into the grey squall where the Reverend had disappeared.

'Jesus, yeh know how tae pick yer friends, don't yeh?'

Preliminary Assessment: Specimen #190321

I sleep untroubled by my victims' faces. Every opponent is an assassin. They wish to murder our ideology. To shatter order and bring chaos. There is no excuse for their actions; no acceptable morality. Their actions are born of bitterness and ignorance. It is our duty to correct that ignorance. We must educate without mercy.

But this specimen is different to the others. It has an unquantifiable belief system. It seems to think that smiling at Death means it will be left untouched. How do we make it clear there is no such extenuation? How do we make it known that however much you may smile at Death, he *will* lay his hands upon you?

This case is also conspicuous in the absence of belief systems that traditionally characterise rebellion - when a fighter's identity fuses with those of his brothers in arms. At no point does the specimen exhibit that essential quality for success: the transcendental fundamentalism that will not be traded for anything. Quite the opposite in fact.

I do not put much store by Professor Spring's amateur diagnosis of Witzelsucht, although the specimen's medical records are incomplete. Nor does the specimen crave power. It may speak of revenge for wrongs perpetrated by its family, but addressing such greed and avarice - which amounts to the theft of a few baubles - is not commensurate with the campaign of terror, nor does it seem to meet its ends.

As such, I remain mystified: what is it that has ultimately brought us here, to this godforsaken corner of the world, my skin burning in the merciless sun?

Perhaps we have become complacent. Perhaps we assume too much. We take for granted that we own the young and, as such, hold the future in our hands. We assume that there is no point in trying to convert the intellectuals – that these people would always cower and yield to the mob. What other assumptions have we made? What errors?

We secured Caledon by substituting subtlety for arguments that were crude, clear, and forcible. But we have long since eschewed this methodology, alongside removing portraits, pictures, and monuments to our leadership, which we deemed unnecessary. We took for granted that the invisible data net would serve all our needs. Have we erred? Brash iconography may be vulgar, but it offers honesty and transparency – a constant reminder of our intentions to the people. Perhaps we must do more to create God in our image, not the other way around.

There remains so much more to learn from this specimen. So much more to understand. The next chapter in the specimen's story will surely lift the veil, for the atrocities dictated thus far, while an affront to that which we hold sacred, pale in comparison to the outrages to come.

I will stay the course until the end. I will endure the privations of this place. I will come to understand this specimen by any means necessary. I will have Macfarlane's mind.

The task that the Masters have given me is long and heavy, but I will perform it with vigour and energy, for it is the path on which Fate has called me.

To find out more about the adventures of Jimmy Mac – and to download your free illustrated digital book, featuring beautiful photography of the places that inspired the world of Caledon – visit www.michaelmillar.info. You can get in touch by emailing hello@michaelmillar.info. Cheery-bye!

A NOTE ON ACCENTS

In this story I tried to convey accents and linguistic quirks wherever I could to help bring authenticity and warmth to the characters. This was particularly true of Archie, as well as others like the lingtowmen employed by the Reverend. I have done everything I can to be faithful to these regional variations, and I write with nothing but respect and affection for the people and places mentioned. Still, spellings and use of particular words and phrases are subjective. On many occasions I also dialled back to make it easier on non-Scots readers. So, if you disagree with my interpretation of different Scots accents, I will apologise and then start making excuses. The easiest excuse is that this story is set in the future and, as language is ever-changing, who's to say my usage won't be right in twenty years' time? On the other side of the coin, I've also used some words that have long since disappeared to help reflect the faux-romanticism promoted by the Marischal's regime. But if you want to put me right, please do get in touch at www.michaelmillar.info or hello@michaelmillar.info.

ACKNOWLEDGEMENTS

Firstly, my family: Susanna, Freddie, and Evie, who put up with my obsessing over and writing this story for a long time, often at the strangest times of day or night. Thank you for your support and your tolerance. A similar message goes out to my Scotland and Africa-based families who, in many different ways, afforded me the stories, experiences, and knowledge needed to write this story. Mum, Dad, Clive, Carla, Ali, Laura, J and Phil, and all the wee ones, thanks! Granny and Grampa, I will never forget our times in the Cairngorms.

Special thanks goes to Grant Nel, a man with an encyclopaedic knowledge of the African bush and the generosity to share it. Others who have helped me along the way are legion and I apologise profusely to anyone I forget. This has been a long journey!

To Adam Sturdy, who lent me a desk in his office so I could pen the first words of this story. To my beta readers, Robbie Knox and Will Paton, for suggesting key changes to the early narrative. To my editors: firstly, Kate Moore, whose work on the original manuscript transformed this story into something worthy of human consumption. Secondly, to Bryony Sutherland, whom I cannot thank enough for her amazing eye for detail, as well as plot and character development.

To the proprietors of the Hestkuk Arms: Desi Olsen, Tim Lovejoy, Fons Cohen, and Robbie Knox, who made social media truly worthy of the name with their support. To Gustav Pegers, who procured the hut in Devon that broke six months of writer's block. To the Arbuthnott family who, hundreds of years ago, took part in the real murder of Sheriff Melville of Glenbervie ('sodden and supped in broo!') and, rather more recently, let me use the text of the real pardon that their ancestors somehow received. Their beautiful home – Arbuthnott House – was the early inspiration for Glenlairig House. It is open to visitors. Check out their website (arbuthnott. co.uk). I can't promise they'll offer you any soup.

If I had to choose one whisky company that inspired Glenlairig's products then it has to be Glenlivet. It's my favourite Scotch and their distillery and visitor centre ooze romanticism and adventure. Do visit if you're in those parts. The inspiration for Robbie Macfarlane and his whisky pits was one Robbie MacPherson, whose trail, by coincidence, runs through the glen of Glenlivet. (If you have time to read about the early whisky smugglers, it will not be time wasted.) There's also a decent chunk of Dauvit Ogilvy of Rashiebog in there, that marvellous smuggler, astronomer and philosopher from the braes of Angus.

I referenced numerous characters at the start of the book by way of dedication, and they give a flavour of the authors in whose shadow I humbly stand. I must also mention Anna Funder's *Stasiland*, which provided detail and inspiration for Loker's secret police apparatus. Much of the background that formed the world of Caledon also came from podcasts, including the brilliant *Behind The Bastards*, *Stuff You Should Know*, and Dan Carlin's *Hardcore History*. Alex Massie and Chris Deerin were first amongst equals, when it came to political commentators who helped shape my view of Caledon's descent into awfulness. The 'Being Scottish' Instagram feed is a riot when it comes to Scots language, idioms, and quirks. Perhaps the most important source of all was the UKBG's *International Guide to Drinks* (1955 edition), which inspired Archie's No. 1 and No. 2 pick-me-ups.

Two final dedications: Firstly to the Cairngorms, a place of unrivalled beauty and happy memories. Secondly, to the original occupants of that horrible concrete prison. (Both it and the confessions on the walls are real; I saw them myself.) I can only hope yours was a happy ending and you won't mind me using your words as a reminder of what people are capable of when we look the other way. *Mwari inzwai tsitsi nhamo ini muno.*

ABOUT THE AUTHOR

Michael Millar was an award-winning journalist before taking his pieces of silver and becoming a political lobbyist and corporate spin doctor. Before turning to the dark side, Michael reported from Iraq during the war; was business editor of BBC Radio 4's *Today* programme; and wrote, broadcast and dissembled for all sorts of programmes, websites and publications, some more august than others.

As a non-fiction author, Michael's previous work includes *The Secret Lives of Numbers* (Random House, 2012), which was a bestseller for the publisher and translated into several languages. In this book, Michael began to hone the writing style that drives his latest story. He is also co-author of *The Five-Minute Failure* (Rock-Hill Publishing, 2006).

Lightning Source UK Ltd.
Milton Keynes UK
UKHW011309261121
394630UK00005B/519

9 781913 532826